James Grant

The Royal Regiment - And Other Novelettes

James Grant

The Royal Regiment - And Other Novelettes

ISBN/EAN: 9783337044305

Printed in Europe, USA, Canada, Australia, Japan

Cover: Foto ©Andreas Hilbeck / pixelio.de

More available books at **www.hansebooks.com**

The
Royal Regiment

The KING OF PHYSICIA.
PURE AIR!

" Former generations perished in ve ignorance of all sanitary laws. When **BLACK DEATH** massacred Hundred Thousands, neither the victims nor t rulers could be accounted responsible their slaughter."—TIMES.

HOUSE SANITATIO

Dr. PLAYFAIR, after carefully consi ing the question, is of opinion that total pecuniary loss inflicted on the cor of Lancashire from *preventible* dise sickness, and death, amounts to *not* *than* FIVE MILLIONS STERLI ANNUALLY. But this is *only* phy: and pecuniary loss, THE MORAL L(IS INFINITELY GREATER.—SMII

TYPHOID AND DIPHTHERIA, BL(POISONS, HOUSE SANITATION. is no exaggeration to state that not (quarter of the dwellings of all classes, l or low, rich or poor, are free from dan, to health due to defects with respec drainage, &c., &c. . These orig defects will inevitably entail a loss of he and energy of the occupants of the hou

and this may go on for years, working insidiously, but with deadly effect. is painful to know that, after all that has been done of late years in the way of sani improvements, persons die almost daily. POISONED by the DRAINS that should (life and not destroy it.—SANITARY CONGRESS, Sept., 1882.

JEOPARDY OF LIFE—THE GREAT DANGER OF VITIATED AIR

How few know that after breathing impure air for two and a half minutes e' drop of blood is more or less poisoned. There is not a point in the human frame has been traversed by poisoned blood, not a point but must have suffered injury.

ENO'S FRUIT SALT is the best remedy. It removes foetid or poisonous matter groundwork of disease) from the blood by natural means, allays nervous exc ment, depression, and restores the nervous system to its proper condition. Use EN FRUIT SALT. It is pleasant, cooling, refreshing, and invigorating. You cannot o state its great value in keeping the blood pure and free from disease.

THE SECRET OF SUCCESS.—"A new invention is brought before the public, commands success. A score of abominable imitations are immediately introdu by the unscrupulous, who, in copying the original closely enough to deceive the pu and yet not so exactly as to infringe upon legal rights, exercise an ingenuity t employed in an original channel, could not fail to secure reputation and profit.—AD/

CAUTION.—Legal rights are protected in every civilized country. Read the follow: —" In the Supreme Court of Sydney (N.S W) an appeal from a decree of Sir Manning perpetually restraining the defendant (Hogg) from selling a fraudu imitation of ENO'S FRUIT SALT, and giving heavy damages to the plaintiff, has, : a most exhaustive trial of two days' duration, been unanimously dismissed with cos —*Sydney Morning Herald, Nov.* 26.

Examine each bottle, and see that the capsule is marked "ENO'S FRUIT SAL Without it you have been imposed on by a worthless imitation. Sold by all Chemis

DIRECTIONS IN SIXTEEN LANGUAGES. HOW TO PREVENT DISEASE.

Pr   Works, Hatcham, London, S

3 PATENT.

THE ROYAL REGIMENT.

THE

ROYAL REGIMENT

AND

OTHER NOVELETTES

BY

JAMES GRANT

AUTHOR OF "THE ROMANCE OF WAR," "THE LORD HERMITAGE,"
"VERE OF OURS," ETC.

LONDON

GEORGE ROUTLEDGE AND SONS

BROADWAY, LUDGATE HILL

NEW YORK: 9 LAFAYETTE PLACE

JAMES GRANT'S NOVELS.

Price 2s. each, Fancy Boards.

THE ROMANCE OF WAR.
THE AIDE-DE-CAMP.
THE SCOTTISH CAVALIER.
BOTHWELL.
JANE SETON; OR, THE QUEEN'S ADVOCATE.
PHILIP ROLLO.
THE BLACK WATCH.
MARY OF LORRAINE.
OLIVER ELLIS; OR, THE FUSILEERS.
LUCY ARDEN; OR, HOLLYWOOD HALL.
FRANK HILTON; OR, THE QUEEN'S OWN.
THE YELLOW FRIGATE.
HARRY OGILVIE; OR, THE BLACK DRAGOONS.
ARTHUR BLANE.
LAURA EVERINGHAM; OR, THE HIGH-LANDERS OF GLENORA.
THE CAPTAIN OF THE GUARD.
LETTY HYDE'S LOVERS.
CAVALIERS OF FORTUNE.

SECOND TO NONE.
THE CONSTABLE OF FRANCE.
THE PHANTOM REGIMENT.
THE KING'S OWN BORDERERS.
THE WHITE COCKADE.
FIRST LOVE AND LAST LOVE.
DICK RODNEY.
THE GIRL HE MARRIED.
LADY WEDDERBURN'S WISH.
JACK MANLY.
ONLY AN ENSIGN.
ADVENTURES OF ROB ROY.
UNDER THE RED DRAGON.
THE QUEEN'S CADET.
SHALL I WIN HER ?
FAIRER THAN A FAIRY,
ONE OF THE SIX HUNDRED.
MORLEY ASHTON.
DID SHE LOVE HIM?
THE ROSS-SHIRE BUFFS.
VERE OF OURS.
THE LORD HERMITAGE.

CONTENTS.

THE ROYAL REGIMENT.

CHAPTER VI.

CHAPTER VII.

CHAPTER VIII.

CHAPTER IX.

CHAPTER X.

CHAPTER XI.

CHAPTER XII.

MILITARY "FOLK LORE."

CHAPTER I.

CHAPTER II.

CHAPTER III.

CHAPTER IV.

THE ROYAL REGIMENT.

THE RUTHVENS OF ARDGOWRIE.

"THANK Heaven, then I am not too late!" exclaimed Roland Ruthven, as he sprung on the horse that awaited him at the door of the hotel where he had arrived but an hour before; "there is no message for me specially?"

"None, sir," said the mounted groom, touching his hat, and shortening his gathered reins.

" My father —— "

"Is living still, Master Roland; but that is all, I fear," replied the old man, with a sigh.

" Come on then, Buckle, old fellow; I think the grey nag knows my voice, though I have not been on his back for four years."

And spurring his horse, "Master Roland," as the grey-haired groom still called him, though he was nearer thirty than twenty years of age, and had held Her Majesty's commission for ten of them, departed at a rasping pace that soon left the stately streets, the spires and shipping of Aberdeen far behind them.

B

The royal residence at Balmoral had barely as yet been thought of, and railways had not then penetrated into the valley of the Dee; thus, all anxious as Roland Ruthven was to learn details of the perilous illness of the fine old soldier his father—the only kinsman he had in the world—at whose summons he had crossed two thousand miles and more of sea, he could only trust now to the speed of his horse, and without further questioning old Bob Buckle the groom, rode at a hard and furious gallop along the old familiar ways that led towards his home among the mountains, behind which the bright sun of a glorious evening—one of the last in June—was sinking.

Closely rode the old groom behind him, marvelling to find that the little golden-haired boy, whom he had first trained to ride a shaggy Shetlander, had now become a dark-whiskered, tall, and handsome man, well set up by infantry drill, and with all that air and bearing which our officers, beyond those of all other European armies, alone acquire, developed in chest and muscle by every manly sport; and he could recall, but with a sigh, how like " Master Roland " was now, to what the old dying Laird his father had been at the same age, when his regiment, the Royal Scots, was adding to its honours in the Peninsula—more years ago than he cared to reckon now.

And vividly in fancy too, did Roland Ruthven see before him the figure and face of that handsome old man, ere the latter became lined with care and thoughts and even his voice seemed to come distinctly to his ear, as the familiar objects of the well-remembered scenery came to view in quick succession, and at last Ardgowrie, the home of his family, rose before him in the distance, its strong walls shining redly in the setting sun.

Situated among luxuriant woods, in all their summer greenery, Ardgowrie presents the elements common to most of the northern mansions of the same age and kind—a multitude of crow-stepped gables encrusted with coats of arms, conical turrets, and angular dormer windows, giving a general effect extremely rich and picturesque, as their outlines cut the deep blue of the sky.

Notwithstanding its age, Ardgowrie is unconnected with the usual memories of crime and violence which form the general history of an old Scottish feudal fortalice, and yet it stands in the glorious valley of the Dee, between the central highlands and the fruitful lowlands, where in former ages it has been said " that the inhabitants of the two districts, thus joined by a common highway, were as unlike each other in language, manners and character as the French and the Germans, or the Arabs and the Caffres."

" At last ! " exclaimed Roland, with a sigh of satisfaction, as he spurred his horse down a long and rather gloomy avenue of genuine old Scottish firs, dignified and magnificent trees, with massive trunks of dusky red, and foliage of bronze-like hue. " Ardgowrie at last ! " he added, as he reined up at the stately entrance

of his home, for to this moment had he looked forward
with intense anxiety during the long voyage from
America, while his affectionate heart had beat responsive to every throb of the mighty engines of the
great Atlantic steamer.

Home ! How much does that word contain to the exile
or the wanderer ! "What a feeling does that simple
word convey to his ears, who knows really the blessings
of a home," says an Irish writer, who found his grave
in a far and foreign land ; "that shelter from the world,
its jealousies and its envies, its turmoils and disappointments, where like some land-locked bay the still,
calm waters sleep in silence, while the storm and hurri-
canes are roaring without."

The sound of hoofs in the avenue brought a number
of domestics to welcome him home in the kindly old
Scottish way, and he had to shake hands with all, especially with Gavin Runlet, the white-haired butler, Elspat
Gorm, the old Highland housekeeper, who had donned
her best black silk, with the whitest of "mutches," in
honour of the occasion : and then, too, came, though
last, certainly not the least in his own estimation, with
eyes keen as those of an eagle, and massive red beard,
a thick-set sturdy figure, and bare limbs brown and
hairy as those of a mountain deer, the family piper,
Aulay Macaulay, whose boast it was that he came of the
Macaulays of Ardencaple, and was a worthier scion of
the clan than the historian of the same name.

Aulay had his pipes under his left arm, but no note of

triumph or salute could come from them, when the Laird was in his dire extremity, and a great hush seemed over all the household. He had been a piper of the Royal Scots during the campaign in Burmah, and, like Bob Buckle and several others of the grand old regiment, had found a home with their loved Colonel at Ardgowrie.

"Well, Elspat, old friend," said Roland, as he leaped from his foam-flecked horse and tossed the reins to Bob Buckle, "how is my father to-night?"

"The doctor will tell you better than I," replied the old domestic, quietly, and with bated voice; "he has, thank Heaven, fallen asleep after a restless day, and, as sleep is like life to him——"

"Let him not be disturbed. I shall see him when he wakens," said Roland, as the servants fell back at his approach, and the butler and housekeeper led the way to the dining-room, where a repast awaited him, and at which they attended upon him in all the fussiness of affection and reverence as the future head of the house.

"Ewhow! but I am glad to see you here again, Master Roland," exclaimed Elspat, with whom we need not trouble the reader much. "Ewhow!" she continued, stroking his thick dark brown hair, as she had been wont to do in his boyhood, "we have had an eerie time o't wi' the Laird in his illness, and last night I thought the worst was close at hand."

"Why, Elspat? why?" asked Roland, pausing over

the liver wing of a chicken, while Runlet filled his glass
with sparkling Moselle.

"Because the dogs in the kennel howled fear-
fully."

"Where was the keeper?"

"A' the keepers in the world wouldna quiet them!"
she replied, shaking her old head.

"Why?"

"Dogs can see and ken when death enters a
house."

"Death!—is my father's case so bad?" asked Roland,
growing very pale, and setting down his glass.

"Bad—it couldna weel be worse," said she, in a
broken voice, as she began to weep; "but the doctor—"

"Is in the house, I understand. Tell him that I am
here. Oh, Elspat, have I crossed the broad Atlantic
only to face death and sorrow?"

"Death and sorrow!" she added, shaking her head,
"and I dread the fifth of August—it has aye been a
fatal day to the Ruthvens. It was on that day your
lady mother died, and on that day your uncle Philip,
that should have been Laird, went forth and returned no
more!

Roland started impatiently to his feet, and something
of a disdainful smile crossed his handsome face.

There is something grand and noble in the position
of such a young man as he was—the descendant and
representative of a long line of stainless ancestry, having
the sense of carrying out its destiny in the future, and

being the transmitter to other times and generations of its lofty traits and distinction.

No gamblers, "legs," or turf transactions ever degraded the line of Ardgowrie (pigeons there may have been, but never hawks), which, in a collateral branch, represented the attainted Earls of Gowrie and Lords of Ruthven, and if Roland had any weakness it was family pride, which he inherited from his father, who had left nothing undone to develop it; and with it grew the idea and conviction, that death were better than for a Ruthven to do aught that was dishonourable.

The second article of Roland's faith, like that of his father, was a profound veneration for the old Royal Scots, in which so many of the Ruthvens had lived and died, that they deemed it quite a family regiment, and many knew of no home out of it, and many, too, in battle or otherwise, had found their graves under its colours in all parts of the world.

As his father's son, Roland was a favourite with both battalions of the Royal Regiment, and he was the life and soul of the mess, and the most popular man in it.

In friendly rivalry with his chief chum and brother-sub, Hector Logan, of Loganbraes and that ilk (of whom more anon), he was the "show man" of the Royals. None occupied the box-seat of the regimental drag, or tooled the team to race-meetings or elsewhere, in a better style than Roland; in the cricket field, when stumps were down, and the runs were growing few, his batting and bowling were the last hope of the regimental eleven; and at hurdle-racing or steeple-chasing he was ever ready to ride any man's horse, however desperate the leaps or wild the animal, if he had not entered one for himself. Moreover, his good figure and social qualities, his known wealth and high spirit, made him a prime favourite with the other sex wherever the regiment went, and none could see any man's wife or daughter more adroitly or gracefully through a crush at the Opera, or anywhere else, than Roland Ruthven of the Royal Scots.

In all this he was exactly what his proud old father had been before him; but the latter indulged in aspirations that never occurred to Roland.

That even at this remote time Queen Victoria might restore the earldom of Gowrie to his family after the lapse of two hundred and forty years, had been the dearest hope of the old Colonel's life, especially in his latter years. It was a child's whim; yet other titles, such as Mar, Perth, and Kellie, had been restored, he was wont to say.

With all his long service he had failed to win great laurels as an officer, and now his hopes were centred on his only son; but as yet the fields of the Crimea had not been fought, and great wars seemed to have become things of the past.

Though ever kind, loving, and affectionate to Roland, the latter found that in his latter years his father had become somewhat of a stern, moody, and morose man, almost repellant to his county neighbours, whom as

years went on he seemed to avoid more and more, and
of this peculiarity Roland was thinking as the doctor, a
spruce and dapper little personage, entered with his professional smile, and warmly welcomed him home,
adding,—

"I have but to deplore the occasion of it, my dear sir."

"But what is his ailment, doctor?"

"I can scarcely say—it seems to be a general break
up of the whole system."

"At his years that can scarcely be."

"He has been sorely changed since you were last at
Ardgowrie, my dear sir; and there seems—there
seems——"

The doctor paused, and played nervously with his
watch-chain.

"There seems what?" asked Roland, bluntly.

"Something that I scarcely like to hint at."

"How, sir?"

"Well, if you will pardon my saying so, he seems to
suffer more from illness of the mind than of the body."

"Of the mind?" asked Roland, haughtily.

"Yes; as if some secret preyed upon him. I have
watched him closely from time to time, for the last few
years, and such, my dear sir, is my firm conviction."

"Your idea seems to me incomprehensible, doctor."

"There is a skeleton in every house," said the other
with a simper.

"Sir, you forget yourself," exclaimed Roland, with
haughty surprise. "What skeleton could be in ours?"

"Pardon me—I used but a proverb. Your father is awake now," he added, as a distant bell rang. And Roland, considerably agitated and ruffled by what had passed, repaired at once to the sick chamber.

CHAPTER II.

THE FATAL DAY OF THE RUTHVENS.

THE affectionate and filial heart of Roland was wrung by the wan and haggard aspect of his father, who looked as grim and pale as that other Patrick Ruthven, whose ghastly visage in his helmet had so appalled the luckless Mary on the night that Rizzio was slain; but the old man's eyes brightened, his colour came back for a time, and his strength even seemed to rally as his son embraced him.

"You have lost no time in attending my summons, Roland," said he, retaining the latter's hand within his own.

"I left Montreal by the first steamer, my dear father, but I got away with difficulty."

"Why?"

"A revolt among the colonists is daily expected; but when I mentioned your illness, the Colonel at once obtained leave for me from the General at Halifax."

"Dear old Geordie Wetherall! I remember him a

sub in his first red coat, when we were ensigns together, in the "rookery," as we called it, in Edinburgh
Castle.   Ah, few of the Royals of that day are surviving
now.   They have nearly all gone before me to the
Land o' the Leal!   But in fancy I can see them all yet."

Then, though ailing nigh unto death, true to his old
instincts, almost the first questions he asked of Roland
were about their old regiment, its strength and appearance, of the officers and rank and file; and then he
sighed again, to think that none remembered him save
old Geordie Wetherall, a veteran of the conquest of
Java; and all these questions Roland had to answer,
ere he could lure his father to speak of himself, and
when the latter did so, his spirit fell, his colour faded,
and the momentary lustre died out of his eyes, though
the glassy glare of illness still remained.

"I hope the alleged danger of this mysterious illness
is exaggerated," said Roland, tenderly and anxiously;
"and that ere I return to the regiment, I shall see you
well and strong—ay, perhaps taking your fences as of
old with Bob Buckle at your back."

The old Laird of Ardgowrie smiled sadly, and turned
restlessly on his pillow—and a handsome man he was,
even in age, with a wonderful likeness to his son,
having the same straight nose and mouth clean cut and
chiselled, "the prerogative of the highly born," as
Lever has it—for Patrick Ruthven belonged to the un-
titled noblesse of Scotland, the lineage of some of whom
stretches far back into the shadowy past.

" I am lying in my last bed save one, Roland," said the sufferer, in low concentrated voice ; " we have not all died in our beds, we Ruthvens of that ilk, but it shall be said that all have died with honour except——"

" Except *who*, father ? "

The old man trembled as if with ague, and closed his eyes, as he said hoarsely—

" I cannot tell you—in time you will know all ! "

" You have been a good soldier to the Queen, father."

" But a bad servant to her Master."

" Do not speak thus ! " said Roland, imploringly.

" The heart knoweth its own bitterness ; and I have been bad, evil, wicked—false ! "

" This is some fancy."

" It is *not !* " said Patrick Ruthven, emphatically.

" Then can I make amends ? "

" You may, if it is not too late, my poor Roland. Oh, my God ! "

These mysterious words filled the listener with genuine grief and alarm. Was it all some hallucination ? What did they import or refer to ? For much in his father's moody and wayward life, in his latter years especially, seemed to corroborate them, and to hint that there *was* " a skeleton in the house," as the doctor had ventured to say.

" I will have no clergyman about me," said the sufferer, petulantly and almost passionately, in reply to some remark of Roland's.

" Why ? "

" I hope to make my peace with God alone. The Reverend Ephraim Howle, to whom I gave the living of Ardgowrie! What can he, or such as he, do for me now ? "

" Oh, father ! "

" No one ever prospered who grew rich by fraud, it has been said—yet have I, in a manner, prospered," added the old man, as if communing with himself.

" You, father ? " exclaimed Roland, whose blood seemed to grow very cold.

" Yes—I."

" How—how ? "

" I cannot—dare not tell you. Hush ! " he added, glancing stealthily about, as Mr. Runlet, the butler, placed two shaded candles, in massive antique silver holders, on the toilet table, and withdrew, and Roland thought—

" Poor old man—his mind wanders ! "

" My mind is *not* wandering."

" I never said so, father."

" But you seem to think so—I can read it in your eyes. I have been successful in life, and leave at death a handsome fortune to one who has *no* right to it—*you*, my son—you whom I love better than my own soul ! " he exclaimed, in a broken voice that seemed full of tears, and a great horror began to possess the heart of the listener.

" Oh heaven—heaven ! he is mad ! "

"Would that I had died at the head of the Royals, when I led them at Nagpore!"

Intense perplexity mingled with the natural grief of Roland, for the whole tenor of this interview was so utterly beyond all that he could have anticipated.

In a half fatuous manner, the patient was muttering to himself, and in great agony of mind, Roland listened intently.

"Live it down, people say—I have lived it down—it was never known indeed! Poor Philip — poor Philip! One may live down a lie, but not the truth—it is the truth that hurts—that never may be lived down. I ever thought a day of retribution would come, and it is coming—fast!"

"Retribution for what?" asked Roland, in a low but passionate voice.

"Could I face the malevolence of the vulgar on one hand, and the scorn of my equals on the other?—no—oh no!" continued his father, speaking in a low voice, and at long gasping intervals, as if to himself. "It has been truly said, that 'manner and tone of voice may be made to give stabs, only less sharp and cowardly than vile and baseless calumny. There is *no* insolence like the insolence of the well-born and well-bred; and the most vulgar and purse-proud wife of the most purse-proud plutocrat is altogether inferior in her capacity to inflict pain and give offence to the patrician lady of title.' I have been spared all that—for I cast the die in secret!"

" What die ? " asked Roland imploringly.

The old man regarded him wildly, as if for a time he had forgotten his presence.

" When I am dead and gone—dead and gone, dear Roland, you will know all."

" Why not now ? "

" Because I—even hovering on the brink of eternity —blush to tell you. Oh, what a thing it is for a father to cower like a very craven before his only son, and yet, Roland, you know how I have loved you. When I am gone and buried, Roland, open the old Indian cabinet that I found on the day when the Royals stormed Scindia's fortress of Neembolah—read the sealed packet you will find there—and—and pray for me."

These were almost the last coherent words his father spoke ; and he uttered them with the veins in his temples throbbing, and as if the most bitter of all emotions, self scorn, wrung his heart, and then he seemed to sink fast. But he lingered for some days after this, and though his words, manner, and injunction, filled Roland with grief and intense curiosity, he resolved to obey him to the letter and not open the cabinet till the end came, and the doctor assured him it was near now.

" Under what hallucination can the poor old man be labouring ? " thought Roland, as he sat alone in the stately dining-room—a veritable hall — and thought how proud he who was about to pass away to a dark and narrow home, had been of Ardgowrie and all its details and surroundings—its stately park where the deer made their lair among the green ferns, its dark blue loch full of pike, and the pine plantations where the pheasant pea-fowl were thick as the cones that lay around them.

Daily by the sun, nightly by the moon, for many centuries, had the same shadows of the quaint old house been cast on the same places, and it was now an epitome of a proud historic past. It had entertained more than one king of Scotland, and everything in the old mansion was on a grand scale, from the portraits by Jamesone and Vandyck (who married a Ruthven of Gowrie, by the way) to the massive cups won in many a race that glittered on the sideboard. Above the latter, a splendid full-length of the " bonnie Earl " who was wont to flirt with Anne of Denmark in Falkland Woods, and who on the 5th of August, 1600, perished in the famous conspiracy, had its place of honour ; and among other portraits of later times, was one by Sir Watson Gordon of the present proprietor, in his uniform as a field officer of the Royal Scots.

The massive mantelpiece of the early Stuart times ascended to the ceiling. It was an exact copy of the famous one in Gowrie House at Perth, and over it in Gothic letters was the same remarkable and apposite legend borne by the former :—

> "Truths long concealed at length emerge to light,
> And controverted facts are rendered bright."

But Roland now perceived with genuine wonder, that

the couplet had been chiselled completely away, and the stone frieze was now smooth and bare.

" By whose orders was this done, Runlet ? " he asked with angry surprise.

" Those of the Laird, your father," replied the butler.

" When ? "

" Just before his last illness."

" Why ? "

" I cannot say, Mr. Roland, but he has done some queer things of late," he added with diffidence.

On that mantelpiece were cut the Ruthven arms, bars and lozenges, within a border flowered and counter-flowered, crested with a goat's head, and above them hung the tattered colours of Ruthven's battalion of the 1st Royal Scots—one of four—which had borne them in triumph from the plains of Corunna to the gates of Paris, covered with trophies, among which are still the cross of St. Andrew and the crowned thistle of James VI.

Off the dining hall opened a long and lofty corridor hung with moth-eaten tapestries of russet and green hues and with trophies of arms, each having its his-tory; such as the helmet of Sir Walter Ruthven who died by the side of King David at the battle of Durham; the sword of Sir William who became hostage for King James I.; the pennon of the Master of Ruthven who fell at Flodden, and weapons of later wars, with trophies of the chase, heads and skulls of lions shot in

C

Africa, tigers in Bengal, bears in Russia, of elephants
from the miasmatic Terrai of Nepaul—spoils wherever
his father had served; and of noble deer from the
forests of the adjacent hills.

From all these objects and the drooping colours of
the grand old regiment, Roland's eyes would wander
again and again to settle on the cabinet of Scindia, and
he would marvel *what* it contained—if indeed it contained any secret whatever!

With a fond, proud and yet sad smile he looked at
the portrait of more than one fair ancestress, and
thought,

"The girl I left behind me is fairer than them all!"

For in Montreal he had left Aurelia Darnel de
St. Eustache, whom we shall meet in time.   A kind of
half-flirtation—something even more tender and taking
had subsisted between them, and but for his sudden
summons home, it would have assumed greater proportions and had a firmer basis; he would have explained to her the nature and extent of his love for
her, and obtained some pledge or promise from her,
with the consent of her mother, for father she had none
now; and when Elspat Gorm spoke apprehensively of
the 5th of August, as being "the fatal day of the
Ruthvens," he would think, with a smile,

"I hope not, as it was on the evening of that day, I
first met Aurelia at our ball in Montreal!   Would that
I could tell the poor old man who is passing away, of
my love, and gain his permission to address her; for

she must know of my love for her and will await my
return; but I would that he could see her, even as I
in memory see her now!"

And before him came a mental vision of a very
beautiful girl, whose dark hair and long black lashes
contrasted with the pale delicacy of her skin, her pencilled
eyebrows rather straight than arched, a calm loveliness
in her face when in repose, but a brightness over it all,
when she was animated, when her soft eyes lighted up
and her lips became tremulous.

"Aurelia!" he whispered to himself, and marvelled
if the time would ever come, when he would bring her
hither to be the queen of his life, and of beautiful
Ardgowrie.

Day by day, his father was sinking, and all the
powers of medicine could do nothing for him; his ailment was not old age but a passing away of the powers
of life. The old Highland housekeeper, Elspat, had
much contempt for the nostrums of the doctor, and
believing her master to be under the spell of a gipsy
woman whom he had sent to prison for theft, maintained that he would never be cured, until the parings
of his finger nails and a lock of his hair were buried in
the earth with a live cock, a remnant of ancient
Paganrie, which the reign of Victoria still finds prevailing in some parts of the Highlands.

So, as she fully expected, the morning of the 5th of
August, saw the old Laird expire peacefully, after
playing fatuously with the coverlet, and muttering that

c 2

he could "hear the drums of the Royal beating the old Scots March," and the lamenting wail of Macaulay's pipe was heard on the terrace without, as Roland closed his father's eyes, and, crushed with natural grief, knelt by the side of his bed, and Elspat placed a plate containing a little salt on his breast.

In due time, amid the lamentations of his tenantry, and while the pipes woke the echoes of the glen, by the March of Gilliechriost (or of the Follower of Christ), one of the oldest airs in existence, he was laid in his last home, in the Ruthven aisle of Ardgowrie kirk, and Roland found himself alone in the world.

CHAPTER III.

THE CABINET OF SCINDIA.

YES, Roland felt himself, most terribly alone now—far from the merry mess and the daily companionship of his brother officers, in that great old mansion, wherein for centuries generations of his ancestors were born and had died, and which stood amid such wild and desolate, yet beautiful scenery.

Expected though his father's death had been, by Roland, the shock of the event when it did occur, was so great, that it was not until two days after the funeral, and when his legal agents and advisers, Messrs. Hook and Crook, writers to Her Majesty's

Signet, came to consult him on certain matters concerning the estate, that he bethought him of the old
cabinet found by the Royals in Scindia's fortress, and he
sprang up with a start to execute the last commands of
his father the old Colonel.

In the latter's desk he found the key—one of very
curious workmanship, and as he put it into the lock a
singular sense of some great and impending evil—a
sense which had never impressed itself upon him so
vividly before—came over him, and seemed to whisper
to him to be prepared !

Prepared for what ?

He had seen the old cabinet years ago ; it was about
four feet square, formed of ebony inlaid with the finest
ivory and mother-of-pearl with many elaborate orna-
ments, and even some precious stones, and it had been
a gift from old Patrick Ruthven to his bride.

With vivid painfulness too, there came before Roland,
the last expression of his father's face, and more than
all, his eyes with their restless feverish expression, and
strangely lustrous glare.

The doors of the beautiful cabinet unfolded and displayed two rows of drawers, the handles of which were
chased silver, and with nervous haste, Roland opened
these in quick succession.

Therein he found old muster-rolls, reports and
memoranda connected with the First Royal Scots ;
letters and orders from brother-officers who had found
their graves in every quarter of the globe ; complimen-

tary addresses from generals and magistrates, and all
his father's medals and orders.   There too were letters
from his mother in their lover-days, faded and brown;
letters of the lost uncle Philip, and letters from Roland
himself, even those he had written as a schoolboy, with
the now withered and dry locks of hair belonging to
those who had been loved and had long since departed.

All the little relics and *souvenirs* that the poor old
man had treasured most in life were there; but what
could the secret be, that he had so strangely and with
such evident emotion and pain referred to, thought
Roland, as in nervous haste and sorrow he drew out
each tiny drawer in succession—sorrow, for the hands
that had touched and the eyes that had seen them last
were cold and still now in yonder dark old vault.

At last he found a packet carefully sealed with his
father's crest, a goat's-head embossed; but directed to
no one.

He tore it open, and found within the cover, a legal
document tied with red tape, and a page or two written
by the hand of his father, and bearing the latter's
signature.

Both these papers Roland read quickly, but he had
to do so again and again ere his startled mind could
take in their contents.

The first was the last will and testament of his
grandfather General Roland Ruthven, and the latter
was a confession written by his father concerning it.

"My God—oh that this could ever be the case!" exclaimed Roland in a broken and hollow voice, as he read them. Philip, the elder brother, had in some mysterious manner incurred the high displeasure of the general, who bequeathed his entire estate and fortune to Patrick, the younger; but, repenting, had executed a second will superseding the first; and this will, Roland's father had found and *suppressed*, while, with a curse upon their father's name and memory, Philip believing himself to be disinherited, went forth into the world and was heard of no more!

Philip who had never loved him, continued the old man's tremulously written confession, was gone he knew not where, beyond all trace, so that rumour even said he was dead; and to denounce himself then as the possessor of the second will, was to cut away the ground from under his own feet, when on the very eve of marriage with a girl, whose family would not permit her to marry a penniless younger son—so he had deemed himself thus not intentionally guilty, and that no one's interests suffered by his silence.

If he had followed the dictates of the highest principles, he would at once have made the document known; but where was Philip? As time went on Patrick Ruthven became conscience-struck, and he now charged Roland with the task of making some amends if possible, by discovering the lost man or his heirs, if he had any.

A bitter bequest indeed!

With a painfully throbbing heart, and hands that trembled, Roland laid the documents down and strove to collect his thoughts. The first dull and stunning emotion of confusion and unreality past, he looked dreamily around him to see if he was not undergoing a species of nightmare; but no! There was the stately old dining-hall, the spacious Scottish fireplace with its silver fire-dogs, and here were the ebony cabinet of Scindia, with the suppressed will, and the signed confession of his father.

It was a terrible shock to Roland Ruthven to find that his father—his father of all men in the world!—whom through all the years of his life he had looked up to with love and reverence, and who seemed ever to him and to all who knew him, the model of chivalrous honour, should have acted thus, and he actually wept over the event. !

Again and again he read the confession that on one hand Philip had never loved him, had exasperated the general; and on the other, there was the chance—nay, the certainty—of a marriage being marred by the production of the will which was now dated nearly forty years back.

" Justice must be done, at all risks and hazards—but justice to whom?" thought Roland.

Ardgowrie seemed no longer his; as if touched by an enchanter's wand, it seemed already to have passed away, wood, wold, and mountain, by this cruel discovery. He felt homeless in a splendid home, his worldly prospects ruined, and Aurelia Darnel, the only girl he had ever loved, utterly lost to him !

Why not destroy the will ?

But no—oh no ! Roland felt his cheek crimson, as something seemed to whisper of this in his ear, and then he recalled his dead father's remorseful injunctions to himself.

He looked up at the portrait of the lost and disinherited Philip—the outcast son of a patrician race, as limned by the President of the Scottish Academy.

It represented a handsome young man, in a red hunting coat and cap, with regular but rather pale features, dark blue eyes and well defined eyebrows, with a pleasant smile that actually, to Roland's then distempered fancy, seemed to light up, as he looked on the portrait.

Roland wiped the beady perspiration from his brow, and a moan as if of pain escaped him, but again and again he muttered—

"Justice shall be done—justice if it be not too late —oh Heaven—too late ! "

He stepped to the sideboard, filled a silver hunting cup with sherry, drained it at a draught, and taking up the two fatal documents, locked the Indian cabinet, and prepared to join Messrs. Hook and Crook, who were busy with certain accounts and papers in the library.

Of lawyers, Roland, as a soldier, had ever a wholesome dread, and he shrank from the horror of disclosing this trickery on the part of his father even to them, whose lives were too probably but one long and tangled yarn of trickery and deceit; but again, he muttered that justice must be done.

His assumed coolness deserted him, his face became livid, and his eyes sparkled with a strange light, when he spoke to them of the papers he had found, and laid them before their legal eyes.

Then his 'proud pale face flushed scarlet, his dark eyebrows were knitted nearly into one, and his nether lip quivered with suppressed emotion and intense mortification, and in some degree the lawyers were also excited, but amazement was what they chiefly felt.

" What did Mr. Ruthven intend to do? "

" Justice," said he hoarsely.

" But to whom ? "

" That is precisely what I have been asking of myself."

" This will revoking the former disposition, is fully forty years old ; but it has never been recorded," said Mr. Hook.

" And none know of its existence, save ourselves," added Mr. Crook suggestively; " and it is a dreadful thing to lose so fine an estate —so noble a heritage—by one stroke of a pen ! "

" But I quite agree with the young Laird, that some attempt should be made to do justice, and endeavour to trace out Mr. Philip or his heirs," said Mr. Hook, seeing in futurity a pyramid of three-and-fourpences and six-and-eightpences.

" To advertise for the lost one would degrade my father's name ! " exclaimed Roland passionately.

"How else are we to go about it, my dear sir?" asked Mr. Hook, pulling his nether lip reflectively; "but enquiries might be made——"

"Where?"

"Well—a rumour did go about at one time that your uncle had married in Jamaica, Mexico, or somewhere."

"I never heard of it."

Neither had Mr. Hook, but he only threw out the hint to suggest difficulty and complication, and in his simplicity Roland rapidly adopted it.

"Prosecute enquiries in both places," said he; "spare no money—collect and pay in the rents as usual—though not a penny of them shall come to me! You understand me, gentlemen?"

They could better have understood his quietly putting alike the will and confession into the fire.

Why had not his father done so, and spared Roland this season of shame and humiliation, of disappointment and sudden poverty?

But his plans were adopted with decision and rapidity.

"All the old servants will be retained as usual, gentlemen," said he, after a painful pause, during which a swelling seemed to have risen in his throat, "but no new ones will be engaged, and the whole revenue of the estate shall be paid into the bank for the benefit of the real heir, or of his children, if they can be found. I leave all in your hands."

"But you must have some little income out of the estate!" said the astounded lawyers simultaneously.

"Not a penny until I am proved to be indubitably the last and only Ruthven of Ardgowrie and that ilk!" exclaimed Roland with emotion.

"My dear sir, you can't live on your pay," suggested Mr. Hook.

"I will try."

"No one does now-a-days. Nor will you be able to marry."

"I do not mean to marry," said Roland, whose voice fairly broke as he thought of Aurelia Darnel; "but perhaps you may help me with a few pounds till I get exchanged into a regiment in India, for meantime I must rejoin the Royals."

By this discovery in the Indian cabinet, Roland now learned bitterly why the old legend above the mantelpiece had become obnoxious to his father's eye, and been obliterated by his order!

He looked at his family motto—the strongly apposite and ancient motto of the Ruthvens—*Facta Probant*, and muttered—

"That of Argyle would suit me better now!"

He felt that under pressure of the sudden change in his circumstances, that to avoid surmises and explanations which it would be impossible to make, his wisest mode of action would be to effect an exchange into some other regiment where he was unknown; but his own honour at that time of expected peril required that he should rejoin the Scots Royals, and he could not yet bring his heart to quit them, for the corps had been the home of his family for many generations, quite as much as their ancestral abode of Ardgowrie.

Moreover, he was well up the list of lieutenants now. He could recal the emotions with which he first joined them in all the freshness of boyhood, and felt, as a writer says, how "the first burst of life is a glorious thing; youth, health, hope and confidence, and all the vigour they lose in after years : life is then like a splendid river, and we are swimming with the stream — no adverse waves to weary, no billows to buffet us, we hold on our course rejoicing."

But all pride of birth, of race, and name had gone completely out of Roland Ruthven for the time.

Cards of condolence poured in upon him from the county people, but he returned none ; neither did he pay any visits ; he felt himself a species of usurper.

"A morose fellow he has become," some said ; "just like his father in his latter years—moping and melancholy."

A letter from his friend Hector Logan roused him a little, and made him think of returning at once to the regiment. It was full of the mess gossip and barrack news generally, and about a ball "where *la belle* Aurelia had appeared with a new and very remarkable admirer, a Colonel Ithuriel Smash, of the United States army. If the row with the colonists comes off," continued Logan, " some of us may lose our chance of picking up a handsome heiress—for heiresses here are to be had for the asking, some think; I don't. But a girl like Aurelia Darnel, with a stray forty thousand pounds, and having also the frankness and good taste to accept a nice fellow with whom to spend it, is just the kind of girl for my complexion. Logan Braes and that ilk, sound very well; but my pedigree is a powersight longer than my rent-roll."

The letter concluded by urging him to rejoin, as an outbreak among the colonists was daily expected.

Apart from Aurelia Darnel, concerning whom a change had come over his future now, he felt in every way the necessity for action, and for returning to America, and he felt, too, as if he would go mad, if he lingered longer in Ardgowrie.

Aurelia! could he go back to the charm of her society again, with that horrible secret in his mind—the secret the cabinet had contained, and which made him a penniless man! Yet, his thoughts would wander again and again to the girl he had left beyond the broad Atlantic, and doubts rather than hopes, fear rather than joy, crowded upon him, all born of recent events.

Perhaps absence might already have erased all memory of him, and he was forgotten; and who was this new dangler—"admirer," Logan called him, with the atrociously grotesque name? He had left her, without any declaration of his love, and dared he make one now? Left her, at that period, when, as Lever says, "love has as many stages as a fever; when the feeling of devotion, growing every moment stronger, is chequered by a doubt lest the object of your affections should really be indifferent to you—thus suggesting all the torturing agonies of jealousy to your distracted mind. At such times as these a man can scarcely be very agreeable to the girl he loves; but he is a confounded bore to a chance acquaintance."

Aurelia Darnel was one of the wealthiest girls in Montreal. Could he speak to her of love *now?* No—no! It was not to be thought of, and in going back, he would avoid her, and devoutly hoped that the expected "row" would come off, and the Royal Scots would have to take the field.

The two last days of his residence at Ardgowrie he spent in solitude beside the Linn of Dee. There was something soothing to his soul in the wild turmoil of the rushing torrent, from whence, the body of any living thing that finds its way into it, can *never* be recovered.

What a change had come over Roland Ruthven, since last, in boyhood, and just before he joined the Royals, he had gazed into those black and surgy depths which fascinate the eye and render the brain giddy, where the dead white of the foam contrasts so strongly with the sombre tints of the turbulent cauldron, and the still blacker uncertainties of the caverns beneath the rocks, as the Dee, there terrible, yet beautiful thunders over the Linn on its passage to the German Ocean.

Roland felt keenly the change that had come over

him, since last he heard the familiar roar of his native stream; a new life, with the regiment had been opened to him; but a blight had fallen upon it now. Out of many a passing flirtation, his love for Aurelia stood prominently forth on one hand; on the other was his father's sore temptation (he could scarcely give it a harder name); yonder grand old house, with all its turrets amid the stately woods, no longer his; his future wasted, his love denied him, and his inheritance lost!

It was a conviction hard to adopt and bear, yet Roland adopted and bore it bravely, and turning his back, as he certainly believed, for ever on Ardgowrie, departed to rejoin his regiment.

CHAPTER IV

"PONTIUS PILATE'S GUARDS."

"Welcome back Ruthven!" cried Hector Logan.

"Ruthven, my hearty, how goes it with you?"

"Glad to see you with us again, though regret that you have crape on your arm."

Such were the greetings of Roland on his first appearance at mess, when he rejoined, warmly welcomed by all; even the usually stolid visages of the mess-waiters brightened as he took his seat.

"A fresh cooper of wine to drink the health of Roland

Ruthven," exclaimed the President, who, though a young sub, had seen powder burned with the Royals in Burmah. "Welcome back to the Guards of Pontius Pilate!"

He had not been very long absent, but after all he had undergone at Ardgowrie it was a relief to Roland to hear the old "shop" talk again—the old regimental jokes and news, who was for guard to-morrow, who was on detachment; a moose-hunting party bound for the shore of the St. Lawrence; how the last time "the Darnel's phaeton was tooled by Logan, the horses "come home with devil a thing but the splinter bar at their heels; the expected "row" with the colonists; the ball or race that was coming off; the buttons of this corps, the facings or epaulettes of that corps, and so forth.

His old chum, Hector Logan, a tall and very handsome fellow, and some others, could see by the deepened lines between Roland's dark eyebrows, that something even more than his father's death affected him; and also, that his old flow of brilliant conversation was gone. They could detect that "something was wrong—a screw loose somewhere," but could not conceive what it was.

Ere he rejoined he had commissioned Logan to sell his horses—even to Royal Scot, with whom he was wont to ride over the raspers everywhere; to withdraw his name from several races and subscription lists; and he had every way curtailed his expenses—shorn down everything to the great surprise of more than one heedless young fellow, and of the mess in general.

D

"What the deuce does it all mean?" they asked of one another.

"What is up, Ruthven?" asked Logan seriously; "is there anything wrong? Your father dies, leaving you a fine old estate totally unencumbered—a deuced deal more than we can say for many old estates—and you sell off your horses, dogs, and so forth——"

"How do you know it is unencumbered?" asked Roland, with some sharpness of manner. "It is loaded—heavily loaded, indeed!" he added, bitterly, as he thought of the long-hidden *will*.

"Are you going in for a new excitement—that of being poor?"

"Oh, Hector, you don't know who it is you chaff! Are the Darnels in Montreal?" he asked, after a pause.

"Yes;" I saw la belle Aurelia yesterday in busy Paul Street, close to the Hôtel-Dieu; I knew her at once by the long glossy ringlet, the *suivez-moi*—come-follow-me-lads—that hung down her back."

"How your tongue runs on, Hector!"

"Pardon me; I forgot that you were hit in that quarter."

"Positively, Hector, I'll punch your head."

"A fellow always makes a fool of himself about some girl or woman at some time, and it is your case now, though I must admit that Aurelia Darnel is one of the most attractive girls I have seen, and does credit to your taste, Roland. Now that you are Laird of Ardgowrie you'll make great running in that quarter."

'Aurelia is too rich to care a straw even about Ardgowrie."

" I don't know that, Ruthven."

But the latter was in no mood for jesting, especially on such a subject, and abruptly spoke of something else ; for now, with all his intense longing to see Aurelia once more, he actually dreaded the thought of meeting her.

" Better that I should avoid her, but in doing so, what will she think of me ? " he pondered, while manipulating a cigar (we had not yet fought in the Crimea, thus cigarettes were as yet unknown among us). " To see her again will be but torture. What course ought I to follow—must I pursue, when, penniless as I know myself to be *now*, her love is denied me ! I must quit even the dear old regiment in time, and begin a life of exile in India."

The latter conviction, which had come strongly home to the heart of Roland Ruthven, filled him with sincere regret, for he loved the Royals, and was proud of them.

A regiment, old in history, is, says some one (Kinglake, we think), like the immortal gods, ever young and ever glorious.

And great, indeed, in fame, rich in glory, and old in history, are the First Royal Scots—the most ancient regiment in the world, for their traditions go back in an unbroken line to the twenty-four Scottish Guards of Charles III. of France ; thence to the Scottish Garde du Corps which saved the life of St. Louis in 1254 in Palestine, and fought in all the wars of France, at

Agincourt, the conquest of Naples, and at Pavia, where they were nearly cut to pieces; even Francis was taken prisoner.

In after years there were engrafted on them the remains of those gallant Scottish bands which served in Bohemia under Sir Andrew Gray, and under Sir John Hepburn in all the wars of Gustavus Adolphus, and as the regiment of the Lords Douglas and Dunbarton—Dunbarton of "the druns"—they returned to Scotland after the Restoration, and now at this day their standards are so loaded by embroidered trophies, that the blue silk—the national colour of Scotland—is nearly hidden, while the *mere list* of the battles and sieges in which they have been engaged—ever with glory and honour—occupy ten closely printed pages of the War Office Records. Even their rivals for three hundred years, the famous Regiment de Picardie, could not equal this, though in the French service they were wont to quiz the Royals as having been "the Guards of Pontius Pilate who slept upon their posts"

In all the armies of Europe we can find no parallel to their annals, for there is nothing like it in the military history of any other country.

Among all our noble British Infantry—that infantry which, as Bonaparte said, "never knew when it was beaten," and which, as Green tells us in his "History of the English People" was first created when William Wallace of Elderslie, drew up his Scottish spearmen, in these solid squares before which the united chivalry of England and Aquitaine went down: Amid all our "unconquerable British Infantry," we say, none have such a brilliant inheritance of glory as the old Royal Regiment.

Hence it was that Roland Ruthven, whose family had served with it for three or four generations, looked forward with extreme reluctance and regret to the coming time when, by exchange or otherwise, he would be compelled to serve in the ranks of another; and that the time was not a distant one was rendered fully evident by letters which he had received from his legal agents, Messrs. Hook and Crook, W.S., Edinburgh.

These assured him that they had obtained some certain knowledge of the movements and marriage of his uncle Philip, and of his having left heirs. They had traced him to Jamaica, and would ere long send proofs of the said marriage, and of there being an heir to Ardgowrie.

"An heir to Ardgowrie!" muttered Roland, through his clenched teeth. Half expected though the tidings were, they sounded like a species of death-knell to him now.

"You look disturbed, old fellow," said Hector Logan, as Roland crushed up and then tore the letter to pieces.

"I am disturbed!" said he.

"What are these—lawyer's letters?"

"Yes, Hector."

"Hah—a lawyer I always look upon as a species of rook with a devil of a long bill. You'll get over it, I hope," he added, rolling the leaf of his cigar round his finger.

"I have got over it already," replied Roland; but his looks belied his words; "but it is hard to have one's first and dearest hopes blighted," he continued, thinking of Aurelia Darnel; "disappointments, however, I suppose we get used to, like the eels to the skinning."

"Can I help you, Ruthven? Logan Braes are not exactly like the Bank of England; but if a few hundreds ——"

"You cannot help me, old fellow—thanks."

"Why?"

"I cannot, and may not, tell you; it is a family trouble—a secret, and a sore one."

Some days elapsed before—under the alteration of his circumstances—he could summon up courage to visit the Darnels; but he felt the imperative necessity of doing so, after all the hospitality he had received; and then he would gradually cease to go near them, whatever view might be taken of his changed conduct; but after all that *had* passed between himself and Aurelia one visit was necessary, and then—what next?

He shivered as he thought of it with sorrow and shame.

CHAPTER V

At the usual hour for an afternoon visit Roland Ruthven, in his blue undress uniform, with the handsome gilt shoulder scales then worn (mufti was forbidden), left his sword in the entrance hall, and was duly ushered into the handsome and spacious drawing-room of the Chateau de St. Eustache, as Mrs., or rather Madame, Darnel's abode was named, for she was a French Canadian, a widow and the heiress of one of those seigneuries which are in so many instances in possession of the families endowed with them by the kings of France.

Over these seigneuries they formerly exercised the rights of *haute, moyenne, et basse justice ;* but these have become obsolete since Wolfe carried the British colours up the heights of Abraham, and they are now reduced to the right of building a mill, at which the vassal must grind his corn at a fixed rate, and a fine if he desires to sell the load which he holds from his overload.

Much of the reserve and pride of the old noblesse of France still hover about these Canadian seigneurs, and Madame Darnel possessed these characteristics in a very high degree.

Neither she nor Aurelia were in the room, so Roland had a little time to collect his thoughts.

How much had happened—how altered were all his views and hopes of life—since last he had sat on that particular sofa, and beheld the view from these windows!

He had come hither from the barracks on foot, as he had sold off all his horses now, and he thought sadly—could it be otherwise—of the stable court at Ardgowrie, with all its excellent stalls fitted with enamelled mangers and encaustic tiles, and the artistic devices on the iron heel posts, and for holding the pillar reins.

This visit over, he thought he would go moose-hunting with Logan and some others : activity out of doors being the best cure for love according to certain writers. "Men try wine and cards," says Yates, " both of which are instantaneous but fleeting remedies, and leave them in a state of reaction, when they are doubly vulnerable ; but shooting or hunting, properly pursued, are thoroughly engrossing while they last, and when they are over necessitate an immediate recourse to slumber from the fatigue which they have induced."

But while making these resolutions Roland, like one in a dream, watched the view from Madame Darnel's windows : Montreal, the largest of the three elevations near the city so named—its base surrounded by country houses, with orchards and gardens, and its summit covered with foliage ; the city itself, with its lofty edifices of dark limestone or of painted wood, its churches, monasteries, its glittering spire, its shipping,

and the St. Lawrence winding far away in the distance,
till he was roused by the rustle of a silk dress, and
Aurelia Darnel stood before him, and her hand was in
his.

"Miss Darnel!"

"Mr. Ruthven!"

The latter was the less self-possessed of the two.

"I knew, Mr. Ruthven, that you would come to
Montreal again," said Aurelia, with one of her brightest
smiles.

"Were it but for a moment like this, I should have
come," said Roland, under the charm of her presence,
forgetting the *rôle* he intended to adopt; "and your
mamma?"

"Is, unfortunately, from home; need I say how
sorry we were for the sad occasion which hurried you
away."

Roland coloured with pain, vexation, and sorrow;
and before him seemed to stand that horrible "last
will and testament," which beggared him! Aurelia
Darnel, who had occupied his entire thoughts since he
left Montreal, was beside him now; but he had only
common places, the merest platitudes to offer her. His
innate pride, tenacity, and over-sensitiveness, now that
he was poor, and she was rich—he little knew *how*
rich—tied up his tongue, and the love, he trembled to
avow, remained unspoken.

We have already partially described Aurelia Darnel
and the character of her beauty. She was a girl of

talent, with many accomplishments. Her French, of course, was perfect, as she inherited it from her mother; she played brilliantly, with a soft yet dashing touch; she could sing little *chansons* in the most seductive way, and was full of those pretty graces and mannerisms which are peculiar to continental girls; she had, too, a way of looking down, drooping her long dark eye-lashes, that was often the cause of more tenderness and admiration in those she meant to dazzle, than when she looked up, or straight forward.

Offers she had had in plenty, and for two seasons she had been the reigning belle of Montreal. By a subtile perception, Roland had been distinctly conscious that she preferred him to any other man of her acquaintance, and that her eye brightened and her smile sweetened at his approach.

He had ever felt a strange joy in her society, and a pride in being seen with her, for is it not something to excite envy and jealousy by being the favoured partner of the acknowledged belle of every ball! In attractiveness her tone and manner were quite different to all that Roland had met before, and yet he had moved in the best society everywhere.

Though but a few months had elapsed since he saw Aurelia last, her figure seemed to have attained more roundness than before, and her soft features a more decided character; most winning and shy was her smile, most graceful her carriage, and sweet was her voice when she welcomed him to Montreal again.

" It is eight whole months since I had the pleasure of seeing you last, Miss Darnel," said he, after a rather awkward pause.

" Eight months—yes, true."

" A gap in life—in my life at least."

" Filled up by sadness ? "

" Exceeding sadness, and much mortification," said he.

" I was but a little girl when papa died, yet I can remember what a wrench it was. In losing your father—"

" I lost more than him."

" More ! "

She looked up at him inquiringly; could he tell her all he had lost—his heritage—his grand old baronial home, a princely estate—even honour itself, for thus, in his over-sensitiveness, did Roland view the matter of the long-hidden will!

" If matters remain quiet here among the colonists, Miss Darnell, I mean to leave the regiment."

" Leave the Scots Royals—the Royal Regiment ! " she exclaimed with surprise; " I thought it was the second home of your family; I have often heard you say so."

" It can no longer be mine."

" Why ? "

" For reasons that I cannot tell—even to you."

" Ah, pardon me; but what do you mean to do ? "

" Soldier still—of course."

" But where ? "

" In India."

" In India ! " she exclaimed, with a depth of interest that made Roland's heart beat wildly ; " oh, how far, far away ! "

" Far away from you ;—oh, Miss Darnel—Aurelia ! " His heart was rushing to his head.

At that moment a visitor, Colonel Smash, of U.S. army, was announced, and Roland withdrew, leaving unsaid all that he ought to have said—that she expected him to say, and what he would have said, but for the secret of that accursed cabinet of Scindia.

Could she have looked into his heart and read his thoughts, through the window which Vulcan wished had been placed in every human breast !

Both Aurelia and Madame Darnel had a right to expect something more to develop itself from the visit of Roland ; but he felt himself a very craven, and retired, leaving her with the most absurd of her many admirers, Colonel Ithurial Smash, a long-legged, hard-featured, and most ungainly New Yorker, whose rivalry was too contemptible for Roland's consideration, though he did marvel whether one could "possibly parade a fellow," for interrupting one's conversation with his cousin—for in this degree of relationship the " Colonel" somehow stood to Aurelia Darnel.

CHAPTER VI.

AFTER this, many days elapsed, and Roland, having ever before him the last crushing communication of Messrs. Hook and Crook, never went near the Chateau de St. Eustache, much to the surprise of Logan, whose mind was sorely exercised on that subject, and on some new and unwonted peculiarities of temper and system which he discovered in his old friend and once jolly comrade.

Aurelia, too, felt some surprise at his protracted absence, and that she never saw him at the promenades and public places where she had been wont to see him before.

She was thinking could he have fallen in love with some one else—she always thought he loved *her*—some one in Scotland where he had been ? If so, what business had he to come to her and talk, and act, and look, too, as if he were free and fetterless? Could he have been playing with her, making a fool of her all along ? How coldly and quietly he had talked about going to India, too.

Ah no ! could she have seen Roland Ruthven at that very time ! He was kissing, looking at, smoothing out, and caressing a tiny kid glove, which he had begged from her at that very ball where they first met, on the 5th of August—the fatal day of the Ruthvens, as Elipat Gorm was wont to call it.

"Roland, old fellow," said Logan, dropping into his quarters one evening when he was dressing for mess, "what is up—you look like the ace of spades? Never saw a fellow so changed in all my life."

"One day you may know all, Hector—meantime, don't worry me," replied Roland, with the hair brushes suspended in action above his thick head of dark brown hair, while Logan smoked and talked. His toilet table bespoke taste and that wealth which he no longer possessed, with its ivory-handled brushes having on them the Ruthven arms; his dressing-case of silver-gilt, with gold-topped essence bottles in nests of blue velvet; rings, jewelled studs, and sleeve-links, lay there scattered about, with pipe heads of rare fashion and costly material.

"You are not using that girl well, Roland—you know what I mean; before you went on leave you were like her shadow, and now——"

"I can't get over my scruples about—about——"

"What, in the name of heaven?"

"Well, about making up to a girl who has a fortune —a very handsome income, at all events—when I am so out at the elbows."

"Out at the elbows—are you mad?"

"The thing would look ill—yet I *could* make a little

running with her," said Roland, with a dreary attempt
to be lively.

"I should think so. Ruthven of Ardgowrie out at
the elbows—why, man alive, what the devil has come
to you? You could marry Miss Darnel without
exciting anybody but her special admirers. There is no
'establishment' to break up; no fair denizen of such
a villa as is proverbial at St. John's Wood to tear her
dyed locks, and demand a monetary kind of 'loot'—
so I say again, what the deuce has come to you?"
asked Logan, with genuine surprise.

"That which I cannot tell."

"Even to me?" asked the other reproachfully.

"Even to you, old fellow, just yet.

"This passes my comprehension."

"The misfortune that has befallen me passes mine."

"She is a delightful girl, Roland," said Logan, after
a pause, during which he had been reflectively preparing another cigar; "she never misses fire in the
way of a repartee or a brilliant rejoinder."

"In that I agree with you," replied Roland, quietly.

"How cold you are."

"I am far from feeling so, any way," said Roland,
with a sigh.

"Can't make you out, by Jove! In the Chateau de
St. Eustache, unless I am very much mistaken, you
have gone in for some very effective bits of flirtation, in
which the inconstant moon played no inconsiderable
part."

" Flirtation, Logan?　I never could flirt with Aurelia Darnell."

" Indeed !" said the other incredulously; " why ? "

" Because I love her too sincerely."

" Yet you never go near that house where you have often acted almost as host to the whole garrison, and where that horrible Yankee Colonel has the field all to himself."

" Oh ! he is a cousin of some sort—but what the devil is he to me ? "

" Well—he is a good shot I hear."

" A shot—d—n him !" said Ronald, with considerable irritation of manner; " I would think very little of parading *him* on the other side of the Canadian frontier."

" I don't doubt that, Ronald, old man ; but he has fought several duels, and successfully I hear."

" With double-barrelled rifles, at two hundred yards' distance, each man posted behind a tree, and dodging every way to dodge the other's fire. Well, I would meet him that way if he wished it.　I have asked the Colonel to mess."

" To mess ? "

" Yes."

" That fellow !　What will the Colonel and others think?　Your reason is, I suppose, to keep up a connecting link with the Chateau ? "

" Perhaps so," said Roland, wearily; and, sooth to say, that was his sole reason.

" Well, if with the rental of Ardgowrie, you can't—— "

" Please not to speak of Ardgowrie," said Roland impatiently, as he thrust himself into his shell-jacket; " there go the drums for mess."

It was impossible that Aurelia could have any regard, even amenity, for this horrible American cousin, the Colonel; yet if she had, Roland felt that the changed circumstances of his own fortune tied up his tongue and would render his attentions an interference; yet it was scarcely possible for him to look on such a dangler or admirer with total indifference.

The Colonel, of whom we shall have more to relate anon, came duly to mess, where his appearance and bearing caused some speculation, and not a little secret mirth among Roland's brother officers, who were all men of a very good style and tone.

Lean, wiry, and powerfully made, he was above the middle height, had sharp aquiline features of an exaggerated type, that might not have been bad but for a chronic expression of vulgar suspicion and 'cuteness that played about his eyes, giving him a rather hang-dog look; moreover, he had lost three front teeth in a row in Arkansas. He was closely shaven all save a long square goatee imperial that quivered when he spoke. Then he had a nervous way of clutching his hat and banging it against his thigh, with a curious but unmeaning energy. His clothes were loosely made, and he wore enormous cuffs, collar and studs. Every way,

E

he looked, as Logan said, "like a man you would rather drink with than fight with, any day."

The Colonel had of course the usual American ideas about equality, and "the sovereign people," with considerable contempt for the little island, from whence "the Britishers came."

Doubtless he had never seen such a dinner-table as the mess of the Royals before, with all its massive and magnificent silver trophies, epergnes, and goblets—even the White House could not equal it; thus his utter bewilderment excited as much amusement as his *gaucherie*, for he picked his teeth with a silver fork, rinsed his mouth with the contents of his finger-glass, and so forth; but he made good use of his time in more ways than one, as we shall show.

"Strike me ugly, but this is a fine set of fixings! and that one in particular," he added, tapping with his knife a magnificent vase presented to the corps by its colonel, the late Duke of Kent.

As a friend of the Darnels, Roland was very attentive to "the Colonel," who was very loquacious on the subject of the local excitement among the Canadians of the Lower Province, then agitated by factious men who sought to dictate to the Government measures which were not deemed conducive to the welfare of the State, were actually preparing to rise in arms, and counted on the sympathy and support of American filibusters and all manner of desperate and broken fellows from beyond the frontier.

During the summer of that year, and while Roland had been in Scotland, the House of Assembly had refused to proceed in its deliberations until the demand for a total alteration of the legislative powers was complied with; and this was followed by the appearance of many of the colonists in arms, and by serious violations of the law.

On these matters, and the prospects of a row with the authorities, "the Colonel" was more loquacious than became a guest at a regimental mess; but more than once his phraseology excited the risibility of even the waiters. When offered wine, he asked if he "couldn't get some egg-nogg." He described the dry goods store he had once kept at Baltimore, and of the two clubs there, of which he was chairman, the "black snakes" and the "plug uglies," and Roland's bewilderment grew very great to think that such a man as this could be even an acquaintance, far less some remote kinsman of Aurelia Darnel.

Like all Americans, he boasted a good deal and had a sovereign contempt for every other constitution in the world save that of the United States, draining all kinds of wine in quick succession, and ever and anon announcing that he "was dry as thunder," till Roland felt as one in a fever for having such a guest, and saw the commanding officer regarding him with a rather mingled expression of face.

In short, it proved in the end that Colonel Smash was a spy of the intended insurgents, and contrived to glean up a considerable amount of information as to the positions and strength of the Queen's troops in Lower Canada, all of which he duly committed to his note-book.

He sat late, or early rather, and never left the mess table till the sweet, low notes of the old Scottish *réveille* were waking the echoes of the lonely barrack-square when he went forth, as Logan said, "like an inveterate soaker, without a hair of his coat being turned."

Assisted by Roland, through the medium of cigars and brandy-and-water, Logan was going over the books of his company, to wit, the ledger, day-book, and the acquittance roll, which is rendered every month to the commanding officer—an investigation to Hector of a very solemn nature, whereat there was much occasional anathematising, twisting of the moustache, appealing glances cast to the ceiling, a secret totting off of sums under the table, much rubbing of the chin, and many references to a ready-reckoner—when they were inter-rupted by the adjutant, who came clattering in with sword and belt on, and his face full of importance.

" What's the row ? " asked Logan, looking up.

" Row enough ! " replied the adjutant, laughing ; " these colonial beggars are up in arms, and four com-panies of ours have to take the field to-morrow in the direction of Chambly, with some cavalry, a howitzer, and two six-pounders ! "

" Bravo—anything is better than *this* sort of work ! "

exclaimed Logan, tossing the books aside. "At what hour do we fall-in?"

"Immediately after the men have breakfasted."

Roland looked at his watch; the November evening was darkening fast; he borrowed the adjutant's horse, gave a few instructions rapidly to his servant, and in a few minutes more was spurring in the direction of the Château de St. Eustache.

Come what might of it, he had resolved to see once more Aurelia Darnel, and bid her farewell.

CHAPTER VII.

"LOVE WAS YET THE LORD OF ALL."

MANY mails had come to headquarters without any fresh intelligence from Messrs. Hook and Crook concerning the lost or rival heir to Ardgowrie, and Roland Ruthven had gathered a little courage from that circumstance, and with it even love strengthened in his heart as he rode on.

What a credit such a wife, such a girl, such a brilliant young matron, as Aurelia would be, representing at balls, dinners, and everything, the married ladies of the regiment! She would be the veritable Queen of the Scots Royals! But that could not—might not be, so far as Roland was concerned if the heir of his uncle

were actually found; and in this mingled mood of mind
he spurred onward the adjutant's horse, in a mode that
must rather have surprised that quiet quadruped, to bid
Aurelia, it might be, a last farewell.

With all the advantages of a highly cultivated mind,
trained in one of the best West End educational establishments, she possessed all the attractive manners of a
French girl, with the honest fearlessness of an English
one, innocent of worldly trickery and the deceits of
society, and yet she was a girl well calculated to shine
amidst that charmed circle.

Roland had shown her innumerable attentions, but,
as we have elsewhere said, till he could arrange with
his father as to his future he had spoken no word distinctly of love to her yet; and now he dared not!

The polite or politic coldness he had displayed of late,
was thus very different to the bearing towards her
which the girl, from his past conduct, had every right
to expect. She was piqued and rather prepared for a
flirtation with Logan or any one else; and thus at
balls or elsewhere a lot of men were always hovering
about her, among whom was too often the obnoxious
Colonel Smash, the low state of whose exchequer would
have made an alliance with the heiress of St. Eustache a
very pleasant speculation.

Roland, with his pay only, or little more—the sum
he accorded to himself out of the rents of Ardgowrie,
and meant to refund—felt that he had no right to ask
her hand, or seek to lure her from amid objects and

associations endeard to her by taste and her earlier
years, and, more than all, from the luxuries by which
she was surrounded.

And yet it was with him, as it is with some others,
barriers to his hopes and wishes only made these wishes
and hopes all the more keen ; and thus whenever he
left her he would pause and commune with himself
from time to time, conning over her words and her
glances, as if to glean therefrom whether he was indifferent to her or not.

The doubts and fears that agitated Roland's heart
were painful and poignant; had he been as he ought to
have been, Laird of Ardgowrie, fortalice and manor,
wood and mountain, with what honest confidence would
he have told her of the love he dared not speak of
now !

Yet it was so sweet to dream on ; for the artless simplicity of Aurelia's manner, and the freshness of her
untutored heart, had led him to know and feel that the
greatest personal attractions may be second to excelling
qualities in the girl one loves.

When he entered the familiar drawing-room, with its
air of culture and wealth, pictures, statuettes, and
bronzes, and saw from the windows the familiar view
he might now be looking upon for the last time,
Aurelia did not hear him announced. She was alone,
seated at the piano, and singing one of those *Chansons
Canadiennes*, as they are named, which she had learned
from her mother, for among the French Canadians of

all ranks there linger yet the *chansons, refrains,* and *barcarolles,* brought from Brittany and La Vendée by their ancestors three hundred years ago; and when Roland suddenly appeared by her side, she started, and arose, surprise mingling with her smile of pleasure, as the hour was an unusual one for a visit.

"I do not ask you to resume your singing, Miss Darnel," said Roland, in a voice that lacked all firmness, "as I have but a few minutes to remain with you, and these may, perhaps, be the last we shall ever spend together."

Her glance drooped, then she lifted her long, silky and most killing lashes, and Roland gazed with unconcealed tenderness into her eyes, which were of that deeply dark blue, which at times and in some lights, especially by night, seem almost black.

"You are, then, going to India?" she asked, in a breathless voice.

"No, Miss Darnel; and yet I am come to say good-bye."

"Good-bye?"

"We take the field to-morrow."

"Against whom?" she asked, growing very pale; "the Insurgents?"

"Yes—the French malcontents and others, I am sorry to say."

"And to-morrow—oh, that is sudden indeed—mamma is from home—and—and——"

Roland could see how her bosom heaved; his heart

was rushing to his head, and he drew nearer to her. A black velvet riband, that hung down her back from her delicate white neck, was awry; he put it straight, and then trembled. No one surpassed Roland Ruthven in confidence with women, or at a little bout of *persiflage* with a jolly flirting girl; but now he was very silent and sad.

The frill of lace that encircled her neck was ruffled in one place, and by a delicate and almost caressing touch he smoothed it as her own brother might have done; then his hands stole softly downward and took each of hers, while his heart beat like lightning.

" Miss Darnel."

She was trembling now, and her sweet face quivered.

" Aurelia."

" Well, Mr. Ruthven."

" I am about to leave, it may be for ever."

" Do not say so! " she said, almost imploringly, while her eyes filled with tears.

" If anything in this world could make me feel like the Roland Ruthven of a year ago, hopeful, trustful, and happy, it is to see that I am not indifferent to you. Aurelia—my love—my darling! "

She looked at him wistfully for a moment, and ere her white eyelids drooped, a long kiss came, and then a silence, full of happiness most strangely blended with an emotion of intense gratitude, while his arm went round her, and her face was nestled in his neck, and he began, at broken intervals, much that was soft nonsense; but "it was the nonsense which every woman loves to hear from one man (at least) during her lifetime."

Then suddenly, while still retaining her hands, and looking at her with infinite tenderness, he told of his great love for her, but how poverty had tied his tongue —poverty brought upon him through a will executed by his grandfather, which deprived him of all he possessed in the world, save his sword, for now the lost heir of Ardgowrie had been found, and no doubt by this time knew of his good fortune.

Roland had to repeat this more than once ere she quite understood him, for Aurelia felt as one in a dream —but a dream of happiness, for " is there any other time," says some one, " like that, when the knowledge comes upon you, that you are singled out, that you are admired most, that one other person is happy only when near you, that eyes are watching for your eyes, that a hand is waiting to touch your hand, when every speech has a new meaning, every word a bewildering significance."

" And you do love me ?" she asked, in a low cooing whisper that filled his heart with rapture; he could only utter a deep sigh, and kiss her again.

" And you are poor—Roland ? "

" As I have told you," he replied, his heart thrilling again at her utterance of his Christian name for the *first* time.

" Well—I am rich—all *I* have is yours; I am my

own mistress, and mamma loves me too well, and you also, to thwart our wishes."

"Darling Aurelia—it is incredible—that—-that——"

Roland knew not what he was about to say, so solved the difficulty with a long caress, from which Aurelia suddenly started back. as she now perceived they had a listener.

Unseen by both, Colonel Ithuriel Smash had been standing in the archway of the outer drawing-room, with a curiously malignant expression on his very marked visage, for he had evidently overheard and over-seen the whole interview. His presence occasionally at the Château de St. Eustache was only tolerated by Madame Darnel because he was penniless, his store in 75th Avenue having been sold up; and now he was foster-ing, on the strength of a very remote relationship, some very bold views with regard to Aurelia.

"Jerusalem, apple-sauce, and earthquakes, my young Britisher, but you make yourself quite at home in the house of my kinsman!" exclaimed the Colonel, who had concocted an effervescing drink in a long tumbler, and was leisurely stirring it with the jack-knife used by him for cutting his pig-tail tobacco; "I wonder blood has not been shed about you before this, Miss Aurelia Darnel."

"Blood!" exclaimed Roland, swelling with indig-nation.

"Jerusalem! but it may be shed soon."

"But, that I am under orders for Chambly to-morrow,

I might condescend to punish your insolence and your daring intrusion!"

Roland pressed the hand of Aurelia again, and in doing so deftly slipped a ring upon her engaged finger; he then kissed her deliberately and withdrew (just as the servants came in with lights), exchanging with Smash one of those unmistakable glances that is expressive of—and rivets for life—a hate that dies not, fired by the secret instinct of mutual enmity; yet Roland despised himself for having a foe so ignoble.

That night, without delaying an hour, Colonel Ithuriel Smash took his departure in the direction of *Chambly!*

Of so little importance had his presence been, that Aurelia never missed him as she sat alone, in a dream of joy that was not unclouded with anxiety for the cause of Roland's departure, and yet it was that event which brought the joy to pass, by laying bare the secret heart of each.

So the girl smiled fondly to herself, as she gazed at and kissed again and again her engagement-ring; and it seemed as if her former life had passed away and a new one of greater sunshine and brightness had begun; and long she sat there looking dreamily at the lovely moon (shining over the spires of Montreal), round as the shield of Fingal, her sweet face wreathed with smiles that no eyes could see, unless they were those of the old man who dwelleth therein.

CHAPTER VIII.

THE INSURRECTION.

ROLAND's heart was brimming with happiness and gratitude for the love and generosity of Aurelia Darnel, and it seemed actually to dance in his breast joyously, when, next morning, the four companies detailed for service marched from Montreal, with the colours flying, the bayonets fixed, and the band playing the old regimental quick-step of the pre-Revolution days, varied by the pipes,—

"Dumbarton's drums beat bonnie O,'

in memory of the Colonel, that loyal and gallant Earl, who followed his royal master into exile and died at St. Germains.

A hundred times Roland asked himself, why had he not tested the great love of Aurelia before? why had he lost so much time and so much happiness? A little time—the insurrection ended, and he would be by her side again, as he had somewhat needlessly assured her in a passionate little farewell note, dispatched that morning.

A little time? Alas, the first day of absence seemed to consist of at least seventy-two hours!

The force which now took the field by order of Lieutenant General Sir John Colborne (afterwards Lord Seaton), G.C.B., Colonel of the Cameronians, a wounded veteran of the Peninsular war, consisted of detachments of the 24th, 32nd, and 66th Regiments, with one howitzer, under the Hon. Colonel Charles Gore, son of the Earl of Arran, and afterwards Deputy Quartermaster-General in Canada, who marched towards St. Denis and St. Charles, with orders to arrest certain armed traitors who were alleged to be in these villages.

At the same time, Colonel Wetherall, with his four companies of the Royal Scots Regiment, Captain David's troop of Montreal Cavalry, a detachment of the 66th, and two six-pounders, was to move on the last-named village to assist a magistrate in executing the warrants.

The month was November, the weather severe, and the roads bad; the men were in heavy marching order, with knapsacks, great coats and blankets, camp-kettles, and with the arms and ammunition of the day, making up a load of seventy-five pounds twelve ounces per man; but all were in the highest spirits. Anything seemed better than moping in barracks, and when the music ceased as they marched "at ease," they made the forests resound to their merry choruses.

All parts of the country thereabout which have not been cleared for cultivation are covered with timber, and he alone, says a traveller, who has visited these

regions of interminable forest can form an adequate
idea of their dreariness, yet there the red oak, the
white pine, the beech, elm, cedar, and maple mingle
their branches *ad infinitum*.

Here and there a lonely clearing was passed, where,
amid lofty trees devoid of lateral branches, their stems
or stumps scorched and blackened by fire, stood the log
hut of a settler, who, with his wild-looking brood, came
forth to gaze with wonder, perhaps hostility, at the
passing troops.

In autumn these magnificent forests assume hues
of every shade—yellow, brown, and red—under sunsets
which present the most glorious assemblages of clouds.
But winter was the season now; the leaves had fallen;
the humming-birds and fire-flies had departed, and the
wild fowl had taken refuge on the lakes or the St.
Lawrence.

The force under Colonel Wetherall crossed the
Richelieu River by the upper ferry at the village of
Chambly, where, in the days of the monarchy, the French
had a strong palisaded fort; but the nature of the roads
and the unfavourable weather seriously impeded his
march, while information having reached him that the
rebels in arms at St. Charles had been greatly increased
in numbers, and had with them a number of lawless
American or Yankee "sympathisers," under his late
guest, Colonel Smash, whom he remembered at the
mess, eating peas with his knife and wiping his mouth
with the back of his hand; so he made a halt at

St. Hilaire, until he could be joined by a fifth company of the 1st Royal Scots under Hector Logan.

On that night it was evident that the country was alarmed. Instead of the stillness usual to the time, the clanging of church bells was heard at intervals, with the barking of dogs, the report of firearms occasionally, the blowing of conches and horns, red alarm-fires blazed up on the dark summits of the distant hills; and more than once horsemen in hot haste dashed past the advanced sentinels without responding to their challenge, and as the troops, as yet, were only acting in support of the civil power, they could not fire upon these strangers.

This was the night of the 24th November, and to Roland, like many others, it was a sleepless one, as he commanded an out-picket and had to visit his sentinels every hour.

On one side of his post rolled the mighty river, reflecting in its ripples the star-spangled sky; on the other, stretched away into darkness and utter obscurity the vast dingles of an American forest, planted and grown by nature.

His mind was full of that last evening with Aurelia and all its sweet details. On his odious rival he scarcely bestowed a thought, and he felt happier than an emperor in his palace, as he lay there, with his cloak around him, his sword and pistols at hand, his head pillowed on a pine-log, and all oblivious of the rattle-snakes, which there are six feet long. Near him was Robert Bruce, one of his sentinels, treading softly to

and fro, with bayonet fixed, and singing to himself the
old Scottish barrackroom ditty :—

> "Poor Willie was landed at bonnie Dumbarton,
>   Where the stream from Loch Lomond runs into the sea,
>   While at home in sweet Ireland, he left Mary Martin,
>   With a babe at her breast and a child at her knee."

The night passed in quietude, apart from the alarm-
ing sounds mentioned; on the 25th November the
march was resumed, and on coming within a mile of
St. Charles, puffs of white smoke spirted out of the
dark jungly brushwood on the opposite side of the
river, as the rebels daringly opened a straggling fire
upon Her Majesty's troops. A Royal Scot was struck
down by Roland's side, and several were wounded.

Rifle shots were also fired from a barn in front.

"Push on, Logan!" exclaimed Colonel Wetherall;
"push on and storm that place at the point of the
bayonet!"

Logan advanced with his company at a rush; his
powerful arm burst in the door; the place was taken, all
in it bayoneted or put to flight, and then it was set in
flames, the whole affair occupying little more than the
time we take to narrate the episode.

Near St. Charles were more than fifteen hundred in-
surrectionists under Papineau and Colonel Smash, posted
in a strong and closely stockaded work from which they
opened a sharp and serious fire, the echoes of which the
adjacent forest repeated with a thousand reverberations,

F

while the whole place seemed enveloped in white smoke, streaked with flashes of red fire.

The Royals responded with several rounds well thrown in; but they had stormed too many such works in Burmah, the land of stockades, to linger in attacking this one.

A breach was beaten in by axe and hammer, and cannon shot together. In three minutes the place was carried by storm and its occupants bayoneted, shot down, or put to flight; but not before seventeen of the Royals, and four of the 66th were killed, and a great number wounded, while Colonel Wetherall and Major Warde had their horses shot under them, and Roland's cheek was grazed by a rifle shot.

The mingled curses and imprecations, yells of agony and rage, seemed to fill the air, when the roar of the firing died away, and the prisoners were disarmed and secured. "Every officer and man behaved nobly," says the dispatch of Colonel Wetherall. "Major Warde carried the right of the position in good style, and Captain George Mark Glasgow's Artillery did good execution; he is a most zealous officer; and Captain David's troop of Montreal Cavalry rendered essential service during the charge."

The murder of stray soldiers from time to time, and particularly that of George Weir, a young lieutenant of the 32nd Cornish Light Infantry, who was bound to a cart, and hacked to pieces with his own sword, by certain miscreants (among whom Ithuriel Smash was

supposed to be one), now began to infuse in the minds
of the troops much of that rancour which adds to the
severity of a civil strife.

After the stockade had been uprooted and destroyed,
the troops returned to St. Hilaire and remained in
cantonments for three days. There a dragoon of the
Montreal Cavalry arrived with the mail, which brought
from Aurelia Darnel the first letter she had ever addressed him, and the sight of her hand-writing raised
Roland at once to the seventh heaven of delight. We
know not whether he kissed it, but think it extremely
probable that he did, if no one was near.

As the contents of love-letters are of interest to the
recipients thereof alone, and the said contents, with all
their half-fatuous endearments and double diminutives,
are at times rather grotesque, the reader need not be
troubled with that of Aurelia, save in one part thereof.

" I told dearest mamma of all that had passed between us, shewed her our engagement ring, and added,
that as soon as leisure permitted, you would write to
her on that subject. She was agitated, the dear old
soul, and tearful at the fear of losing me; but kissed
me many times, and said she was certain we would be
happy together, and that she loved you with all her
heart. Oh, think of that, Roland! But we shall have
mamma to live with us, won't we dearest, when I am
your own—your very own? She will be a comfort to
us both, and not at all like the proverbial ' mother-in-
law ' of the novel and play. But I must now conclude,

as we are both on the eve of starting for our Seigneury
of St. Eustache, where the French people are taking up
arms; but they love mamma so much, that she hopes
she may prevail upon them to refrain from breaking the
Queen's peace. So adieu till I write you from there,
dearest, dearest," &c., &c.

And then, of course, there was a postscript, containing
"cartloads of kisses."

Had she told Madame Darnel about the long-hidden
will and his changed circumstances?

Roland rather supposed not; she was generous and
loving enough, in her love and joy to have forgotten all
about the matter!

Roland found an entire day's occupation in reading
again and again the letter of Aurelia, nor was it fairly
consigned to that breast-pocket in his uniform which
contained her glove, till the warning drum beat on the
28th, when the troops marched to attack another body
of the rebels, who had taken post at Point Oliviere, and
had actually constructed there an abatis of felled trees
for the purpose of cutting off the retreat of Wetherall's
entire force!

But when the Royals came in sight, with their brass-
drums beating and fixed bayonets gleaming bright and
keen in the cold winter sun, and deployed from the
line of march with coolness and confidence into companies for attack, after exchanging a few shots, the
rebels lost all heart, and fled, with the loss of their
cannon, which Roland captured at the head of his com-

pany, sword in hand, together with twenty-five prisoners, and then rescued his captain, a brave fellow, who in the first advance got entangled among the branches of the abatis and ran thus the serious risk of being shot down helpless; and for all this, Roland was elaborately and honourably mentioned in Colonel Wetherall's dispatch to Sir John Colborne.

On the same day the Colonel's force returned to Chambly with the captured guns and prisoners; but though elated by their success every officer and man was suffering greatly from the heavy and chill rain which turned into mud the wretched roads that were already knee-deep in snow.

Meanwhile tidings reached them that the Queen's forces, under Colonel Gore, had encountered such formidable obstruction and opposition, and, moreover, endured so much from the severity of the Canadian winter, which had set in with all its bitterness, that they had been compelled to fall back from St. Denis, and retire.

Marching was now laborious work, for when frost came, the troops had to wear *creepers*, or plates of spikes strapped to their feet.

The snow lay so deep that one might almost imagine no power of the sun would ever melt it; and, at times, when the leafless trees are coated on every branch and twig with ice, whole forests seem to be turned into crystal, when the rays of light produce ten thousand prisms, and most wonderful is the effect if there is a slight breeze to set them in motion.

Wetherall had partially, by his great success, arrested the rebellion in his own quarter; but it was in all its strength elsewhere, and the troops had many severe and harassing duties to perform amid the frost and snow of a very severe winter. It has justly been said that the British officer is essentially a dandy, that "the neatly and closely cropped hair, the well-trimmed mustache, the set up figure, the spotless gloves, boots bright as a mirror, and the general air of dandyism are the outward symbols of those qualities which make men good soldiers."

It no doubt is so. The set up figure remained, but in Canada at that particular juncture, the dandyism had nearly departed, as much as it did in the Crimea.

Amid these duties, Roland could have no letters from Aurelia; neither could he write, for the postal arrangements were completely suspended, or could only be carried on by parties of armed men.

At last there came a day—one of horror—and Roland never forgot it!

"Look here, old fellow," said Logan, with a bright expression on his handsome face, bringing him a copy of the *Montreal Gazette* some weeks old; "as Byron says, 'pleasant 'tis to see one's name in print—'"

"Even in the 'Army List?'"

"Yes, and proud was I when first I saw my name there," said Logan.

"Well, whose name is in print now?"

"Yours."

"Mine!" A sickening thought occurred to Roland of the story of the concealed will, Ardgowrie, and the discovered heir or heirs, for though he had schooled himself to face the idea, it was a bitter one; therefore, it was only a relief to his mind to find, that the matter referred to, was the fact that he was favourably mentioned and thanked in General Orders by Sir John Colborne, commanding Her Majesty's forces in Canada, "for his gallantry displayed on the 28th of November last, at the abatis of Point Oliviere."

As he read it he thought of Aurelia, and the pleasure such a notice would afford her; and was carelessly running his eyes over the columns of the paper, when they caught her name—*her name*—and mentioned in a way that made his blood turn alternately cold as ice, and hot as fire!

When proceeding in her sledge, with her daughter Aurelia, Madame Darnel had been stopped and surrounded near her own seigneury "by a band of rebels under the notorious Colonel Smash, for whose arrest a reward is now offered."

The old lady had been subjected to such violence, that she had fainted and been borne to the house of the curé insensible, while her beautiful daughter was brutally carried off by the "Yankee Sympathiser," and was now, if alive, a helpless prisoner in his hands at St. Eustache.

Roland was petrified with grief and dismay by intelligence, so deplorable—so terrible! Logan, full of just anger and great indignation, was speaking to him, but Roland knew not what he said.

The former was recalling the views "the Colonel" had with regard to Aurelia; he recalled, too, his eaves-dropping, his rancorous hatred, threats, and jealousy; he recalled, also, the whole character and bearing of the man, and when he thought of the soft, gentle, and beautiful Aurelia being helpless in his power, at such a time, when the whole of Lower Canada was rent by civil dissension, outrage, and bloodshed, and when the Queen's troops were menaced everywhere, the heart of Roland seemed to die within him!

Again and again had Roland thought, while angry pride mingled with love and gratitude, that in marrying Aurelia, he would deprive her of no luxury to which she had been accustomed,—horses and carriages in summer, the sledge in winter, a dressing maid, or the thousand and one little things which wealth can procure, because *she* had that; but he had longed to make her mistress of Ardgowrie!

Now—now, when he had lost her, perhaps for ever, how pitiful and minor seemed all such considerations.

CHAPTER IX.

THE ABDUCTION OF AURELIA.

In the main, the newspaper report was correct.

Madame Darnel, with the amiable object in view stated in the letter of Aurelia, had been proceeding with her toward her own estate, which was near the pleasant and well-built village of St. Eustache, in Lower Canada. It consisted then of about a hundred houses, a handsome church and parsonage, and is situated near the mouth of the river Du Chine.

Her sledge was a handsome and fashionable one; the day was clear and bright, the snow, though deep, was frozen hard, and the sledge glided along delightfully. It was drawn by two fine horses, with showy harness, set off by high hoops with silver bells on the saddles, with rosettes of ribbon and streamers of coloured horse-hair on the bridles; and Aurelia—her charming face flushed and pinky with frosty air, a cosy boa round her slender neck, her hand, through gloved, inserted in a sable muff,—was enjoying to the utmost the gay jingle of the bells, the nice crisp sound of the runners of the sledge, when suddenly and involuntarily a shrill scream broke from her, when at a turn of the road near the river, where the cuttings in the banked-up snow lay deep between two rows of picket-fencing, a musket was fired, and their driver fell forward, a corpse, shot through the head, and the vehicle was surrounded by a mob of men.

Infuriated or sullen, but all ruffianly in aspect, these men nearly all wore fur caps, with large flaps down their cheeks, enormous pea jackets or blanket coats patched and tattered, with India-rubber shoes, or moose-skin mocassins, or thick cloth boots with high leggings.

All were armed with pikes, pitch-forks, swords, and pistols; many had fowling pieces; many more had muskets and bayonets, and wore cross-belts stolen from Government armouries or stripped from the slain; and some carried their ammunition in hunting pouches and shot bags.

One who seemed the leader wore a huge coat of buffalo hide, and looked like some great wild animal, for of the human face, nothing was visible, but a long blue nose and a pair of red and blood-shot eyes.

"Jerusalem and ginger nuts, but that was a shot well put in!" exclaimed this personage, whose voice there was no mistaking, and the two horrified and help-less creatures found that they were in the hands of that gang of the insurgents—the most dastardly and lawless —led by Ithuriel Smash.

Their first emotions on finding themselves in the centre of such a savage throng, were undoubtedly those of extreme terror and shrinking delicacy; but Madame Darnel for a time forgot her naturally womanish apprehensions, collected the powers of her mind, and throwing up her veil, confronted the whole band, which mustered more than a hundred men.

Among that mob were many on whom Aurelia and her mother had conferred countless acts of kindness and charity in sickness and health; but, like low-born and ungrateful cowards, they hung back now, when they should have rushed to her defence.

Certainly, to some of the French insurgents, the appeal of Madame Darnel, a handsome woman about forty years of age, with an intelligent and sweet expression in her well-cut features, and every way a person of refinement and delicacy, was not without a little effect; but the announcement of Smash that her daughter was his affianced wife who "intended to slope with one of the 'tarnal Britishers," against whom they were in arms, deprived poor Aurelia of all sympathy, and a roar of menace escaped his hearers.

"Is this conduct your return for my kindness and charity to a creature so immensely beneath me?" asked Madame Darnel.

"As whom?" asked Smash.

"You, fellow!"

"D—n your cussed impudence! Now then, Aurelia, come along, white face. You look as if you required a box of our New York 'Never-say-die or Health-restoring pills,'" said Smash; and a shriek burst from the girl as his coarse fingers with their long spiky nails grasped her tender arm, and she was literally torn away from her horrified mother, who fainted, and was borne off by some of the better disposed to the house of the curé.

Followed by the armed rabble, the helpless Aurelia incapable of all resistance, was dragged through the village of St. Eustache, and taken a literal prisoner, or victim, to her mother's house which adjoined, the seigneury of the Darnels, wherein Colonel Smash had established his headquarters.

For a moment or two she thought to conciliate her chief captor.

Tears big and bright were welling in her dark blue eyes; her bonnet and veil had been torn off, and her dark hair all unconfined rolled over her back and shoulders, as she stood with clasped hands and pleading looks before the so-called Colonel.

"Do shake hands with me," she condescended in her first fear to say; "shake hands, Ithuriel—let us be friends, and send me back to mamma, or bring her here."

"Friends—friends be darned!" roared Ithuriel, whose plug of pigtail dropped out of his lantern jaws, after which he proceeded to air it on the point of his jack knife, while eyeing her with mingled malevolence and admiration, and seated himself on a table. "You won't give me a kiss, I suppose; but I can take as many as I like, I reckon; and you look as if you scarcely remembered me—Ithuriel Alcibiades Smash. Strike me ugly, but that's a bad compliment. But," added the bantering ruffian, "I calculate I'll survive it! Flirtation

and courtship are two very different things, Miss
Aurelia, and I ain't disposed to flirt with *you*, as you'll
find out before long."

Smash did not yet molest her; but she knew not what
he might do if he imbibed much brandy, as he had a
bottle beside him, and was helping himself liberally
to the contents thereof, while he talked; and she eyed
him with fast-growing alarm.

That he had shot the poor sledge-driver, an old and
faithful domestic whom she had known from childhood,
Aurelia never doubted; and that deed added to her un-
fathomable loathing and horror of him. She shivered
in his presence, and shuddered whenever he drew near
her. She glanced wildly at the room door, but escape
was hopeless. He saw the glance and laughed aloud.

Was she acting in a melo-drama with the ruffian, as
the heavy villain of the piece? Was it all a dream?
It almost seemed so, the whole situation with all its
contingent horrors and future uncertainties, appeared so
new, so unnatural and unreal! He seemed to read her
thoughts, for he said,—

"Was it not to spite that tarnation Britisher, who
used to come into the room with an opera hat under his
arm, like a roasted fowl with its gizzard, I might give
you a little time to think of marrying me."

"Marry *you!*" exclaimed Aurelia in a peculiar tone,
that filled him with rage and caused him to indulge in
much language that was "more pagan than parlia-
mentary" till he roused her scorn and anger.

" Coarse fool, and worse than fool! how dare you use language that is unfit for me to hear ? "

" 'Guess your Britisher will never see his wretched little island again—too many rifle bullets flying for that," said he irrelevantly, as he saw how every reference to Roland affected her. " You encouraged that 'ere Britisher," continued the Colonel, still airing his quid on his jack knife.

" Encouraged—how dare you say so ? "

" Dare—there is no daring in it, my dear. Who commands here—you or I ? "

" Sir, you presume upon your relationship in some way with mamma, to talk to me thus, surely."

" I presume only on my own love for you, and would keep you, a daughter of Canada, as I would a daughter of America, from the contamination of that 'tarnal red-coated British slave ! "

Still, as yet, save when dragging her to the house— her own father's house—he had not laid hands on her. With all his roughness and innate brutality, he felt that there was an undefinable something in the grand hauteur, the excessive delicacy, the tone of refinement, in the general aspect and bearing of Aurelia, that quelled, while it secretly " riled " him.

He noticed the very expression of her nostrils, the quiver of her proud lip and the flash of her dark blue eye—the flash of scorn and loathing when she replied to him, and he quailed under it—he, the utter American rowdy ! But this emotion began to die as he drained another bumper of stiff brandy and water, and he took to blustering and swearing again.

"Do not use language such as this—and to me," said Aurelia, putting her trembling hands to her ears; "surely you do not know the nature of oaths."

"Don't I? I calculate I've sworn enough to sink a seventy-four-gun ship," said he, with a mocking laugh; "but surely," he added, drawing nearer her, and adopting a coaxing tone and bearing, "in time you'll forget all about that fellow, and see the necessity of quietly becoming Mrs. Ithuriel Smash, when you cannot make a *better of it.*"

The girl's heart seemed to give a great bound, and then to die within her, at these words, the look that accompanied and the dreadful inference to be deduced from them.

"Anyhow, I calculate that I shan't forget the evening I saw you and that yaw-haw beast of a Britisher giving each other such nice tokens of your mutual good-will—he giving you what he calls his heart—and you making a free gift of the whole seigneury of St. Eustache! If once he comes within the reach of my rifle !"

The Colonel was unable to express what would happen then. He clenched hands and set his great yellow teeth with such force, that his quid slipped down his throat and nearly choked him.

Two or three days were passed by Aurelia in extreme misery and captivity, and almost hourly she was warned by Smash that his patience would soon be exhausted, and he would " send for the parson."

She secluded herself in her own room, and found for a little time a temporary protector in Papineau, one of the rebel leaders, a dapper little French colonist, who had now come to concert measures for the defence of the village, and urged that the young lady must not be intruded upon,

" Snakes alive ! man, don't I tell you she is to be my wife ? " roared Smash.

" *Mon Dieu*, my dear Colonel, that may be so," replied Papineau, taking a pinch in the old Parisian fashion ; " win the heiress, but woo her gently. A lady can only receive in her own apartment a clergyman or a doctor."

" And a hairdresser," added the barber of the village who was there, armed to the teeth.

" By Jerusalem, then, I'll go as a hairdresser and scalp her, if she gives me more trouble ! I'll teach her that I'm half-horse, half-alligator ! " exclaimed Smash, who by this time was intoxicated to a dangerous extent.

A violent illness—the fever of great fear—had prostrated Madame Darnel.

Separated from the latter, Aurelia was without the little protection her presence might have afforded. She was glad to keep beside the female domestics of the seigneury, from among whom she was often haled forth shrieking to endure the extraordinary love-speeches of Smash; at last the women quitted the house in terror, and she was left there alone—alone with a man whom she now loathed with a fear indescribable!

CHAPTER X.

THE END GROWING NEAR.

THE sea was frozen now for miles upon miles along the coast, there were no electric cables as yet, and inland all postal communication was cut off by concurrent events. No news came to Roland from Messrs. Hook and Crook, and for all that he knew to the contrary, the newly-found heirs might have eaten their Christmas pudding and drunk the new year in, at Ardgowrie!

But Roland gave not a thought to such matters now! He had become changed in appearance, too; he was thinner, and two or three lines appeared about his eyes, where none had been visible before; and times there were when he thought himself going mad, with the bitter strain upon his thoughts.

He had but a wild, clamorous craving and gnawing at the heart—a fierce longing to quit Chambly and set out for St. Eustache. But Roland Ruthven was a soldier of the Queen, and was chained to his post. His place was with the colours of the Royal Scots.

The cold at this time was intense; in the village

G

market-place were masses of beef, sheep, and deer frozen hard as they had been for months, having been killed when the severe weather first set in. There, too, were plucked fowls, fish of all kinds frozen hard, and eels as stiff as walking-sticks. Even the milk was sold by the pound, and the loaves of bread, frozen hard the moment they left the oven, had to be literally sawn into slices, and half-and-half grog froze.

The snow was deeper than it had ever been seen by that proverbial party who is to be found everywhere, "the oldest inhabitant," and military operations were out of the question. Guards, when relieving others, frequently took over the arms of the old guard being unable to carry their own; and once Roland found a sentinel frozen dead, hard and stiff and pale as the snow around him, in his sentry-box, with his glazed eyes glaring horribly out of their sockets. He was Robert Bruce, already mentioned, who, poor fellow, would sing upon his post no more.

But amid all this, the mess often thought and talked of punkahs, of Bengal curries, green chillies, devilled biscuits, and other "up-country" memories, as if the very mention of such things would keep them warm! And at that merry mess-table Roland always felt himself to be now—how different from past times!—the skeleton at the banquet.

But there comes an end to all things, and relief came ere long to the agonised mind of Roland. He was seated in his billet—a miserable wood-cutter's hut

at Chambly,—when, one morning, Hector Logan burst
in upon him like a gale of wind, bringing a tempest of
snow with him.

"News for you, Ruthven!" he cried, shaking himself like a Newfoundland dog; "splendid news! We
are to march at once."

"For where?"

"St. Eustache, my boy."

"St. Eustache!" exclaimed Roland, starting to his feet.

"St. Eustache it is. I have just seen the Colonel
with the General's order in his hand."

"Thank God!" exclaimed he, with great fervour;
"we shall soon gain tidings now—you know of
whom?"

"True, old fellow!"

"Yes—and vengeance too, perhaps!" added Roland,
but his heart sank at the thought of how unavailing
might be all human vengeance *now!*

Never did soldier prepare to take the field with
greater alacrity than Roland Ruthven. The chances of
Fate or of war might have compelled him to remain
where he was, like Tantalus, in his pool, or to move in
some other direction than St. Eustache!

It all came to pass thus.

The severity of the weather had abated a little, and
even while it lasted rapine and outrage had reigned
supreme in the disaffected districts. Sir John Colborne,
on the 13th December, with all his disposable forces,
set out on his march from Montreal, and Wetherall's

little column was to join him on the way to St. Eustache
to seize that place and scour the country about the Lake
of the Two Mountains, where the insurgents under
Papineau, Smash, and others had barbarously driven
out all the loyal inhabitants, leaving many of them to
perish miserably among the snow; and a vast extent of
country was ravaged and pillaged.

Sharing Roland's anxiety, Hector Logan was in the
highest spirits, when the troops moved off and turned
their backs on Chambly, as they devoutly hoped, for
ever.

Evening was approaching when the march began,
without music, and the drummers had their drums slung
behind them. The soldiers had their buff belts above
their great coats. The musket-locks had been inspected
and fresh ammunition served to all, which, as the men
said to each other smilingly, "looked like business."

" No ' beauty and the bowl' for us to night, Roland,
by Jove," said Logan, as he set his face to the fierce
northern blast, which came sweeping from the Pole
itself over half a world of snow, rasping the cheek like
the roughest file.

Roland commanded the advanced guard, which consisted of two sections, with detached files, and as they
were penetrating into disturbed districts, Colonel Wetherall repeated to him the usual orders and cautions
to be observed when entering defiles or hollow-ways,
ascending hills, with flank objects, and so on, and never
did the young officer feel more sternly zealous in his life.

After proceeding some miles, just as the moon rose and the guard entered a hollow-way, where the cutting in the drifted snow was deep, Roland heard his first advanced file challenge some one and cock his musket. Then a man on horseback appeared, who replied in broken English.

Roland drew his sword, and on hurrying to the front found that his next advanced files had stopped the stranger, who appeared to be a peasant—a French settler. He wore an old-fashioned *capote* and mocassins of cow-hide, and had a rifle slung across his back.

"You are a Frenchman, I perceive?" said Roland.

"Monsieur l'officier," replied the man, saluting him, "je suis Canadien."

"Why are you armed?"

"For my own protection, monsieur."

"That may or may not be. Where do you live?"

"My farm is on the Rivière de Chine."

"Has it been burned?"

"No, monsieur."

"That in itself looks suspicious," said Roland, while the stranger glanced uneasily at the dark mass of the grey-coated and cross-belted column, now descending the slope in the moonlight.

"From whence came you last?" asked Roland.

"The village of St. Eustache, monsieur."

Roland's heart leaped; it was with difficulty he could ask the next question.

Did he know aught of a young lady who was in the hands of the insurgents?

"Mademoiselle Darnel—yes, monsieur. She is still in the house of the Seigneur with Colonel Smash, or perhaps in the church which is fortified. She is married to him, people say—or, rather, *he* has married *her*," added the fellow, with a grin, which nearly tempted Roland in his then mood of mind to run him through the body.

He felt sick, sick at heart; but in a little time he would know all—the worst!

"Corporal Burns," said he, with a voice strangely broken, as the listening soldiers told, "take this fellow, with a file of men, to the rear. The Colonel may wish to question him. Forward, lads!" he added, as the peasant was taken, in great tribulation of mind, towards the column, and once more the march of the advanced guard was resumed, and Roland Ruthven tramped on, so full of agitating thoughts that he never knew his cigar had been cold and out for half an hour or more.

The junction was duly effected with the column of Sir John Colborne; the Royal Scots Regiment, the Montreal Rifles, and Globinsky's Volunteers, were formed in one brigade under Colonel Wetherall. The latter force was dispatched through the forests that border the upper road leading to the point to be attacked, with orders to drive back and disperse all pickets and parties of the insurgents, while the remainder of the brigade crossed the Ottawa, or Grande Rivière, on the ice on the 14th of December.

There along the Ottawa, the then snow-covered country is undulating, thickly covered with fine wood, except on the western bank of the river, where for some twelve miles have been laid out townships, chiefly occupied by Irish and American settlers. Below that of Chatham the old French Seigneuries begin.

The advance on the enemy's stronghold now began from several points.

In Roland's heart much of the ardour and fierce excitement incident to the march had died away, or rather taken the form of unspeakable anxiety and grief, especially when on the 14th of December he saw before him St. Eustache, with its wooden houses and orchards of bare apple-trees, the cold winter sunlight tipping the spire of the church, and the vanes of the large white house, wherein Roland knew that she might be, though the man taken over night informed Colonel Wetherall that it was not improbable she might be in the church, which the rebels considered the key of their position.

" Patience—patience ! " he muttered, "patience yet awhile ! "

No magistrate being with the troops, Sir John Colborne, while still at a little distance from the place, resolved to send forward an officer with the printed proclamation. For this service Roland at once volunteered. Tying a white handkerchief to the blade of his sword, in token of truce, he borrowed his friend the

adjutant's horse, and galloped forward to the first line
of stockades or outer defences, behind which the dark
forms of armed rebels were seen clustering thick as bees,
and at the windows of the seigneur's house.

The whole troops watched with anxiety the brief
parley that seemed to ensue; then it was suddenly cut
short by a lamentable crime. A stream of smoke came
from the window of a house, the report of a musket
rang out on the clear frosty air, Roland's horse was
seen to rear, with its rider lying back on the crupper,
but his knees still in the stirrups, to all appearance a
corpse, as Nolan's was borne back from Balaclava !

A shout of rage burst from the Royals; the artillery
opened, and all pressed forward to the attack, intent on
dire vengance, at a well-ordered rush.

By barricades, palisades, trenches, and loopholing
the houses, the church, and its presbytery, Papineau,
Smash, and their bands of rebels, had left nothing undone to render St. Eustache a somewhat formidable post;
and they were encouraged by the knowledge that other
bodies of their compatriots had fortified themselves at
St. Benoit and elsewhere.

These preparations had, luckily for poor Aurelia,
occupied much of her ungainly suitor's time, but he
found himself at full leisure on the eventful 14th of
December, and he began his system of annoyance
again.

"The Colonel" had never sacrificed much to the
graces, and his late occupations in St. Eustache had

effectually prevented him from doing so at all; thus his appearance was every way the reverse of prepossessing.

In her own house, surrounded by familiar objects, though havoc and wanton destruction were visible on every hand, Aurelia had after a time gathered a fictitious courage, for was she not at home! But what struck her as curious was, that in this fellow's strange love-making he had never spoken of *love*, for, sooth to say, he knew not what, in its purer sense, the sweet emotion meant; and by partial successes, particularly the failure of Colonel Gore's column before St. Denis, he was now so swelled and inflated with pride that he threatened to explode like a Woolwich torpedo, and ever and anon he would say to Aurelia,—

"Snakes! I could scarcely expect you to marry me right off the reel, slick at once; but I may grow weary of giving you time, so listen to me!" (here he registered one of his awful oaths) "rather than that blazing Britisher should succeed, I'd job my bowie into you!"

If St. Eustache were attacked, and the Queen's troops defeated, then indeed did Aurelia know that one way or other her fate would be sealed. Indeed, it might be sealed either way!

Cold though the season—it could not well be colder—so hot was the constitution of the Colonel (or his "coppers," as he phrased it), that he was always compounding curious effervescing drinks in long tumblers from the contents of Madame Darnel's cellars; but on the morning in question he said,—

"Aurelia, my dear, I have a bumper of that old mydeary, which belonged to your dad, old Darnel! Snakes! but it *is* the stuff. Not the mixtour of hickory and Jamaikey rum we get in New York," he added, draining a tumbler of the late Mr. Darnel's most cherished Madeira, much to the alarm of his shrinking listener, as intoxication always added, if possible, to the Colonel's vulgarity.

"Ah—ah!" said little M. Papineau, regarding him with a smile, snuff-box in hand, "the ancient Persians— if we are to believe history—never undertook any great matter, and never discoursed of aught that referred to policy or public interest, till they were at least, as the sailors say, three sheets in the wind, and you seem to be of their opinion. And now I must go round our posts."

And, bowing with mock courtesy to Aurelia, he took his sword and pistols, and withdrew, stuffing them into the belt that girt his buffalo coat.

Afraid almost to close her eyes at night, the poor girl had now an unslept, wild, and hunted look in them, with black circles round them; her face was deadly pale, and her once beautiful dark silky hair, never dressed now, was twisted in one great uncombed mass at the back of her head. Smash saw all this plainly enough, but he was pitiless as a Canadian bear, and only muttered,—

"Darn me, but I'll tame her yet, and break her spirit or her heart!"

A little cry escaped her—a cry of joy, but more she

dared not utter, for lo! from the windows of the room
she could see, advancing over the waste of far extending
snow through which the great Montreal road lay, the
dark masses of the approaching troops, dark because all
were in their grey overcoats; but the fixed bayonets
glittered like a grey steely forest; the bright colours,
crimson, blue, and gold, were waving in the sun, here
and there the rays of the latter were reflected from a
brass drum.

The heads of the infantry columns halted, and a
distant flash or gleam seemed to pass along the ranks
as the arms were "ordered" and the men stood "at
ease;" the artillery were all well to the front, unlimbered
and wheeled round, the horses untraced and taken to the
rear, and while one solitary officer was seen galloping
towards St. Eustache, a ferocious interjection escaped
Ithuriel Smash, and a roar of voices burst over all the
place, when some thousand men grasped their arms—
weapons of every description.

How wildly with hope beat the heart of Aurelia at
this moment! But she closed her ears to the cries she
heard around her, from the colonists and their American
sympathisers.

"Sacré Anglais! Blood for blood!"

"Down with the Red slaves of Queen Victoria!"

"Death to the island savages!"

"We'll whip the 'tarnal Britishers into the sea!"

And so forth, the phrases only alike in their spirit of
ferocity. Meanwhile the solitary and adventurous

officer was coming galloping on. At last he drew near that portion of the rudely-constructed works or fortifications (that connected all the houses and gardens of St. Eustache) which was immediately overlooked by the windows of the room in which she was compelled to remain with Ithuriel Smash, who, on the officer reining in his horse and waving his flag of truce, threw up a sash to hear what he had to say.

" Listen, my good people," he cried, displaying a paper, " to the proclamation of Lieutenant-General Sir John Colborne, G.C.B. and G.C.H., Commander-in-Chief of all Her Britannic Majesty's forces in Canada :—

" Our Sovereign Lady the Queen chargeth and commandeth all the persons here assembled in Eustache, immediately to disperse themselves, and peaceably depart to their habitations, or to their lawful business, upon the pains contained in the Acts made in the 27th year of King George the Third, to prevent tumultuous risings and assemblies."

A yell of scorn and defiance responded to the reading of this brief document. Meanwhile a moan escaped Aurelia, and a fierce chuckle Colonel Smash ; and so occupied was the former in looking at her lover, that she took no heed of the Colonel, who softly and silently cocked a musket, took aim, and fired.

Then a piercing shriek escaped Aurelia, as Roland, to all appearance dead or dying, prostrate backward on the crupper of his horse, was borne by it to the rear.

"Jerusalem and earthquakes!" said the assassin, laughing. "No need to waste a second bullet now!"

"Oh Father in Heaven, but this is too much—too much!" cried Aurelia, as she fell on her knees and covered her face with her hands.

"Is it?" said the ruffian, with another fiendish laugh, while proceeding to reload. "Now I think the game is in my own hands in more ways than one, Aurelia Darnel. We've dug up the war-hatchet, and ain't going to smoke the painted calumet of peace now!"

She fell prone on her face in a swoon, and thus Ithuriel Smash had to leave her, to come round as best she might, as other work was cut out for him now, as the troops were closing up fast on every hand, and already the guns of Glasgow's artillery had begun to knock everything in the village to pieces.

CHAPTER XI.

ST. EUSTACHE STORMED.

WE have no intention of keeping the reader in suspense.

The shot fired at Roland had missed him, and only barked a tree; for though he was so close, recent potations had rendered "the Colonel's" aim a very unsteady one; but his intended victim, inspired by a sudden idea born of his own coolness and decision of purpose, gripped the horse with his knees, and, feigning death to escape further firing, fell back on the crupper of his saddle, and in this way was carried safely to the rear, followed by the yells and derisive laughter of the insurgents.

Believing their favourite officer slain, a shout of rage burst from the Royals, and every man made a forward step in eager anticipation of the order to advance.

" A flag of truce fired on ! " exclaimed old Sir John Colborne, starting in his stirrups with honest grief and indignation. " Forward, Wetherall, to the attack and lead your column up the central street ! "

" I have escaped, General, by a miracle and a ruse," said Roland, reining in his horse and sitting erect in his saddle, to the surprise of all who saw him; "and now I shall rejoin my company."

He resigned the steed to its owner, and the attack at once began—indeed it had begun, for the artillery had already opened fire, and stone and timber were alike going crashing down beneath it.

Covered by the Montreal Rifle Corps, the First Royals advanced, steadily firing up the central street, and seized all the most defensible houses. Logan was then despatched by Colonel Wetherall, with orders to bring up some of the artillery; but he was driven back by the fire of the rebels from the lower windows of the church of St. Eustache, till the officer commanding the artillery had promptly conceived where his services were wanted, and galloping into the village by the rear, endeavoured to blow or burst open the door of the sacred edifice, but completely failed to do so, so dense and heavy was the barricade of earth behind it ; but some companies of the Royals and Rifles from the neighbouring houses opened a terrible fire of musketry upon the occupants of the church, whose shrieks and yells came through the windows, which were almost instantly divested of every vestige of glass.

After an hour of heavy cross-firing, and the door still defying every effort of our troops, the Scots Royals attacked the presbytery, which was full of men, forced an entrance, led by their officers, sword in hand, and now ensued a terrible scene, for they bayoneted nearly every man in the place, and then set it in flames, while scores of desultory combats were going on in the streets without.

There, in many places, streams and pools of crimson blood dyed the pure white snow ; in others, by repeated footsteps and struggles, it was trod to slush and snowy mire, wherein the dead and dying lay weltering—the breath of the latter, in many instances their last respiration, curling away like steam upon the frosty air of the keen Canadian winter day, while on all hands were heard strange cries, oaths, and yells.

" Vive la République Canadien ! A bas les Anglais !" cried the French Colonists.

" A bas la Reine ! A bas la Ligne !"

" Vive Papineau !"

"Down with British rule; death to old Colborne and his red-coats!"

Such were the shouts on one side; on the other, only the din of the heavy file firing, and at times that ringing united cheer, the import or instinct of which there is no mistaking.

By this time the smoke of the blazing presbytery had enveloped the whole church, which, as a wooden edifice, it was supposed would soon catch fire. Now Roland remembered the supposition of the French peasant, that Aurelia might be there, and we may imagine the sensations with which he beheld the dark smoke-wreaths eddying around its taper spire!

"Carry the church by storm!" was now the order of Sir John Colborne; and while a straggling fire was poured upon the column, from the house of the seigneur and others, Wetherall ordered his grenadiers —we had such soldiers still—to lead the van, the post of honour and peril being ever theirs by traditional right.

The blood of all the troops was fairly up, and as the column went forward surging and storming, and firing with the bayonets pointed upward at an angle, the soldiers of the Royal Regiment raised the shout of "Scotland for ever!"—a *cri de guerre* first used by the Greys at Waterloo, and last by the Duke of Albany's Highlanders at the storming of Kotah in 1858.

Pouring in by the shattered windows, leaping over every obstacle, and plunging like a torrent among the armed crowd within the church, the Royals made a terrible havoc, and among those who fought here was Roland, as yet untouched, and amid all the carnage and mad confusion around him, having but one thought in his heart.

At the same time, some other of the battalion companies, led by Major Ward and Captain Bell (afterwards Sir George and colonel of the regiment in 1868), a Peninsular officer who in this war commanded the fort and garrison of Coteau du Lac, an important post on the frontier, and received the thanks of Sir John Colborne for his exertions in recovering all the 24-pound guns and 4000 shot from the bottom of the river, and getting them in position amid the winter snows to face the rebels—led these and other officers we say, the rest of the Royals gradually fought their way into the church by the rear, and bayoneting all who resisted, set it on fire, and the corpses were consumed in the flames.

One hundred and eighteen men taken prisoners.

" *Quartier! Quartier! Je me livre à vous!* " (I yield myself up to you) was now the cry of the French colonists.

" Quarter for the love of God, and her Majesty the Queen!" echoed the British rebels, on finding that all was over.

Papineau, if there, was nowhere to be found; and Smash, though seen often, had disappeared.

In the apartment where we left her, Aurelia Darnel

H

had heard all the dreadful uproar around her—the myriad horrible sounds of a combat on which she dared not look, and she lay in a corner, gathered, as it were, in a heap, though on her knees, unable even to form a prayer, stunned, crushed, and bewildered, with but one thought—" Roland dead ! "

Steps, sounds rather, drew near the room; the door was flung open and Ithuriel Smash, pale as death, bleeding from more than one wound in his body, and with a dreadful rattle-snake expression in his eyes—an expression of agony, madness, and rage, staggered in; then he fell on his hands, and came crawling slowly, panting and groaning, towards her, leaving a track of his own blood—" the trail of the serpent " behind him on the floor.

His long knife was clenched in his teeth; his murderous intention was plain—to slay her would be his last effort, and in the corner where she crouched, Aurelia could not escape him !

She uttered a low wail of despair, ending in an involuntary shriek for help—help for the love of God ! And help came.

Poetic and dramatic justice would require that the obnoxious Colonel Smash should perish by the hand of Roland; but responsive to her cry, there burst into the room, Logan of Logan Braes and a few of the Royals, by whom he was speedily bayoneted like a reptile or mad dog, and he died, biting at the bayonets, like a dog or a savage.

Logan tenderly raised the half-dead girl from the floor, and in a few minutes after, the caressing arms of Roland, caressing and reassuring, were around her—and she felt safe then—doubly safe with him and her mother.

CHAPTER XII.

CONCLUSION.

WITH the civil war in Canada, our story has little more to do.

Suffice it that for a brief time, Roland Ruthven, after seeing Madame Darnel and her daughter safe in their château of St. Eustache at Montreal, had again to join the troops, who advanced to St. Benoît, where, so great was the terror excited by the recent victorious assault, that no opposition was offered, and the rebels sent delegates to say humbly, that they would, without conditions, lay their arms down, and they were conveyed under escort to Montreal, to meet the meed of their crimes.

The good result of all these operations was the return of the colonists to their homes, and the disappearance of all armed parties of insurgents. About the same season, however, in the following year, when the deep snows of the Canadian winter began to fall, there was a second rising in Lower Canada; but it was again crushed by the energy and gallantry of Sir John Colborne at Napierville, and for these and other services, the Queen created the fine old soldier a peer of Great Britain.

Prior to these events some startling changes occurred in the history of the two principal characters in our little narrative.

The Darnel estate at St. Eustache was utterly destroyed; the mansion had been ruined or burned, the lands ravaged, and the circumstances of the once wealthy widow were sorely impaired; her horses, carriages, and many other luxuries had to be dispensed with and economy become the new order of the day; but now, safe at her own home at Montreal, all the beauty and gaiety of Aurelia returned, and after all she had undergone, even poverty seemed a slight matter to face—as yet.

"O Roland darling!" said she, with a little laugh, as they stood together in a window of the château one evening in the spring, looking towards Montreal steeped in the sunset, and where the greenery of the woods was deepening faster than it ever does in Britain at the same season, vegetation maturing with wondrous rapidity the moment the snow disappears; "O, Roland—I am poor as yourself now, and yet you still talk of marrying me and going to India; but could I take my poor mamma there?"

Roland's loving countenance fell.

"You lost your noble estate by a will; I my seigniory—or nearly all of it—by civil war; our fortune is ruined."

" Yet—we must not—cannot part, after all—after all ! "

" Oh no—no ! " murmured the girl, fondly and plaintively, with her sweet face pillowed on his breast.

Next day Roland arrived with a face full of such excitement, wonder, and so many varying expressions, that Aurelia knew not what to make of him and his incoherences for some time at least.

That morning the regimental postman brought him a letter, the first words of which, however much expected, made a lump rise in his throat.

It was from his legal agents, Messrs. Hook and Crook, Writers to the Signet, and dated from Edinburgh :—

" Dear Sir,"—(It used to be *my* dear sir once) "We beg to acquaint you, with much regret, that we have now traced out and learned authentically who are *the heirs of the marriage of your deceased uncle*, the late Mr. Philip Ruthven, eldest son of General Roland Ruthven, who went to Jamaica."

Roland felt very sick as he read, and paused ; then summing up courage, he resumed the obnoxious epistle, and read on.

" From the latter place that gentleman went to Canada, where he married a lady of Montreal, by whom he had several children, all of whom are dead save one,

Miss Aurelia Darnel de St. Eustache " (" Oh, my God ! " thought Roland, " what miracle is this ? "), for he took the name of Darnel to please the family of his wife, who was the daughter of a wealthy French seigneur.

" We regret to be the medium of such very bad news, but of course are now taking the usual legal measures to execute the will of the late General Ruthven, according to your own instructions."

So Aurelia was his cousin, the daughter of the lost Philip, who had quitted Scotland in disgust, never to return, and she was the heiress of Ardgowrie !

And he—what was he ? For weal or woe her affianced husband. It was all like the plot of a drama ; and some time elapsed before Roland could realise the whole situation ; but there was the prosaic letter of the lawyers, which, under *other* circumstances, might have seemed to cut his very heart-strings.

Now how innocuous it was !

Another hour found him by the side of Aurelia, and to attempt to record all the explanations and loving incoherences, astonishment and joy of *that* particular interview would be a difficult task indeed; but even while speaking to her, and while her voice was in his ear, Roland seemed to see before him the cabinet of Scindia, with the now baffled secret it contained.

If Roland had now, in a modified sense, to blush at, and feel shame, for his father's duplicity in the matter of the will—a duplicity born of the various emotions we have already described, dislike between brothers, temptation offered on one hand, the dread of losing the ambitious girl he loved on the other—and then the total disappearance of Philip, he had to blush before one who had accepted him as a husband when their positions were very different, when all the odds of wealth and landed property were, as once again, in her favour, and he was still the penniless soldier with his sword alone.

And Roland, as he looked on Aurelia again, recalled the youthful portrait of his lost uncle Philip at Ardgowrie, and saw, or thought he saw, how closely she resembled it.

We have little more to add.

The Darnel estates, we have said, were ruined; but Ardgowrie was yet in all its baronial glory; to Ardgowrie they would go, and sell the former, so it was all settled ere the Canadian summer came swiftly on; thus the reader may be assured that they were married long before the month of August, so old Elspat Gorm's "fatal day" of the Ruthvens was fully evaded. Nor need we add, though we do so, that jolly Hector Logan was groomsman, and old General Colborne gave the bride away.

In winning Aurelia, Roland regained his inheritance, but he never left the old Royal Regiment, or returned finally to Ardgowrie, till he had, like his father before him, been long a popular colonel of the corps.

THE SECRET MARRIAGE.

In famous old Cornwall, known as "the Land of Tin," in the days of Solomon—the land of Druid Cromlechs and Celtic circles, of those mysterious sarcophagi named Kistvaens, wherein lie the bones of a race unknown—the land of many wondrous relics of a vanished past, lies the scene of the following events.

Not far from that part of the coast which is washed by the British Channel stands Restormel Court, at the time of our story—a few years ago—the seat of Sir Launcelot Tredegarth Tresilian, Bart., a proud old gentleman, whose chief, if not only failing was an inordinate pride of family; and hence whose principal regret was, that though he had heirs to succeed him in his estate, there was none to follow him in his title, which had been bestowed upon him by the late King William IV for certain political services. His two sons had been killed in the service of the country. One had fallen in Central India and the other in the Crimea, and as the baronetcy was limited by diploma "to the heirs male of his own body," he had to rest him content with the knowledge that he was the first and last baronet of Restormel Court.

Occupying the site of a castle demolished by the French when they landed in Cornwall during the reign of Henry VI., the latter is an edifice much older than it looks.

The whole house was an epitome of the past ; trophies of war and the chase—coats of mail and stags' horns—decorated the hall, and some of the rooms had remained untouched since the days of the " Virgin Queen," hung with tapestry, which was lifted to give entrance ; hearths intended for wood alone, and andirons—heraldic griffins—to support the logs ; and there were curious cabinets, Cromwellian chairs, and carved *prie-Dieu* of all kinds.

On one evening in autumn, the present lord of Restormel Court was lingering over his wine—some choice old Madeira, which had been carefully iced for him by the butler—in company with his two nephews, the eldest of whom was understood to be, and acknowledged by himself and all, as his future heir.

Sir Launcelot, verging then on his eightieth year, was a pale, thin, and wasted-looking man. He was toying with his wine-glass, and from time to time contemplating his wasted white hands, on each of which a diamond glittered ; and then he looked at his nephews, who were intently conversing near the fire.

They were both men about thirty-eight and forty years of age respectively. Arthur Tresilian, the eldest, and ever the prime favourite, was remarkably handsome, with fine, regular features.

His brother, Basset Tresilian, who followed the legal profession with success in London, was less athletic, but quite as striking in figure.

Somehow people, especially in Cornwall, did not like Mr. Basset Tresilian; and his periodical visits to the Court added no brightness to the circle usually to be met there.

" Well, boys " (for though men, the old baronet, by force of habit, called them boys still), "fill your glasses, and don't leave me to drink alone. Egad! in my time fellows didn't shirk their wine as you do; but it is all cigars and odious pipes now. Well, Basset, what does he say? Is he inclined to follow the example you so boldly set him some sixteen years ago, and take unto himself a wife?"

" I cannot say, sir. It is of a horse we were talking."

" A horse—pshaw! You were wise to marry young, Basset. *I* did so!" said Sir Launcelot.

" I have had no reason to repent me thereof," replied Basset, complacently. "My family are charming; Mona is a fine girl in face and figure."

" Quite a Tresilian—eh?" said the old man, proudly.

" And your nephew, Lance, is as handsome a boy as any in London. I have, indeed, prospered every day since I placed the marriage hoop on Marion's finger."

"Egad! you sing your own praises well, nephew Basset," said the baronet, after a pause. "But you, Arthur—why have you not imitated this fine example? I cannot last for ever, and I don't want my estates to go begging for owners."

Arthur coloured with too evident vexation.

"They cannot beg far, dear uncle," he replied, "while I have the good fortune to be your heir; and, then, Basset——"

"His sons, you would say?"

"Yes," replied the other, with a faint voice; for Basset was regarding him so keenly that he felt his colour deepen.

"What is the booby blushing for?" asked Sir Launcelot, laughing. "Blushing at forty! By Jove! I was cured of it at fourteen! Will you ride with—I mean, drive over with me to Carn Mornal to-morrow? My friend Trelawny has three fine daughters, and I should like you to make their acquaintance. Tresilian and Trelawny would quarter well on a shield; or would it be *impaled?* Will you go, Arthur?"

"I regret to say it is impossible, sir."

"When—why?"

"I have been a whole month at the Court, and am now due at a friend's house near—near London."

"London again? The last time you started for London, Trelawny gave me some hints that you never went in that direction so far as the borders of Devonshire. I can't understand your total indifference to the

society of ladies, and this resolute celibacy at your time
of life. D——n it, sir, it don't look well! and I only
hope you hav'n't conceived some unworthy attachment—
I mean unworthy the name of Tresilian."

"I have not, sir," replied the other, almost angrily
for he still felt the keen legal eye of Basset upon him.
"I shall never, I hope, do anything unworthy of the
name we bear in common."

"Thank you, Arthur boy.　Give me your hand."

"And now, uncle—leaving you and Basset to the
Madeira—I'll smoke a cigar in the stable, and look at
that horse I mean to take away with me to-morrow."

And anxious to close a conversation, the subject of
which pained him deeply, Arthur Tresilian left the
stately dining-room, and strolled over the beautiful
lawn towards the stable court.

"Can Basset suspect me?　Does he know anything?
No! no!—he cannot!　My poor Diana!" he muttered;
"still this humiliating concealment, and no hope save
through the death of that poor old man.　Accursed be
this silly pride of birth!"

*　　*　　*　　*　　*

"How long papa has been away from us—a whole
month!"

"When will papa be home, mamma dear?　The
cottage seems so dull without him!"

Such were the questions two handsome boys—one
was now quite a lad of eighteen—asked of a lady on

each side of whom they stood caressingly, while she hastily read a letter which had just come by post.

"In four days, dearest boys, he returns to leave us *no more!*" she exclaimed, with joy, as she fondly kissed them both, and once more turned to her letter.

"Restormel Court, Sept. 8.

"My Darling Diana,—My uncle, Sir Launcelot, is gone, poor man! He was found dead abed by his valet this morning. No cause is assigned but old age, yet he was hearty as a brick last night over his Madeira, rallying Basset and me. Well, he has gone, with all his overstrained and old-fashioned ideas of birth, and all that sort of thing. And now for our marriage, dearest —now all justice can be done to you, my much enduring one! I am the sole heir to Restormel, and your Arthur after me. I have written to the curate of H——, Jersey, for the attested copy of our marriage left with him, and expect it by return of post. Kiss our boys for me, and believe me, dearest Diana, your affectionate husband,

"Arthur."

Yet she remarked that it was addressed, as usual, "Mrs. Lydiard, Carn Spern Cottage," forgetting that she was unknown by any other name.

"It is well named Carn Spern—the Carn of Thorns —for in some respects, with all our happiness, such has it been to me; but now—now all that is at an end!

and blessed be God therefor! Yet it is through death
—the death of an old man, however—a very old man!
My boys—my innocent boys!—they are so young—they
must never know our secret! Yet—how to explain to
them the change of name from Lydiard to Tresilian?
I must be silent as yet, and consult dear Arthur about
this."

And now to go back a little way in the private life of
Arthur Tresilian. The favourite nephew and acknowledged heir of his paternal uncle, he had ever been
supplied by the latter with a handsome allowance.
When travelling or sojourning for a time in Jersey, he
had there made the acquaintance of Diana Lydiard,
then a girl barely done with her schooling. Her rare
beauty fascinated him; but, unfortunately, she was the
daughter of one who, at Restormel Court, would have
been deemed as a mere tradesman. Arthur knew that
he should mortify, offend, and disoblige irrevocably
the proud old Sir Launcelot if he made such a *més-
alliance* as to marry Diana Lydiard openly; for he
knew that his uncle's immense fortune was entirely
at his own disposal, and that he was quite capable of
cutting him off with the proverbial "shilling" and
leaving the whole to Basset—the careful, plodding, and
thrifty Basset.

So they were married; but wherever they went they
passed as Mr. and Mrs. Lydiard, the maiden name of
Diana. The marriage was duly registered in his name
in the book of the little Jersey church, and an attested

copy of it was lodged with the incumbent who performed the ceremony.

Arthur Tresilian took his girl-wife to the Continent, as he could then with a safe conscience write home for remittances.

Amid these wanderings two boys were born to them —Arthur and Ralf, whom she so named after her father, and each boy seemed a reproduction of either parent: for the eldest had all the personal attributes of the father—was bluff, bold, and manly; while the latter had all the dark beauty and gentleness of his mother. On the education of these boys Arthur Tresilian spared nothing, and both were already highly accomplished. Everywhere they had the best masters money could procure; but no profession was decided on for Arthur, the eldest, as the *false name* and the expected wealth raised alike doubts and objections as to what should be done.

Diana Lydiard was the daughter of a tradesman— true; but amid the love she bore her husband, and the luxuries by which his wealth enabled him to surround her, she had ever felt her position to be anomalous, and with it the pride that struggled against shame—a shame that at times became blended with vague fear and sorrow for the future.

And now for the last three years the secret family of Arthur Tresilian had been settled in a little seques-tered spot named Carn Spern, near Trevose Head, a rocky cape that juts into the sea westward of Padstow,

and some thirty miles or so distant from Restormel
Court. There he was known simply as Mr. Lydiard,
and by the frequency of his absence was supposed to
be a commercial traveller; but as the little family lived
quietly, made few acquaintances, and incurred no debts,
their lives glided by unnoticed and uncared for by all
save the poor, to whom the charity of Mrs. Lydiard
was a proverb, and something more solid too.

Through some unseen agency a whisper of an
alleged improper connection formed by Arthur did
reach the ears of Basset Tresilian, and through him,
those of old Sir Launcelot, and in the fury and indignation of the latter, his lofty and aristocratic scorn, he
had a foretaste of what awaited him, and the three
beings he loved most on earth, if the reality became
known.

And now the proud old man was dead, and all necessity for concealment was at an end. Arthur Tresilian
succeeded to Restormel Court, with thirty thousand
pounds a year; Basset to eight thousand pounds, the
baronet's gold repeater, and all the legal works in his
library.

"It is well the boys have gone to fish, I have so
much to say to you, Diana darling," said Arthur, as
he flung his hat away, and clasped his little wife to his
breast. "And about the resumption of our name,
Diana, they must simply be told that I have succeeded
to an estate which requires a change in our designa-
tion."

" Excellent, Arthur."

" To-morrow I must start for St. ——."

" For Jersey ? "

" Yes, Diana, I am anxious personally to get the attested copy of our marriage certificate by the curate who married us, or a new one from the records. I shall fill up the time of absence by writing my will in your favour and the boys, to make all sure, for one never knows what may happen. When you see me again, Di, both documents shall be snug in this old pocket-book my father gave me."

And laughingly he tapped the heirloom, a handsome scarlet and gilt morocco book, on the boards of which were the Tresilian arms, surmounted by a griffin stamped in gold.

" A strange little episode, almost a romantic one, has occurred during your absence, dear," said Mrs. Tresilian, for so we must now call her; " Arthur has quite fallen in love with a young lady, whom he has met riding her pony among the green lanes near Padstow."

" Arthur—that mere boy. It won't last long, Di."

" I hope not, and so will you, perhaps, when I tell who she is, and the risk we have run : Mona Tresilian ! "

" What, my brother Basset's daughter ? "

" Yes, Arthur."

" But the girl has gone to London with him, and that will end the affair. And now to-morrow, darling, I must leave you by the train for Falmouth, whence I

ı

shall take the steamer to Jersey.   When I return the
carriage shall be sent on here for you and our two dear
little fellows, as I wish you to enter Restormel Court
in the state that befits you, though my uncle's hatch-
ment still hangs above its *porte cochère.*"

Next day she was alone once more, and he had sailed
hopefully on his errand.

The hour she had pined for during eighteen years—
never so much as after the birth of her boy Arthur—
when she should sink the dubious name of Lydiard and
be acknowledged as the wife of Arthur Tresilian, had
come at last, and a thrill of the purest joy filled her
heart.   In her anxiety for her children's future she felt
small sorrow for the death of the octogenarian.   How
should she feel more ?

His absurd pride had kept her under a species of
cloud for eighteen years, as a person unknown to the
world, and as one even now to be recognised with
wonder—yea, perchance with doubt.

The period of her life so longed for, not for its
wealth, but when she and her children should take
their place in the world as Tresilians, had come at last.
There are times when an hour seems long.   Oh, then,
how long must days, and weeks, and months appear,
when they roll into years ?   All time passes inexorably,
however.   While she sat reflecting thus her eldest son
was engaged elsewhere, but not, as she thought, with
his fishing-rod.

"And you are going to London with your papa ? "

said he to a fair-haired and blue-eyed girl, who was clad in deep mourning, and who had pulled up her pony in one of the grassy and shady lanes near the unsavoury old fishing town of Padstow.

" Yes, and we leave by the train to-night."

" And I shall see you——"

" Perhaps never again, Arthur," replied the girl, with her face full of smiles and tears, for she was less affected than her lover. " I shall never forget you, Mr. Lydiard, or all the pleasant walks and meetings we have had, by these green lanes, by the Bray-hill above the sea, and ever so many places more."

" And you call me Mr. Lydiard ? Oh, Mona, can you leave me so coldly ? " he asked, sadly; " may I not write to you in London ? "

" Ah, good heavens, no ! " she exclaimed, with all a school-girl's terror. " What would mamma say ? And then there is papa ! "

It was delightful to have a lover; but not delightful that the fact should come to the ears of such a papa as Mr. Basset Tresilian.

" Then I have no hope ? "

" Yes, you have," said she, playfully tickling his face with her riding switch.

' Oh, name it, Mona ! "

" I have an uncle named Tresilian down here in this country."

" He who succeeded to Restormel Court, or some such place ? "

" Exactly, Arthur—the same."

" Well ? " asked Arthur, little thinking that she referred to his own and well-loved father.

" Papa thinks we shall spend our Christmas holidays
with him—he is so jolly !—and, somehow, it will go
hard with me if I don't get an invitation for Mr. Arthur
Lydiard."

An expression of thanks and quietude spread over
the young man s face, mingled with great sadness, for
she added,—

" I must go now—must leave you, Arthur."

" Oh, Mona ! Mona ! it seems so hard to lose you
now ! "

" My darling Arthur !" exclaimed the girl, giving
way to a shower of tears, as his arms encircled her
slender waist, and she permitted her soft, bright face
to fall upon his shoulder.   But at that moment they
were rudely interrupted.

Arthur felt himself seized by the arm and thrust
violently aside by a grave and stern-looking man about
forty years of age.   This person was in mourning, and
instinct told the lover that he must be Mona's father.
He seized her pony by the bridle, and—after darting a
furious glance at Arthur, a glance not unmingled with
surprise, as he saw in his face a likeness to some one,
he knew not whom—led the young lady away through
a wicket in a thick beech-hedge and shut it.   Ere he
did so, however, he turned and said to Arthur,—

" Whoever you are, young fellow, let such tomfoolery cease. This young lady leaves to-night for London. Attempt to write to, or follow her, at your peril; and I may add that we shall dispense with the pleasure of your distinguished society at Restormel Court in the Christmas week."

Arthur's spirit was proud and fiery. He made a spring towards the little gate, but checked himself; he felt that he dared not confront, in wrath, the father of the girl he loved, and so he turned sadly and hopelessly away, like a good, simple-hearted lad as he was, to tell his mother all about it, for he concealed nothing from her; but, somewhat to his surprise and chagrin, instead of sympathising with his disappointment, or betraying indignation at the "flinty-hearted father," she laughed merrily, smiled, and kissed him, thrusting at the same time into her bosom a letter she had just received from her husband.

"But I shall never see her more, mamma," urged Arthur, piteously.

"You shall, Arthur—you shall! be assured of that. Did your own mamma ever deceive you?"

"No, no, never!" replied Arthur, hopefully.

"And she is to be at Restormel—is that the name of the place?"

"Yes, mamma; Restormel Court—a grand place, they say."

"At Christmas? Well, Arthur, and you shall be there too, or your mamma is no true prophetess."

Diana's husband had reached Jersey in safety, and

gone to the little secluded church of St. ——, where
they had offered their mutual vows to heaven on that
eventful morning, so well remembered still, when their
only witnesses were the parish clerk and sexton.

"The poor old curate"—so ran his letter—"you remember his thin, spare figure, with a long black, rusty
coat, diagonal shovel hat, gaiters, and white choker—
has gone to his last home under the old yew-tree that
for centuries has guarded the burial-ground. By a
destructive fire in the vestry the whole of the marriage
registers, and some of the baptismal ditto, have perished
before the copies thereof were transmitted to headquarters—wherever that may be; but I have, most
fortunately, oh, my Diana! by the special providence
of heaven, secured *the attested copy* of our marriage
lines, which the old curate made at my request from
the now defunct register. It was found among his
papers by his successor, and is now in my possession—
in the old scarlet pocket-book, together with my will,
which I have carefully drawn up in favour of you and
our boys, and signed before witnesses. I mean to
spend two days here with an old friend, and shall
return by the steamer *Queen Guinevere*, which leaves
Jersey for Falmouth on Friday, and which, by-the-bye,
has on board a large sum in specie coming from France
to England."

"Friday? On Saturday I shall see him!" thought
the wife in her heart, with a sigh of relief, and a
prayer of thanks to heaven.   "The register of their

marriage had perished! *What if the attested copy had been lost?* Oh, what then would have been the fate, the future, of their idolized sons—her tall and handsome Arthur, her merry little dark-eyed Ralf?"

Thursday passed; Friday, too; then came Saturday, but no Arthur Tresilian, or Lydiard, as she had to call him still at Carn Spern. There came tidings, however, that the *Queen Guinevère* had left Jersey duly, but had never reached Falmouth. Great was the anxiety, grief, and terror of the little family at Carn Spern; for there had been a severe storm in the Channel, and many ships had been driven ashore about the Lizard and Land's End; but none of these were steamers, and a whisper began to spread abroad that the *Queen Guinevère* must have foundered and gone down at sea, or some trace of her would have been found upon the coast. But all doubts were speedily resolved, when, on the third day after she was due at Falmouth, Derrick Polkinghorne, coxswain of the Padstow life-boat, discovered her shattered hull sunk and wedged in a chasm of the rocks near the lighthouse on Trevose Head. How she had come to be stranded there on the other side of Cornwall was a mystery to all, unless she had been blown by the late tempest completely round the Land's End, and been forced to run for shelter by St. Ives and Ligger Bay. Much wreckage and many bodies were cast on the beach; but, though none of them proved to be that of Arthur Tresilian—or Mr. Lydiard, as he was called—no doubt remained in the anguished mind of Diana that

he had perished, and she at once wrote to his brother
Basset, announcing the event, her existence, and the
legal 'claims of herself and her children.

All this complication proved very startling to Basset.
He knew nothing of his brother's Jersey journey,
though he always suspected his secret ties; but, ignor-
ing the latter, he at once put his household in super-
mourning, and took possession of Restormel Court as
his own, leaving, however, no means untried to prove
the death by drowning of Arthur Tresilian, though
the name of Lydiard was borne on the list of pas-
sengers.

The following day saw Diana and her sons, attired
in deepest mourning, at the Court, requesting an audience with Mr. Basset Tresilian—her close cap and concealed hair, her long crape weepers, and face deadly
with pallor, announcing her recent widowhood, which
Basset viewed with a sneer, as with a haggard eye she
looked at the stiff ancestral portraits, the cedar carvings
of the stately library, the blazing fire, the gleaming
tiles, and picturesque furniture of white and gold and
crimson velvet.

She announced with quiet dignity, yet not without
doubt and much perturbation, that she came as the
widow of the late Mr. Tresilian, to claim her place, and
the places of his children, at Restormel Court.   He replied, calmly—

"You have proofs, I presume, of all this, Mrs.—Mrs.
Lydiard?"

"Mrs. Tresilian, sir!" said she, while her Arthur, in silence and bewilderment, recognised an uncle in the father of his Mona.

Alas! Diana had neither the certificate nor the will; both had gone down into the deep, with her hapless husband. She had, however, the letter referring to those documents: but Basset, after a furtive glance at the fire, tossed it back to her contemptuously, saying—

"I have heard of you before, madam—years ago, too. My brother is drowned, and you are now poor. I dislike death and poverty, and all that sort of thing; but I'll do what I can in the way of Christian charity, and have your hulking boys bound to trades. But you must leave this place at once; the ladies of my family must not come in contact with—such as you."

She rose, and left the stately house mechanically, with one hand on Arthur's arm and the other on the neck of Ralf; and she looked at them in agony—the latter her little pet, the other the stately king of the playing fields, and captain of the school eleven, to be tradesmen!

Deep in the hearts of both boys sank their mother's grief; but deepest in the heart of Arthur, who felt himself called upon to do something—he knew not what.

He spent hours and days upon the solitary rock above where the wreck lay, looking at the spot with haggard eyes. Oh, if that shattered hull had a voice—had the dead that came ashore the power of utterance, the secret of his father's fate might be revealed; but three months had passed, and who could doubt it now? One morning early, as he came to the accustomed spot, under the grim shadow of Trevose Head, he found the puffins scared away, and the solitude invaded by others —one of whom he knew well, Derrick Polkinghorne, a bold and hardy native of the Scilly Isles, where people spend so much of their time on the boisterous ocean that for one who dies abed nine are drowned; and, by order of Lloyd's agent, he was preparing a diving bell to examine the wreck, as much specie was known to be on board of her.

"Mornin', Muster Lydiard," said he, for he and Arthur had frequently boated together; "that's a smart yatch outside the Lines. Sir Launcelot Tresilian's she was—Master Basset's now "

"What is her name?"

"*The Bashful Maid.*"

"She sails like a duck!"

"She does. Ah, there's ne'er a craft out o' Cowes like that 'ere *Bashful Maid!*—'specially when she's got a dandy rigged astarn; then she hugs the wind beautiful! Just goin' down to 'ave a squint at this here wreck."

"Take me with you, Derrick; for heaven's sake do" implored the lad.

"What on earth do you want down there?"

"Only a scrap of paper, perhaps, Derrick."

" Then you ain't like to find it, you ain't."

" I should like to see the deck my father stood on last."

" I understand that, I does. Come, then. I wonders as he went to sea in that craft, for last time she left Falmouth the rats rushed out of her in thousands; and they never does that for nothin' But as for finding paper here, you'll be like them as mistook the mild reflex of the lunar horb for a remarkably fine Stilton. But here we goes ; and now take care on yourself."

With a thrill of awe and horror, oddly not un-mingled with delight and a sense of novelty, Arthur took his place beside Derrick on the seat that was placed across the bell, which at once began to descend. Light was admitted by convex lenses, through which were seen the long trailing weeds, the creeping things of ocean, and now and then the sea-green faces of the blackening dead !

They passed downward into the water, which surged against the sides of the bell, and rippled over the lenses till they were close to the bulged wreck. Her starboard bow was completely smashed upon the rocks; the cargo had been washed out, and was still oozing forth by degrees. Already barnacles and weeds were growing on it, and dreary, dreary and desolate looked that shattered hull at the bottom of the sea; and Arthur surveyed it with tears of the keenest grief.

" Suppose a shark stuck its nose into the bell ? " said Polkinghorne.

"I don't care if one did," said Arthur.

"A dead body? and, by Jove, here's one coming in grim earnest. On his face, it's a man. Women allus floats on their backs; how's that, Muster Lydiard?"

"My name is——" but he checked himself, for now a corpse, which Derrick had roused with his pole, came slowly athwart the stage at the bottom of the bell, and remained there.

Suddenly a cry escaped Arthur! The grey great coat upon it, all sodden and studded with weeds and limpets, he recognised as one usually worn by his lost father, and, longing to know more, he implored Derrick to examine it; for himself, he dared not move, or breathe, or think! Oh, could it be, that those poor remains, half devoured by fish, and floating face downward in the sea, were all that remained of his handsome and beloved father?

"Hold on, lad, shut your eyes; and I'll soon see," cried the resolute diver, as he lowered himself to the loathsome task of examining the remains.

Arthur dared not look; but ere long a cold metal watch was placed in his hand.

"It is not papa's," said he, with a sigh of relief, that ended in a cry of horror, for as those in charge of the bell began to raise it, the water surged within it and dashed about the corpse, which came against him again and again, till Derrick, who was investigating its pockets, thrust it with his pole out of the bell, which in another minute was suspended over the sunny surface of the sea.

" See, Muster Lydiard, I've found a pocket-book into that ere poor fellow's overcoat," said Derrick.

" It is my papa's ! " shrieked the lad ; his old scarlet book, with his arms and crest upon it."

And in that book, safe and dry, were the lost will and certificate of marriage.

" But, oh," moaned the lad, when he had told his mother this startling occurrence, as he sank half sick upon her breast, " if that was poor papa I saw, he came from his grave in the sea, mamma, with those papers for you ! "

But the body was soon known to be that of a channel pilot.

Ere the end of that week Basset Tresilian had to change his tone, and Diana and her sons took legal steps to make her the mistress and them the masters of Restormel Court. So autumn drew towards winter ; but ere the sad widow quitted Carn Spern, one night a carriage drew up, a man alighted, full of bustle and excitement; a well-known voice was heard, and Arthur Tresilian, the elder, was clasped in the arms of his half-fainting wife.

Washed overboard from the steamer, he had been picked up by a vessel bound for Cuba; his coat had been donned by the pilot, so there was an end of all the sorrow and mystery.

THE STUDENT'S STORY.

It is a ghastly tale I have to tell, in some respects; but so far as regards its close, I have some reason to congratulate myself, and to feel, that " All is well that ends well."

It is almost an old story now, though I was an actor in it ; but the world is ever reproducing itself in some form or fashion. Was there not an instance, in the August of 1870, of a resurrection taking place at Harrington, when all that quiet locality was startled from its propriety by the discovery of a body cast in its shroud beside its grave, which had been violated to procure the jewellery with which the deceased had been interred? My adventure, however, refers to the regular old " body-snatching " times, before unclaimed subjects were supplied to the anatomical theatres from our public hospitals, and when houseless ruffians of the lowest and vilest type made a livelihood by their loathsome and almost nameless trade.

I had graduated at the great medical school of Edinburgh, after a hard tussle with Hunter and Fyfe's

Anatomies, Bell on the Bones, the cell theories of Schwan, and even grappling with some of the abstruse and now exploded speculations of Gall and Spurzheim. I had mastered all; I had been solemnly "capped" in the old Academia Jacobi VI. Regis Scotorum, by the Reverend Principal L.—— (now in his grave); I had undergone all the jollity of the graduation dinner, and with *Frederick Mortimer, M.D.*, duly figuring on my portmanteau, found myself, with my college chum, Bob Asher (who, by the way, had *not* passed), sailing from the harbour of Leith for London, in the Royal Adelaide, one of the only two steamers which then plied between these ports.

Though "plucked" for the third time, poor Bob was in no way cast down. With him, study at Edinburgh had been all a sham. He had duly "matriculated," and sent the ticket as a proof thereof to his father, who duly paid for classes he never attended, and expensive books he never read. But Bob had always plenty of money then, at least, while I had barely wherewith to pay my class fees and lodgings in Clerk-street, a quiet place near the University.

At last I had the letters "M.D." appended to my name—those magical letters which open the secrets of households, the chambers of the fairest, the purest, and most modest and refined to the perhaps hitherto wild, and it may be "rake-hell" student, who is thereby transformed suddenly into a member of the learned profession, and a grave and responsible member of society.

A comfortable home, board, and washing, with forty pounds per annum whereon to enjoy the luxuries of this life, were the inducements which drew me back to London, where I became duly inducted as assistant to Dr. Crammer, in Bedford-street, Strand, one of those old-fashioned practitioners who always had a lighted crimson bottle flaming over the door by night, and had a dingy little room off the entrance hall, with a skull or two on a side table, snakes in "good spirits" on the mantleshelf, and which by its appurtenances seemed laboratory, surgery, and library in one.

The doctor's practice was more fashionable, however, than one might have expected from his locality, and many a patient of his I visited in the statelier regions of Piccadilly and those pretty villas that face Buckingham Palace and the Green Park. Dr. Crammer was a fussy and pompous little man, with a bald head, an ample paunch, and a general exterior like that of the well-known Mr. Pickwick. He was vain of his aristocratic practice, and more vain of none than of the family of Sir Percival Chalcot, whose eldest daughter was said to be one of the handsomest girls in London, and whose son was in the Household Brigade.

I flattered myself then that I had rather a taking manner and gentlemanly exterior; and that old Crammer was a little vain of me as an assistant, especially after I passed at Apothecaries' Hall—an absurdity necessary then for graduates of the Scotch Universities, who otherwise, in London, were liable to imprisonment.

I soon remarked, however, that he never sent me to the baronet's. Every visit there he made in person, and by himself; every dose of medicine, however infinitesimal, was conveyed there by his own hand; for he liked to have it to say to a friend *en passant*, "I am just going to," or, "have come from Sir Percival Chalcot. Lady Chalcot is unwell;" or, "Miss Gertrude over-danced herself at the Palace last night." So that great house, near where now the stately arch is overtopped by that hideous statue of Wellington, was to me as a sealed book. I soon ceased to think about it, and gave all my attention and skill to the smaller fry in the neighbourhood of the Strand; and between St. Clement's and St. Martin's there is scope enough, heaven knows!

One day a professional visit had taken me farther westward than usual, and I was sitting wearily on a seat in Hyde Park, near the statue of Achilles, watching the occasional carriages rolling past—I say occasional, for it was an hour or two before the fashionable time—when a cry roused me, and I saw a spirited horse coming along the drive at a terrific pace. Its head was down, and it had evidently the bit between its teeth; while the reins, which had escaped the hand of the rider, a lady, were dangling between the forelegs. She seemed a skilful horsewoman, and kept her saddle well. I saw her floating skirt, her streaming veil, her pale face, and wild, imploring glance as she came on.

One or two men attempted to catch the bridle, but were instantly knocked over.

K

I leaped the iron railing, and by the greatest good fortune contrived to snatch the reins, to gather them together at the same instant, to twist the curb behind the horse's jaw, thus arresting his progress; and then, with a strength I did not think myself possessed of, to bear it furiously back upon its haunches. At the same moment that I thus mastered it, I was conscious of hearing something snap; a dreadful pain shot through my left arm, which hung powerless by my side; but the lady, who was both young and beautiful, with a charmingly minute face, and large dark hazel eyes, gave me a glance expressive of intense relief and gratitude.

"Thank you, sir—thank you. Oh, how shall I ever sufficiently thank you?" she muttered hurriedly with pallid lips.

"It was well done, miss—splendidly done of the gentleman," said her old gray-haired groom, who came up at a rasping pace. "Another instant and the blind brute would have dashed you ag'in yonder gate."

"My papa shall thank you for this, sir; at present I am unable to speak," she added.

So also was I; but she knew not the extent of the injury I had suffered, as she bowed and rode away, her horse being now led by the groom, who had taken its bridle; while I was left there with my broken limb, and without any clue as to who she was, save her handkerchief, which I had picked up on the walk, and in a corner of which was the single letter "G."

For a time I felt very faint; but at that juncture Bob Asher drove past in his phaeton, and took me home. Old Crammer set the bone, which progressed favourably, and after a few days I was able to go abroad a little, with my arm in a leather case and black sling.

The face of the girl I had saved—a haunting face, indeed—dwelt in my memory; and now that danger was past, I thought of the episode with pleasure, for I had scarcely a female friend in London; and I wondered in my heart if she ever thought of the humble pedestrian to whom she owed so much, and who had so suffered in her cause. I could scarcely flatter myself that she did so, for she was evidently by her air and bearing, and by the mettle of the horses ridden by herself and her groom, one of the "upper ten thousand;" one in wealth, if not in rank and position, far above an assistant to a sawbones in the Strand. She might be married, too; yet she had nothing of the matron in her appearance.

But often, when I had the opportunity, I went back to the place where I had checked that furious horse, and looked, but in vain, for it and its bright-eyed rider; so I kept the little lace-edged handkerchief as a *souvenir* of the occurrence.

About a fortnight after this, Crammer was summoned to attend the deathbed of an aunt at Gravesend —one from whom he had some monetary expectations that were not to be neglected. The whole *onus* of our

K 2

practice thus for a time fell on me, and I was worked very hard. Among many other visits to pay, was one at the house of Sir Percival Chalcot, from whom a message came for Crammer, urging his attendance without delay. Ordering the little "pill-box," as we called his brougham, I drove off in state to explain about his absence, and offer *my* professional services.

A tall servant, in showy livery, with the invariable whiskers and calves of his fraternity in London, ushered me along the marble vestibule up a stately staircase, adorned by pictures and statuary, into a beautiful little library, where Sir Percival, a tall, thin, and aristocratic-looking old gentleman, received me politely, but somewhat pompously, and with an air of puzzle and surprise.

"It was Doctor Crammer I most particularly wished to see," said he; "and he may be absent some days, you say? Very awkward—especially as he, and he alone, knows the general constitution of my family. I dislike to consult a young man on the nervous disorder of a young lady, but I may mention to you that my eldest daughter has been engaged for a year past to a friend; the settlements are all drawn out most satisfactorily, I assure you; everything has been adjusted for the marriage, even to the line of their continental tour; but for the last three months she has sunk into exceedingly low spirits. She suffers from nervous depression, and at times is quite listless. Now, I think that something bracing—some system of tonics—you understand?"

"Sir Percival, could I see Miss Chalcot?"

"Well — yes, certainly; that, of course, will be necessary first."

"What is her age, may I ask?"

"Twenty. Please to follow me."

He led me into a magnificent drawing-room, through the festooned curtains of which I saw another beyond with the buhl and marqueterie tables, easy chairs, couches, mirrors, and glass shades, peculiar to such apartments. There was a pleasant odour of flowers and perfume; and there, seated on a low folding-chair, was a young lady, in a maize-coloured silk dress, the tint of which well became her rich dark beauty. On the soft carpet we approached unheard, or, if noticed, she never deigned to move, and I could observe the superb development of her figure, which looked more like the maturity of twenty-eight than twenty.

Her attitude was expressive of perfect listlessness; a book lay on her knee, but her eyes were bent on vacancy. The purity of her profile was most pleasing; her eyelashes were long and black, and curled at the tips. The masses of her dark chesnut-coloured hair were looped up on her head in such a manner as to show the delicacy and contour of her throat and cheek, the complexion of which was pale and clear. Her nose was straight, with nostrils deeply curved; and the lips were full, as if with a fixed pout.

"It is the doctor, my dear girl," said Sir Percival.

But she only raised her shoulders and eyebrows a little, and became again still and quiet.

"Gertrude, dearest, 'tis the doctor. I told you that I should send for him."

"He is welcome," replied the girl, as she raised her large, dark, and at that time sullen-looking eyes to mine; and then added, "But this is not Dr. Crammer, papa."

"It is his assistant, Dr.—Dr.—Colliner."

"Oh, papa!" she exclaimed, suddenly starting to her feet, as the whole expression of her face changed; "it is the gentleman who saved me in the Park, when that horrid animal——and your arm, sir—was it injured on that occasion? Oh, I hope not!"

"It was broken——"

"Oh, good heavens!—and for me!"

"In such a cause I should have risked the arms of Briareus, had I possessed them!" said I, with enthusiasm.

"Permit *me* to thank you, sir," said the baronet, stiffly and grandly. "I always thought that the gentleman who had rendered my family a service so important would have done us the honour to have left his card, at least."

"But I knew not whom I had aided, sir, or where to call."

"Most true," said Miss Chalcot; "I left you in such rude haste; but, then, I was so alarmed!"

"And now, Miss Chalcot, permit me to feel your pulse."

I put my fingers on the delicate wrist. Her pulse

was going like lightning for a time; then it became in-
termittent; then feeble, as the old listless expression of
inquietude stole over her fine face again, as her mind,
probably by the object of my visit, reverted to its old
train of thought, whatever it was.

Sir Percival regarded us dubiously over the point of
his high, thin, aristocratic nose. I was evidently too
young, perhaps too good-looking, or had too great an
air of *empressement* about me, to suit his ideas of a
medical adviser for his daughter, so he said, coldly and
loftily—

"Without disparagement to you, sir, I think I should
rather have Crammer's opinion, Dr.—Dr. Lorimer."

"Mortimer," I suggested, mildly.

"Ah, yes! If he don't come soon to town, I'll have
Clarke or Cooper to see her."

"Then I shall bid you good morning," said I, assum-
ing my hat; but turning again to the daughter, while
he was ringing the bell for the servant—he of the calves
and whiskers—to order the "pill-box," I said, "I have
often gone to the scene of your accident, at *the same hour*,
to look for you. Pardon me saying this; but your face
so dwelt in my memory."

"At the same hour—it was about *two* in tho afternoon," said she, with a bright smile.

"Yes—good evening, Dr. Short," blundered the
baronet.

My name was evidently not worth his committal to
memory.

And I drove away, feeling happy in the conscious-
ness that I had seen her again, and that, though *engaged*, as I had been told, I should see her again where
we first met, for her bright glance of intelligence told
me *that*.

Her father had shown pretty pointedly—with all his
punctilio, almost rudely—that he had no further use for
my professional services; but I felt deeply smitten by
the beauty of the girl. I strove in vain to thrust her
image from my thoughts, and recalled again and again
the galling information that she was the betrothed bride
of some beast—I rated him "a beast"—unknown; but
strove in vain; and found myself going to sleep that
night in my den above the surgery in Bedford Street,
with her laced handkerchief under my pillow, like a
lover of romance, with all the roar of the prosaic Strand
in my ears.

Next afternoon—Crammer was dutifully at his rich
aunt's funeral—saw me in the park, and occupying the
same seat from whence I started to arrest the runaway
horse. Every fair *equestrienne* I saw in the distance
made my heart beat quicker; but how joyous were its
emotions—how high its pulses—when, exactly at the
hour of two, I saw her come trotting slowly along the
walk, accompanied by the same old groom, and draw
up, with her little gauntletted glove tight on the bridle
rein, just before me. I came forward, and, after rais-
ing my hat, presented my hand, which I felt to be
trembling.

"Somehow, I thought you would be here," said she, with charming frankness, "and how is your arm? Better still, I trust."

"I shall have the splints off to-morrow, Miss Chalcot."

"That is good—I'm so thankful! Do you know that though this is only the third time we have met, Dr. Mortimer, I feel quite as if we were old friends? You must have thought my reception of you rather ungracious yesterday."

"Nay; but for what does your papa think you require medical advice? You seem perfectly well."

Her face fell—her features, or the expression of them, changed as I spoke.

"That is my secret. No doctor can cure me, or 'minister to a mind diseased;' not that mine is precisely so," she added, with a merry, ringing laugh. "Neither papa nor mamma can understand me. I lack decision and firmness, I fear. Dark women are imagined to be fiery, and all that sort of thing; but it is the fair little women of this world who possess the firmest will and greatest strength of character."

"But you are subject to low spirits, your papa hinted."

"Not naturally; but for a year past my heart has begun to fail me in hopes of the future, why, or how, I cannot tell you; and now, dear Dr. Mortimer, good morning," and away she trotted, with a pleasant smile and a graceful bow, leaving me rooted to the spot

with admiration of her beauty, the craving to see her
again strong in my heart, and conflicting with the
fear that she was fickle, and wearied of her engagement,
or had conceived a fancy for some one else, a year
ago.

From that period she had begun to date her emotions
of sadness.

A year ago, I had been a hard student in my little
den in Clerk Street, Edinburgh, a dim shadow in the
distance now.

"Go it, old boy," said Bob Asher, who came suddenly upon me a-foot—the phaeton was gone now—
"that's not one of old Crammer's patients surely. You
are getting on, Fred, and if you wish to continue doing
so always talk most to the women, and middle-aged
ones; flatter the young girls, but on the sly only; and
make a most fatherly fuss with the babies, however
ugly or squally, at all times."

Rashly heedless of what the old groom might think
or report on the subject, I had an interview there
almost daily, for a few brief minutes; at times it was
but a bow and a smile, if she was accompanied by
friends, or more especially by her brother; and it went
hard with me but I made my professional visits and
old Crammer's practice suit my plans—if plans I had
—for I had given myself up to the intoxication of—
yes, of loving Gertrude Chalcot, though she seemed
placed above me by Fate as far as the planets are above
the earth; but with the conviction came reflections that

were not in my mind when the charm of her presence
absorbed every other thought and feeling.

When I was alone came calmer thoughts. She was
engaged, though to whom I knew not, and she might
just be amusing herself with me for the time, while I
was laying at her feet the purest love of an honest
and affectionate heart.

> Why did I love her? Curious fool, be still!
> Is human love the fruit of human will?

Engaged to another—whose ring was doubtless on
her finger—another, who had the privilege of kissing
and caressing her, while I had but a formal interview,
a park rail between, and the eyes of an observant old
groom upon us. I felt as jealous as a Turk or Spaniard
at the idea. One day I briefly implored her to meet me
a-foot in another part of the park. She agreed to do so,
and we had the opportunity of an explanation. I shall
never forget how charming my dark-eyed and dark-
haired beauty looked in a yellow crape bonnet—that
tint ever so suitable to a brunette—with violet flowers
between it and her pure complexion.

In language that was broken, but which the emotions
of my heart inspired, I told her of the enchantment her
society was to me; of the love that was becoming a
part of my nature, the love that had been so almost
ever since I had seen her, and led me to treasure her
handkerchief (which I then drew from my breast); but,
I added, that as she was plighted to another—more than

all, as she was so rich and I so poor, I had come to the bitter resolution of seeing her no more, and quitting England for some distant colony.

"You love me then?" she asked, calmly, and with downcast eyes.

"Love you! Oh, words cannot tell you how fondly, Gertrude."

"Then I, too, am the victim of circumstances. By the manœuvres of mamma, who is a great matchmaker, in the very year of my *début* in London she contrived, I scarcely know how, to have me engaged to a man for whom I cared nothing then, and, oh, how much less now! A young girl of eighteen, his presence dazzled, his attentions flattered me, and that was the whole matter. I tolerated him. I have done all I can to delay the marriage for many months by feigning illness; but papa and mamma say that to make a regular break off will prove such an *esclandre* in society. Yet is my life, all my future, to be sacrificed for the myth we call society? I foresee too clearly what my fate will be, to pass through existence unloving and unloved; but it is heaven's will, or rather mamma's pleasure."

"Oh, that I were rich, Gertrude, or that men could not stigmatise me as an adventurer and fortune-hunter, as they will be sure to do, if I—I——"

"Did what?"

"Proposed the alternative."

"Fear nothing, Fred, but speak. I need advice."

The sound of my name on her lips, the intense sweet-

ness of her eyes and sorrow of her air, rendered me
blind to all but her beauty, her love, and the passion
that was in my own heart, and oblivious of those who
might be passing near—and afterwards we had soon
cruel reason to believe that we were not only seen, but
watched, as it was quite unusual for her to be out a-foot
and alone—I told her that if she would rely upon my
affection and honour, on the love with which she had
already inspired me, it would be the duty of my life to
render hers happy; that I would save her from the
delusive snare called "society," and the thraldom of her
proud old father and calculating mother. Of course, I
didn't call them so to her. I spoke with boldness,
decision, and facility, for love and passion lent me
power. I looked into her eyes and saw an answering
light; but she answered, pale and trembling the while—

"You are poor, you say, my dear Fred. Now papa
is rich, and ambitious of being richer. Alas! you
must be satisfied with——"

"What?—your friendship? Oh, Gertrude, can you
speak so coldly, and to me?"

Her tears fell fast.

"You overrate my powers of endurance. To be your
friend, and even that only in secret—to see you, after
your avowal to me, the wife of another perhaps, rendering all my existence hereafter a blank."

"I do not mean that, Fred. Alas! I know not what
I do mean," she added, weeping so bitterly that my
heart was pained.

"Mean—say that you will be mine, and not the wife of this mysterious other."

"To-morrow I shall be here again—to-morrow shall end all!"

She held up her sweet face; no one seemed near. With the speed of thought I pressed my lips to hers—for the first and the last time on this side of the grave, as it proved—and we separated in a tumult of joy.

Next day I kept my appointment without fail, but not without difficulty, as I had a long and troublesome operation to perform in a totally different direction, near Wimpole Street. I waited till I could linger no longer, and quitted the park slowly, filled by doubts and dread, and by the hope that visitors—something unavoidable—anything but illness, caprice, or change of mind—had prevented my bright Gertrude from meeting me.

If her beauty, humility, and sweetness dazzled and won me on one hand, her father's insolent *hauteur*—for, like her brother, the Guardsman, he always "cut me dead" in the street—piqued me on the other. I was a gentleman by birth and education as well as either, and what was more, I was the graduate of an ancient university; yet I disdained to risk being stigmatised as a fortune-hunter, which would surely be said of me, as Gertrude had some eight thousand pounds yearly of her own. But the girl loved me, and the conviction of that rendered me blind to everything.

The morning of the second day brought me a note from her, dated from St. George's Place.

A note !

We had met again and again by arrangement, but never had I got a note from her, and I read and kissed it a score of times, and committed many other absurdities while studying the bad writing, which somehow seemed totally unlike that of a lady; but then poor Gertrude had never ventured to write to me before.

It contained but three lines, saying that she was unable to meet me as usual, for reasons I should learn if I would call, and see her after luncheon time, as papa and mamma had left town, and she should be quite alone.

The boldness of this proceeding was so altogether unlike her, and so strange, that my mind became filled with vague fears of some impending calamity, and I counted every moment till, with a heart, the pulses of which certainly beat fast, I rang the sonorous bell at the door of the lofty house in St. George's Place, *then* a more fashionable locality than now, for the house itse... is changed into a public building. I had never before entered it but once, though many a promenade I had made before its stately plate-glass windows, in hopes of obtaining a glimpse, however brief, of her I loved so dearly.

" Jeames "—ne of the calves and whiskers—opened the door rather wider, I thought, than before, and his usually stolid and stupefied visage wore a strange ex-

pression. That might all have been fancy, for *he* could
not know the secrets of his mistress. I warily did not
ask for her ; but on giving my card, inquired for " Sir
Percival Chalcot, or either of the ladies," certain that
she I wanted alone was " at home."

The tall loafer in livery bowed, and ushered me up
the great staircase once again ; but instead of opening
the door of the glittering drawing-room, where I expected to be met by the beaming face, the tender eyes,
and radiant figure of her I loved, I was shown into the
library, and found myself face to face with the baronet
himself.

He looked as high-nosed and aristocratic as ever,
and, moreover, as grim and pale and stern as death.
He barely acknowledged my somewhat bewildered bow
—I felt conscious that I had not been sent for profes-
sionally—and instead of asking me to be seated, he
took a chair himself, and left me standing opposite.
Folding one leg over the other, and putting the tips of
his fingers together, as he lay back, and mostly looked
up to the ceiling—

" Sir," said he, " my son has, doubtless, informed
you in his note of this morning that I wished to see
you ? "

" Your son, Sir Percival—I received no note from
him ! " I replied, in utter bewilderment. " If Miss
Chalcot is indisposed—— "

" Do not dare to name Miss Chalcot, fellow! She is
by this time in France."

"In France?" I repeated faintly, and with a sinking heart.

"Yes; and beyond the reach of beggarly adventurers and *chevaliers d'industrie.*"

(So the letter had been a forgery by the brother—a lure for me.)

"Listen to me, sir, and attend," said the old man, gravely and calmly, "for it is the last time I shall ever degrade myself by addressing so contemptible a trickster!"

"Trickster, Sir Percival!" I exclaimed. "Your injurious language——"

"I said trickster," he continued, with a mock bow. "All has now been discovered; the secret meetings in the Park, the artful plans you have laid to worm yourself into the affections of a silly and *wealthy* young girl, luring her heart from the man—the gentleman, I mean —she is to marry; causing the delay of that marriage; making scandal and gossip even among the menials of my own household. Miss Chalcot, sir, has been sent to the Continent, and I hereby inform you that if you venture to follow, to trace, to speak with, or to write to her, THIS is but a small instalment of what is in store for you!"

And ere I could think or act, the savagely-proud old man had snatched up a heavy riding-whip that lay at hand, and dealt me two severe cuts fairly across the face, almost laying it open, as if with a sword blade.

L

"Madman!" I exclaimed; "dare you strike me?"

"I *have* struck you twice, sir," said he, with a disdainful smile, as he reseated himself.

"You are old, and your white hairs protect you; but you have a son, and I'll have him out at Chalk Farm"—it was really Chalk Farm *then*—"and—and —but, oh heaven!—he is the brother of Gertrude!"

"Bah! I thought so, you presumptuous beggar! Go—go! or I shall chastise you again. Go, I say! and remember well my words and my warning!"

I was trying to say something—I know not what —when the door opened and his son appeared with several servants, and before I could speak, I was thrust, dragged, beaten by many clenched hands, and forcibly expelled—yea, literally spurned—into the public street —I, Frederick Mortimer, M.D., &c., &c.

Right well did they know—old Chalcot and his son —that the very magnitude and depth of the insult to which they subjected me would protect them, and that, for her sake, they might have torn me limb from limb without revenge on my part. Yet every nerve and fibre tingled with shame and passion as I crossed the street, and while endeavouring to conceal my discoloured and lacerated face by my handkerchief, sought the seclusion of the park opposite, going to the very place where I was wont to meet my lost Gertrude, and where the charm of her presence seemed to hover still.

But where was she?

There I remained for some hours, in a state difficult to conceive. The insults to which I had been subjected drove me to the verge of insanity. My situation was unique, and I cannot now analyse or describe all the emotions that surged through my brain—memory furnishes nothing that will connect them. But there were rage and shame, grief, hatred, and love, and sorrow. It was here but yesterday she had said, prophetically, " To-morrow should end all ! "

And all was *ended, indeed !*

France !—she was in France ; there would I follow her, and yet be revenged upon them all. I started up to seek old Crammer, and resign my situation as his assistant.

The afternoon was far advanced, and many a patient must have been sorely neglected by that time. But what cared I if the world had burst like a bomb-shell beneath my feet ? I sought the house in Bedford Street, with the red bottle in the fanlight, to find that its crimson glow paled beside the hue of Crammer's face. He was literally boiling and choking with indignation at me.

He had received due intimation of my " insolence and presumption " from Sir Percival ; was desired to send in his account, and appear at the house no more. Thus his most aristocratic patients were lost to him for ever.

Ere I could speak, he took the initiative, and dismissed me, and that night found me in a humble resi-

L 2

dence, near the Temple, with a few pounds in my purse, my worldly goods a portmanteau and a few medical books ("Bell on the Bones,") seeking to soothe my thoughts by the aid of an execrable cigar and a little weak brandy and water.

The bright bubble had burst! I had lost Gertrude, and she, being facile, or having little will of her own, on finding that she had lost me, would too probably make peace with her own family by fulfilling the engagement that was so odious to her.

As this conviction forced itself upon me, I could have wept; then I would start up, and mutter of going to France ere it might be too late; but I had no money, and travelling in those pre-railway times was not the cheap luxury it is now. Moreover, I knew not how or where to seek her; and while doubts grew thus, and time went on, I might lose her for ever.

The result of all this was that the next day saw me in a raging fever, and months elapsed ere I was convalescent. For some time after sense returned I knew not where I was, or what had happened to me. Close by a table sat a familiar figure in his shirt-sleeves, smoking, and occasionally taking a pull at a pint of stout. These pleasures he varied by reading aloud from a medical work, on pharmacy apparently, and breaking into a scrap from a song, thus:—

" 'Plumbi subacet: an aqueous solution of the salt produced with the acetate and oxide of lead. A dense, clear liquid. Colourless, odourless, and slightly alka-

line in taste. Produces a white coating on glass.'
Plumbi subacet—that's the ticket!

> " ' He was a jolly old cock, and he cared not a d——n
> For the laws or the new police,
> And he thought mighty little of taking a lamb,
> If he only fancied the fleece.'

" ' *Sodæ chloratæ :* a solution of carbonate of soda,
after the absorption of chlorine gas. A clear liquid,
and colourless. Odour——' "

" Bob—Bob Asher!" said I, in a faint voice, and he
started at once to my bedside; and from him I got a
history of how ill I had been, and how he had been my
chief attendant; how sore trials had come upon himself,
and that, by his father's failure, he was at the lowest
ebb now for funds, but had betaken himself to study,
and meant to pass now.

" But who the deuce is this Gertrude of whom you
have been raving for weeks past? Not she ' of Wyo-
ming '—eh, Fred ? "

I told him my story, and he was excessively in-
dignant.

" Why, death alive ! " said he, " Chalcot is only a
baronet, and in the civil line of precedence—that is
pretty like a full corporal in the army—the second round
of the long ladder of rank. I'd have chucked the old
beggar over his own window ! "

" Not if you loved his daughter, Bob," said I mourn-
fully.

" Well, no, perhaps."

" And you are reading up ? "

" Hard, Fred. I am doing the ' Modified Examination' in pharmacy, and think I shall pass now."

I had been three months ill. Three months! Bob told me that the Chalcots' town house was still shut up, and no one knew in what part of the Continent they were travelling. Our separation seemed confirmed now. The dread of never again beholding that sweet face, with the bright eyes and the pretty crape bonnet, grew strong within me, and the idea that she might already have become the wife of another added to my torture of mind.

But lack of funds compelled me bestir myself anon, and through Bob's kind offices, and my own known skill while attending in the hospitals, I was fortunate enough to obtain temporary employment with Professor Sir ——— ———, then the most celebrated anatomical lecturer in England, as an under demonstrator, my duties, as I may inform the uninitiated, consisting to a great extent in the preparation of the various subjects for minute dissection prior to his lectures; and during the hot weather in London, I know of no task more nauseous, repulsive, or typhoid in its chances and nature. However, such work is as necessary for the progress of science and the conservation of life and health in others as the terrible task of procuring the necessary subjects was then—when the tables of anatomical theatres and dissecting-rooms depended mostly, if not solely, on the results of felony—often of murder—

and the abduction of the tenants of the tear-bedewed grave—an abduction in many instances, happily, never known to relatives.

The duties assigned to me at the rooms of Sir—— —— brought me in contact, under cloud of night, with wretches whose character was revolting, and caused me to shudder. Scores of bodies were brought me—valued at from five to twenty guineas each.

Use and wont is everything, and by me at that time they were viewed as coolly and callously as we may the fish that lie on marble slabs in the curer's window.

Weary with a long day's work at the dissecting-room, I had retired to my little lodgings, and thinking sadly over the bright past that could come no more, I felt disposed to ask heaven, upbraidingly, why I had ever been cast under the spell of Gertrude, when I was startled by the unusual sound of carriage-wheels stopping before my humble place. There were steps on the rickety stairs, and to my astonishment the professor entered, and shutting the door, said he wished to speak to me alone, as he had suddenly "an expedition" to suggest to me—one that would require decision and care to carry out, as so many morbid and vulgar rumours of violated graves were abroad, and the *suspected*, if caught, had but small chance of mercy from the mob.

"But, Sir —— ——, surely you don't expect *me* to go on such an errand?" I asked, with an incredulous smile.

"By Jove, but I do!" said he, laughing. "I have frequently done so, when a student here, in many a fetid London burying ground, now closed up or built over; but this is a most particular case—a subject we must positively have for demonstration, and, if possible to skeletonize afterwards."

"Is it peculiar, then?"

"Most peculiar!"

My curiosity was excited.

"Where is the burying-ground?" I asked.

"At R——, eight miles from town. No 'outrage,' as they call it, has occurred there. The place is un-watched and open. Would go with you myself—but two, you see—should be just in the way. Yesterday an old woman was buried there. Cholera, they say, caused her death; but anything is called cholera now. She was fifty-eight years old, and known well in the neigh-bourhood for a singular malformation of the spinal column, and I must have that portion of her for my museum; but as the old dame will not be very heavy you may as well bring the whole of her. Young Phosfat, so long my assistant, who has the practice there, has written me all about it. Take a trap and Bob Asher with you—he's game for anything—to-morrow afternoon, and, if you can, manage the matter without fuss. We'll call her an old Dutch woman in the class, say she came pickled in a cask from Holland."

The whole affair was a little exciting, so the high spirits of Bob Asher, who had frequently been engaged in such affairs in the churchyards of Edinburgh, decided me at once. We hired a dog-cart, took large overcoats with us, as the nights were chilly, a cloak, a coil of rope, heavy sticks, and even a brace of pistols for an extreme emergency, which I prayed devoutly might not occur, and we soon left London behind us.

Tom Phosfat was duly prepared by a letter from the professor for our arrival. He was a bachelor, and made us thoroughly welcome, so we had supper and a glass of grog with him : I should rather say several glasses of grog—too many for the work we had to do. However, we set out at midnight for the churchyard, which stood apart from the village, on the borders of a wide waste common, dark, secluded among trees, and lonely.

The night was gloomy and starless, and not a sound was heard—not even a withered leaf whirled by the passing wind—as we left the horse and trap under the shadow of a high hedge and vaulted over the low churchyard wall. My heart beat quickly, all the more so that Tom's brandy had been pretty potent.

The mouldering tombstones, half sunk in the long reedy grass, and tossing nettles, studded all the mournful place. God's acre seemed very solemn that night. The lonely old church, old as the days of the third Edward, half hidden by ivy, and spotted by lichens, raised its square Norman tower against the vapour-laden sky, and quaint heads and demon faces were peeping out of the mouldings and gargoyles upon us.

" You know the grave, Phosfat ? " said I.

"Yes—hush—this must be it. There is no other new one in the ground," stuttered Tom, who had imbibed too much.

"This seems the burial place of wealthy people," said Bob Asher. "The old dame must have had money and to spare."

"By Jove, it is open!" said I, in a low whisper.

"It has not been quite filled up—boards are over it; only some branches and soil thrown in. How is this?"

"The bricking of the vault has been postponed till to-morrow," said Bob Asher, shovelling out the *débris*. "We have no time to lose, Fred. Shall we break open the top of the coffin, and use the rope to pull up the subject by the neck? That was the way with Knox's fellows in Edinburgh."

"Nay," said I, "by such a process the spinal column may be disturbed; and that won't suit the professor's purpose."

"Look round, and listen well; here goes then," and half turning the coffin on its side, Bob and Tom, by inserting their shovels under the lid, burst it up with a hideous jarring sound, and then the ghostly tenant was seen, enveloped in a shroud of white from head to foot; and even to us, prepared as we were for it, that figure had something horrible in its angular rigidity. Muffling *it* in the dark cloak, I cast it over my shoulder, and deposited it in a sitting position—the *rigor mortis* had passed away apparently—between the seat and splashboard of the trap. My companions meanwhile re-arranged the grave and coffin as we had found them. Voices and lights now scared us. Phosfat was so tipsy that I had to leave Bob Asher to take care of him; and casting our shovels and rope into a clover field, I drove at a break-neck pace towards London, intensely anxious to reach the professor's house before day should dawn, lest the police or a passer-by might detect something weird in the person who was my companion.

It seemed to me that we had not proceeded a mile townward, between hedgerows, when the waning moon, hitherto invisible, began to glimmer over Hampstead Heath, shedding a ghostly farewell ray upon the silent country, where not a dog barked.

A strange sound, like the murmur of a voice, came to my ears at times. Was it a pursuit? I looked anxiously back, and even pulled up for an instant. Behind all was silent—but, oh, almighty heaven! what was this?

The old woman was moving—her feeble hands essayed to lift the cloth that covered her face! A wild spasm of terror contracted my heart; and any one but a medical man, I am assured, would have abandoned the trap and an adventure so terrible; but the idea of a recovery from trance immediately flashed upon my mind, and my first thought was, the professor would not get the prized vertebræ after all. I lifted the almost inani-mate woman beside me, and felt that she was warm, fleshy too, and had a returning pulse, which the motion

of the trap accelerated.   I uncovered her face that
she might respire, and a wild cry escaped me—a cry
that rang far over the heath.

Heavens!   Was I going mad outright?   She was
Gertrude!—Gertrude Chalcot!—pale as death could
make her, yet living still, her hazel eyes lurid and
sunken, her dark hair falling about her face.

All that followed was like a swift nightmare: the
drive to town, muffled in my overcoat and cloak; the
abandonment of the trap in the street; her conveyance
in secret to my lodgings, and placing her cosily in my
own bed till I could get her other quarters and attendance.   Luckily, Bob Asher, and the professor too, came
about mid-day, or I should soon have been fit for
Hanwell.

   *   *   *

How all this came to pass was very simple.   Unwedded
still, she had returned with her family to England in
wretched health; her illness took a more serious form,
and would seem to have culminated in a species of
trance, with the medical technicalities of which it might
be wearisome to trouble the reader.   Suffice it, that the
alarm of cholera was abroad, and the local terror at
R—— induced her interment, as, perhaps, in too many
other cases, hastily and prematurely; hence the vault
being left unfinished, permitted her to respire, and our
adventure—a mistake by the way—ended in her rescue,
though a great horror of what her fate might have been
filled my heart, and for a long period we were compelled

to conceal from her the awful place in which she was found.

Under our united care she recovered fast. But my space is short.

Sweet is the union of lovers after a separation; but, with all its charm, much that was sad, startling, and even terrible, mingled with ours. She was mine now. Not even that proud and cruel father, who had so fiercely spurned me, could dispute the claim, I thought. Mine —oh, how strangely and how terribly mine !

The close of the year saw us married, Bob Asher acting as groomsman with great *éclat*. Sir —— —— took me as a partner, and for a month I went with my bride to Baden. There, one day, at the *table d'hôte*, she found herself face to face with her own parents. The alarm, the consternation, the scene, proved frightful; but all ended in a complete reconciliation, and Christmas-day saw us all happy at Chalcot Park, and I felt, on seeing my blooming Gertrude, in all the splendour of her beauty, opening the yearly ball, that I could with a whole heart forgive even her father for his pride and fury on the day that saw us separated.

CLARE THORNE'S TEMPTATION.

CHAPTER I.

" After all that has been, and is no more—after all
that has passed between us, but never can pass again,
why are we fated to meet—and *here?*" wailed the
girl, Clare Thorne, in her heart (for though a wedded
wife, she was but a girl yet, being barely in her
twentieth year), as she suddenly saw, with strangely-
mingled emotions of joy, fear, and sorrow, the face of
Fred Wilmot.

It was on a Sunday morning early, ere the East
Indian sun was quite up, and in the cantonment church
of Mirzapatam, a few miles from the Jumna, that this
unexpected recognition took place.

The girl heard not the voice of the preacher, her
husband Cecil Thorne, the chaplain of the station ; she
forgot for a time where she was, and her thoughts fled—
fled away from that strange-looking cantonment church,
with its long punkahs pulled by nut-brown coolies (who
watched with amazement "the white man's *poojah*")
moving alike over the head of the preacher and his

congregation, when even at that early hour the air was
breathless, and when the ring-necked paraquets, green
pigeons, and other birds twittered in and out at the
open jalousies—fled home, while her heart seemed to stand
still—home to a quaint old English church in beautiful
Kent, with its low broad Norman arches, its stained
glass windows, its sculptured effigies, above which old
iron helmets hung, and spiders spun their dusty webs
undisturbed—for there it had been that she had last
seen the face she now looked on, breathlessly, the face of
her first love and *then* betrothed, Fred Wilmot, ere
misfortune separated them, and a cruel fate sent her to
Central India, to become the wife of the Reverend
Cecil Thorne.

On the preceding day a new regiment had marched
in, but she knew not till that moment at the morning
sermon, that among its officers was Lieutenant Frederick
Wilmot, till she saw him with his men, in his braided
white kalkee uniform, carrying under one arm his pith
helmet, encircled by a blue veil, and looking with his
lithe form, embrowned face, dark grey eyes and heavy
moustache, handsomer than ever, and so unlike her
husband, Cecil Thorne, in his flowing white Indian
cassock.

Square in figure, grave, massive, and commanding in
form, the latter was a man, who, though all kindness
and gentleness, seldom smiled and never laughed, and
was one all unsuited to the volatile Clare ; yet she had
married him for a home ; though knowing that every

thought and impulse of her mind were at variance with
his, and had given herself to him because she was
heart-sick with the struggle for daily bread as a gover-
ness, and feared her hopeless future when left alone in
India. A few years before—for he was much her
senior—Cecil Thorne had been a hard-working curate
on £80 per annum in one of the most squalid parts of
the English metropolis, and was thankful to accept from
the Bishop of Calcutta the post he held at the remote
and sun-baked station of Mirzapatam. He was a good
man, truly a soldier of Heaven, and among the sick and
the dying, did many a task of mercy, from which even
the doctors, and all, save the sisters of charity, shrank,
especially in the times of famine and cholera.

Intent on his sermon, he saw not the glance of
mutual recognition between Clare and Wilmot, the
grave bow exchanged, and the paleness that came over
the two young eager faces, whose troubled gaze sought
each other from time to time, as their thoughts went
back to their past—

> " The love that took an early root,
>   And had an early doom."

" Why are we fated to meet again, and *here?* " was
the ever-recurring thought of Clare, as she strove to fix
her eyes on the grave face of her husband and listen to
his eloquence, but she heard it not.

Her face was not a beautiful one, but it was sweet,
earnest, and most winning in all its varying expressions.

India had paled it already, but the light of her dark hazel eyes, the warm tint of her rosebud lips, and her rich brown hair, almost black in hue, were all unchanged as when Wilmot had covered them with kisses and caresses, in the sad hour of their severance that seemed so long ago.

In due time the service was over, the congregation dispersing and departing on horseback or in buggies, while the new regiment, to the clangour of its band, was marching into its lines, and Fred Wilmot, she knew, was with it. Fearful that he might address her ere the column was formed, she remained nervously in her seat, striving to pray for strength of purpose, or for her past dull content, and then, when she deemed herself safe, drove home alone, for her husband, though hot the coming noon, had sick and other visits to pay.

Clare feared that Wilmot might call at their bungalow on the following day, as every one calls on every one else on arriving at a new station in India; so she resolved to take her horse and be out of his way in the cool of the evening, and also early on the following morning, but to evade him always in the narrow European circle at Mirzapatam she knew would be impossible.

That day her husband was long absent on his parochial duties, and Clare was not sorry; she wanted time for thought—but thought only took the line of repining, and a comparison of what was now the inevitable, with what might have *been*.

Clare was formed by nature for excitement, society,

M

music, and gaiety, she did not like to be left to mope as
a parson's wife "in the station to which the Lord had
called her," as her husband constantly phrased it; and
she had been wont to writhe under his advice as to how
she was to comport herself, what she was to wear and
not to wear, and to avoid the groups of young officers
about the "Band Stand," and all risk of *gup* or gossip.
His intense goodness, his awful sense of propriety, even
his fervid piety, had bored and wearied the young wife
ere their dull honeymoon was well over; for though a
good girl in every way, Clare was not pious, as Mr.
Thorne understood piety. She went, per order, to
church twice on Sunday, but flatly refused to teach
"little niggers" in the mission schools, and he groaned
in spirit over her contumacy The excitement she
wished, was not to be found in visiting old Hindoo
women and teaching naked little boys that the precepts
of Menou, the lawgiver, were idolatry.

"Oh dear, for what did you marry me, Cecil?" she
asked one evening impatiently, when she heard the
strains of military music coming from the forbidden
band-stand, and knew that all the little gaiety of the
place was centred there.

"To be a helpmate to me, Clare," he replied
gravely, "and to share with me, so far as becomes my
wife, my labours in the vineyard of our Divine Master.
In our little Bengali church are regular Sabbath services and weekly prayer-meetings; there are four
patshalas or elementary schools; but to not one of these

have you gone; there are much evangelistic work and colportage work to be done, yet you assist in them not, and will not even sing the hymns I have translated from the *Tembarani*."

"If I did, Cecil—dear Cecil, would you let me go even once a week to the military promenade—I do so love the band?" she asked, with her eyes full of tears.

"No; such frivolity becomes not my wife," was the firm reply.

Repiningly she obeyed his dictum in every respect, and when other ladies ventured to remonstrate with her, Clare, to do her justice, ever upheld her husband, and treated him with respect and honour.

CHAPTER II.

NEXT day, ere the sun had risen, Clare Thorne, attended by Chuttur Sing, her native groom, went forth for her morning ride while the air was yet cool and delicious, and in every European she saw dreading to meet Wilmot, left the station behind her at a canter. She was clad in a light brown holland habit, trimmed with red braid; she wore a broad hat and long feather, and looked strikingly handsome.

Once or twice she looked back to the cantonment, and murmured to herself how strange it was to think that *he* should be there—he, after all! The civilians'

M 2

bungalows were built on the little hills, where a puff of
wind might be caught; but the barracks and sepoy lines
occupied the centre of an arid and unsheltered plain,
where never came a breath of wind to fan the withered
cheek, or to drive away the fever and sickness for ever
lingering there. As usual, the *site* of the cantonments
was a blunder, and there our soldiers were doomed to
languish, swelter, and perish by cholera or sunstroke, for
the barracks had been built, and being so, had to be
occupied.

"Poor Brown is down with cholera this morning." "Poor Brown! another told off to die. There
are four doctors with him; but all in Europe couldn't
give him another day in this world." Such were
usually the first morning greetings in Mirzapatam when
the bugles blew "the assembly." "And Smith of the
1st Bengal died about gun fire." "But that trump,
Thorne, the chaplain, never left him till, with his own
hands, he had closed his eyes." "When is the
funeral?" "In orders, for sunset—the cool of the
evening; *cool* at Mirzapatam!"

"Would Wilmot escape, or be going forth soon on a
gun-carriage, as so many went, from that horrible
barrack!" thought Clare, as she rode on towards the
Jumna, where she knew the country grew beautiful;
and she shivered as she thought of the life she led
now.

Though her husband was chaplain to a military
station, officers seldom or never, except when on duty,

entered his bungalow; so the male visitors there consisted only of eurasian and native catechists, col-
porteurs, and teachers.   To Clare it was an intolerable
existence, and as she saw, when fever abated, the gay
and happy lives led by the other ladies of the garrison,
she repined sorely, and thinking of all these things, she
rode slowly toward the Jumna.

Down from the Ghaut of Etawah the river was rolling
in its beauty amid the most wondrous greenery in the
world.   There were oleanders (the pride of the jungles)
sending forth their delicious perfumes from clusters of
pink and white blossoms; the baubool, with its bells of
gold, the sensation plant, and thousand others all growing together, while the *byahs*, or crested sparrows, looked
like clouds of gold as they floated in flocks over these
and the waters of the river.   Yet, lovely though the
scene, the English girl, as she reined up her horse,
thought she would rather have looked upon the Weald
of her native Kent!

The same idea was in the heart of another, who was
slowly approaching her, an officer in undress, with pith-
helmet and loose white patrol jacket.   He urged his
horse close to Clare, and a little exclamation escaped
her.

" Oh, fatality! " she murmured, on finding herself
face to face with Fred Wilmot; and fatality it seemed
indeed, that they should by chance have chosen the
same hour and the same pathway, amid the many that
diverged from the breathless cantonments.   He sprang

from his horse, and grasping the bridle with one hand, presented the other to her.

"Mrs. Thorne—Clare!" said he, in a broken voice, and as he uttered her name there came into his face a light, an almost divine tenderness, such as she had never seen in it, even in their sweet past time—the light of love, the joy of a great passion.

"I *am* Mrs. Thorne, and we must remember that now, Fred," said she; but without drawing back her hand. None was near but Chuttur Sing, who certainly thought he would not have liked to have seen *his* wife *tête-à-tête* with the *sahib-logue*, in that solitary place, for to the Bengalees the ease of European society is an enigma they fail to understand.

"Till I saw you yesterday, I knew not in what part of India you were," said Wilmot, with his gaze fixed eagerly upon her now pallid face, "and now they tell me that you are the wife of that man—our chaplain, a morose and gloomy fellow——"

"My husband, Mr. Wilmot," said Clare, now withdrawing her hand, and shortening her gathered reins.

"Mr. Wilmot!" he exclaimed, almost reproachfully.

"My husband!" she repeated, with sorrowful emphasis.

"I beg your pardon, Clare. I am not likely to forget the fact," said he, with deep dejection; "but changed though the relations—broken the tie—between us, may I not be still your friend? I—I," he continued, in a voice so pathetic that her soul was moved, " I who was once so much dearer than any friend could be ? "

" We must forget all that—friends ? No, it is impossible ! Better not—better not—oh, what fatality sent you here ! " she added, restraining with difficulty her tears, and aware that the black-beady eyes of Chuttur Sing were upon her—Chuttur Sing of the spindle legs and huge red turban.

" You have not forgotten the past, then, Clare ? "

" No—but I have sought to love my husband as a wife should."

" Sought ? " he asked, inquiringly.

" Well—I have striven."

" But oh, Clare, we can neither love nor forget at will," said he. " May I come to visit you ? "

" No—decidedly no ! "

" Why, Clare ? "

" My husband ! " she replied, firmly enough.

" He knows nothing of our past—he never heard of me. Think how dear we were to each other, Clare—how much we have to remember."

" All the more reason to study the art of forgetting," replied Clare, whose hot tears were falling fast now, " and to show the necessity for your not coming near our bungalow."

" But if all our fellows, from the colonel down to the youngest sub, leave their cards for you and Mr. Thorne, save me, what will he think ? "

" I cannot say," sighed Clare, wearily.

" I must come, then, to avoid remark. May I ? "

" If you must, you may."

" Thanks, Clare—thanks ; may I escort you home ? "

" No—oh no—let us return separate," said she, nervously, and they parted, she urging her horse at a hand-gallop back to the arid plain, where the lines of Mirzapatam were now quivering, and to all appearance vibrating, in the hot rays of the uprisen sun.

So when Fred Wilmot called that evening at the Rev. Mr. Thorne's bungalow, he was cordially received by that gentleman, and by his wife politely, as a— stranger ! Clad in a thin dress, through which her delicate arms and the contour of her bosom were ap- parent, she was reclining in a long-armed Indian cane chair, with all her dark-brown hair cast loose over her back and shoulders, just as her ayah had left it for coolness ; and very charming and girlish she looked, especially when her colour heightened. The fragrant odour of the recently wetted *tatties*, or window-screens, pervaded a large uncarpeted drawing-room. An hour and more was passed in pleasant conversation. No reference whatever *could* be made to the past, so from that hour each of those *two* felt that the game of duplicity was beginning. The piano—which had its feet immersed in saucers of water to save it from creep- ing in sects—was more than once resorted to ; and Mr. Thorne was surprised to find how many airs and duets his wife and the new comer knew in common. He could little dream how often they had practised them *together*, in that sweet Kentish village so long ago, it seemed now. That night Fred Wilmot slept little. He had more than the mosquitos to keep him awake, while in the verandah without the *wallah* pulled drowsily at the cord of the punkah.

"Innocent, pure and artless as ever—poor Clare—poor darling!" thought he; "oh, what avail my money and position now—now that she is that sombre fellow's wife—yet all men speak well of him here. What are her dark eyes, her rich hair, her sweet English beauty to me now!"

CHAPTER III.

CLARE THORNE's life had been so dull, that one can scarcely wonder if she found the advent of Wilmot at the cantonment, and his visits, most welcome, though they filled her with a vague alarm—an undefined fear of violating trust and propriety. We have said that the Thornes had few visitors; this arose from the distaste the chaplain had of society and the general gravity of his demeanour; but Fred Wilmot cared little for all that; it was not him he came to see.

No thought of evil was in the innocent heart of Clare; nor was there in the heart of Wilmot, to do him justice, though he abandoned himself to the perilous charm of seeking the society of the girl who once loved

him so well—from whom he had been separated, and
who felt with him in common "that *death* in life, the
days that are no more." A little time the regiment
would be moving further up country, and all would then
be at an end. Meanwhile both were playing with edged
tools !

Clare and her husband could not understand each
other. His nature, which with all his apparent gloom
was a passionate one, had no outlet save his great love
for her, and his greater for religion. For him the dull
routine of his daily life was enough ; but Clare longed,
like the girl she was, for amusement, excitement, display, society, and yet in gay British India she was condemned by this good and amiable, but fervid ascetic,
to lead a life which, to one of her temperament, was one
of unspeakable martyrdom.

She might, perhaps, under better auspices, have forgotten her first love in time, and learned to like, as
much as she respected, her husband, had he only made
some allowance for her weakness and foibles, and not
judged her so hardly and set before her a standard of
excellence which she was unable to attain.

But the crisis of her life was coming fast to Clare
Thorne.

Her husband began to dislike the frequent visits and
the somewhat brotherly familiarity of Wilmot with his
wife ; there was something in it undefinable. It was
the reverse of flirtation, for his demeanour was grave,
respectful and sympathetic, and in these elements the

danger seemed to lie. Clare's bearing and tone were
irreproachable; yet a suspicion, at which he blushed,
was roused in the honest heart of Cecil Thorne.

"If it should be!" he muttered, with his firm white
teeth clenched. Then he would watch and dissemble;
but even that seemed a stain on his own rectitude.
Thus one day he said, abruptly:

"Clare, that officer—Mr. Wilmot, has been here
again. I see his music strewed all over the piano."

"Well, Cecil?"

"I forbid his visits—that is all!"

"Forbid his visits!" repeated Clare, startled, crushed,
and blushing crimson; "then you must tell him so
yourself."

"Why, madam?"

"He is an old friend of my family, and—and——"

"You, and he too, never said a word of this before!"

"I thought you knew it," faltered Clare, who found
that she had made a sad mistake.

"Old friend—he is about five-and-twenty only. What
brought him here to-day?"

"To give us these tickets for the garrison ball."

"Ball—you know I never go to balls."

"But may I?"

"No—you may *not!*"

Poor Clare repined bitterly and wept profusely, but not
for the first time in her life, and her husband, who knew
that all Mirzapatam was on tip-toe about the forbidden
ball, eyed her with a lowering expression. But he knew

that he must exert his authority, or scandals might ensue, and he felt that Wilmot must cross his threshold no more. Indeed, the ball-tickets were returned to him, and when next he visited the abode of Mr. Thorne, that gentleman, who never did things by halves, and who deemed he had a duty to perform to religion, to himself, and society, gave the young officer a pretty distinct hint that his visits could be dispensed with, and Fred retired, his heart swollen with rage, mortification, and sorrow.

Shame and anger mingled with the sorrow of Clare. How tiresome of him to go on this way to her in their present abode, of all places in the world! Scandal—the thing he dreaded—would be sure to come of it. A great gloom now fell upon Clare, and the ball—girl-like—the forbidden ball rankled in her heart; Thorne supposed this gloom was caused by the banishment of Wilmot only; but that had merely something to do with it.

Was she, that he loved and trusted, wronging him cruelly in her heart? Was he nursing a traitress in his bosom? Sooth to say, the hitherto placid and plodding Cecil Thorne began to think, and sometimes say, all manner of desperate things to his scared and shrinking little wife, whose changed manner he attributed to Wilmot's influence, and he cursed the hour that ever the new regiment marched into Mirzapatam.

Loving his wife as he did, he would rather have seen her lying in her grave and himself reading the burial service over her, than living as a disgraced woman. Then, if there was great sorrow, there would be no shame, and she would be gone where never more dishonour could menace, or shame assail her.

"Clare, child," said he, "my little wife is my all to me. The soul that sinneth shall pay the wages of sin."

"But I have not sinned!" she exclaimed, passionately.

"As yet," said he, pointedly and coldly; "thank Heaven, my eyes were opened in time! Think of what would be my misery and our conjoint dishonour—I, a priest of the Church! Think of how our once happy home might have been desecrated and the bitterness of a love that is slighted!"

"You make too much or too little of all this!"

"I do not!"

"Oh, Cecil—Cecil—my dear husband—I have no forgiveness to ask of you; I only seek your pity."

"I *do* pity you," he replied, grimly, and thought the while,

"She can speak to me thus—with that fellow's kisses fresh upon her lips!" For he had undefined suspicions that Wilmot saw her yet, from time to time.

"How tiresome—how absurd is this jealousy!" thought Clare; yet her own conscience told her it was neither absurd nor mistaken *now;* and all this passed on the night of the forbidden ball!

CHAPTER IV

Mr. Thorne's suspicions were right; they *had* been meeting, without design at first; ample though the cantonment, how could it be otherwise?

"Dear, good Fred," she said, one day, as they met among the baubool trees near an old ruined tomb—the tomb of Abu Mirza—"I want you to help me—you alone can do so."

"In what way?" he asked, looking at her in his old tender manner.

"To be good and proper—to keep in the straight path of propriety, and avoid all chance of scandal."

"You are quoting some sermon of Thorne's now."

"I am not—I mean it; we must speak no more; *will* you help me?"

"Yes," said he, in a choking voice; "yes—if I can," and his mode of beginning was pressing her to his heart, and covering her face with kisses.

From this it may be inferred that the threads of the old, old story had become strong as cables again! She had been rent from Wilmot by Fate, and revenge at Fate made him selfish to her and pitiless to all, especially to her husband, who had, by forbidding his visits, at once given their intimacy a colouring it did not then possess. Now things were said that they had never said before, and wild schemes of plainly running away together—where, it mattered not—were more than openly hinted at by Wilmot. Be it sinful or not, she felt that she loved him better than her own life; his was the only mind that could hold dominion over hers; yet it was one infinitely inferior to that of Cecil Thorne; and his was the only hand whose touch thrilled the smallest fibres of her frame. She worshipped Wilmot, who, as he gazed into her eyes, could read there the struggle that was passing between conscience and passion, and how the latter was certain to triumph.

"Trust me—trust me," he whispered in her ear.

"I will trust you—I will, Freddy!" she replied, choked in tears.

"My own darling—to be my own at last—and after all!"

Clare knew what scandal and gossip were in England; but "gup" in India was fiercer, deeper, more trumpet-tongued, and already in fancy she saw every public print teeming with the story of her elopement and her husband's shame.

"He thinks too much of the other world to care much for this, or me!" she thought; but in that she wronged Thorne, who loved her dearly and devotedly, though in a cold and undemonstrative way, while Wilmot was all passion and energy.

"Oh, the scandal—the scandal we shall give!" said she, wringing her hands.

"Scandals die!" said he; "the world goes too fast

now-a-days for anything—even for a wonder—to live long; and we shall seek a land where none shall know our names or the miserable story of our past."

"Oh, Fred!" wailed the girl, "I was brought up by my mother, in the careful avoidance of all evil, all that was sinful and unholy; and now I am sinking into an ocean of unholiness in loving you, better than I love my own soul!"

"Do not thus upbraid yourself, my innocent darling," said he, in a quiet but passionate tone.

"Innocent? Oh, my God! who will call me innocent, good, or pure to-morrow? Yet, the life I bear maddens me."

"That life will soon be a thing of the past. I am wealthy now, my darling; the bar that poverty put between us is removed. I can give you a home like a palace, in any part of Europe, far, far away from this breathless India; and once my wife——"

"Oh—Wilmot!"

"My darling—I will give you all the love a human heart can render you—the dearest of love and a new life."

"But not with that which makes life alone worth having."

He regarded her passionately, anxiously, and entreatingly.

She felt that if she hesitated—deliberated—she would be lost, and must become, in any land, even though unknown, a social outlaw, a virtual outcast.

All this rushed upon her mind, though she said it not, and with all its minor details of mortification and bitterness, as she lay with her face hidden on the breast of Wilmot.

He smiled fondly, yet sadly, down upon her bent head, and clasped her trembling fingers in his stronger hands, and turning up her white and desperate little face, he dared, in the excess and blindness of his passion, to call on heaven to hear that she would never have cause to regret the step she was about to take.

And so they separated with reluctance, though in haste, aware that when they met again it would be to part no more!

CHAPTER V

Fred Wilmot had obtained a year's leave from the general commanding at Mirzapatam, and had taken all his measures for their mutual flight.

He was to meet her at evening gun-fire, near the old ruined tomb in the baubool grove, when Aloodeen, his native valet, would bring his buggy. In this they would proceed to the branch line that joined the greater line at Allahabad, from whence they could take the great Peninsular Railway to Calcutta, long before reaching which all traces of them would be lost!

N

It was early morning when the scheme was planned ;
a whole day was to elapse ere it could be put in operation ; yet it seemed to pass with frightful rapidity to
Clare, who felt like one in a dream, or as if it was some
other person, and not herself, who was to meet Wilmot
at the tomb of Abu Mirza.

Her silence, her pre-occupation, her nervousness,
more than all, the whiteness of her little face, could not
fail to attract the attention of her husband who, with
unwonted tenderness, bent over her, and, taking her
cheeks between his hands, said,—

"Look up, little woman—why, what is the matter
with you ? "

She closed her eyes, which dared not meet his earnest,
honest, and searching gaze.

He then took her little hands caressingly in his, and
felt, with alarm, that though the atmosphere without
was stifling, they were icy cold and trembling.

"Is there anything wrong, Clare ? What is the
matter with you, my darling little wife ? "

Still she was silent, for her tongue clove to the roof
of her mouth, and she could only sigh in her heart
secretly.

"Oh, heaven—what *am* I to do ? Avoid the temptation—flee the sin—yea, even confess all—ere it be too
late ! "

Then she thought of her husband's frigidity of
manner, his intense sense of morality, religion, purity,
and rectitude, and her timid heart died within her.

"God help us, child," said Cecil Thorne, "I hope that no illness has seized you."

He thought wildly over the several fever and cholera beds he had been beside of late, and the strong man felt his soul die within him with fear, as he saw alternately the wistfulness and wild excitement in his wife's eyes.

"A doctor must be summoned," he exclaimed; "qui hi —hollo, there, Chuttur Sing!"

"Oh, no, Cecil, dearest," said she, with something between a sob and a hysterical laugh; "it is only the heat that affects me—and the thunder," she added, as a peal went hustling through the sultry air overhead.

A storm came on; the rain fell in torrents, and Clare, while in the act of selecting the garments and necessaries she would have to take with her, and while carefully selecting and putting aside, for some *other* and worthier wife, it might be, the few jewels her husband's moderate means had enabled him to give her (Delhi bracelets of champac-work, and so forth), actually began to hope that, if the tempest of falling rain continued, the very flight for which she was preparing might be arrested, ere it was too late, and thus that her sore temptation might pass away!

The innocent words, the tender anxiety and trusting goodness of the man she was about to abandon and deceive, and the knowledge, that in time to come, there would be an amount of grief, shame, and sorrow for her, that would be known in its degree but to God and

N 2

himself, wrung her heart, and filled her eyes with hot and blinding tears.

But the storm passed; the thunder died away beyond the hills that look down on the Jumna; the rain cooled the atmosphere, and the arid soil around the sun-baked cantonment soon absorbed it, to the last huge, warm drop that had fallen; and Clare knew that her lover would be truly, tenderly, and inexorably awaiting her at the old tomb, when the time of their fatal tryst came.

The cantonment ghuries—little gongs that hung near the guard-house doors—clanged the hours in succession, and in *one* more Clare knew that the sun would set. She was alone, for her husband was away, attending some sick beds; when he returned, she knew that her place would be vacant, and that she could never look upon his grave, earnest, and handsome face again. She sunk on her knees beside her bed, buried her face in her cold hands, and while she shivered in the agony of her conflicting thoughts, she prayed for strength to avoid her temptation, or that she might die in her mingled remorse and yearning love.

But her prayer was unheard: the hour came, and saw her, with a little travelling bag in her hand, stealing like a culprit from her husband's home, and taking the most unfrequented path to the tomb of Abu Mirza, the tiny white marble dome of which was glistening in the last rays of the sun above the golden bloom of the baubool trees. The brain of Clare seemed to reel; her temples felt on fire; all within her soul and around her seemed a mass of chaos, she could arrange, disentangle nothing; and almost in despair gave up the attempt to do so; but not the fatal design of meeting her former lover; for the die was cast!

In the distance she could hear the soldiers' children and some of the Christianised natives singing in the Mission School; their united voices came through the open windows on the calm pure air of the Indian night, and she could hear her husband accompanying them on an indifferent harmonium, so earnestly and humbly in the service of his Master, in the hymn he had translated from the *Tembavani* :—

> " Whilst Thee, with tongues of splendour,
>   The orbs of heaven praise,
> Whilst groves to Thee their voices,
>   With tongues of brilliance raise :
> Whilst Thee, with tongues of joyance
>   All gay wood-warblers sing ;
> Whilst praise to Thee, wood-flowerets,
>   From tongues of fragrance fling :
> And whilst with tongues of clearness,
>   The water-floods applaud Thee,
> With the tongue that Thou hast given,
>   Shall I not daily laud Thee ? "

' Poor Cecil—how unworthy I am of you! " thought she, and tears started to her eyes afresh as she thought of him and the *morrow!*

Her heart gave a convulsive leap and she stood still for a moment as the evening gun boomed over the cantonments when the sun set, and then the darkness fell instantly, as it always does in India where there is no twilight, and she saw Fred Wilmot instantly approach her, but from what point she scarcely knew He was attired in plain clothes, for travelling evidently, but he was bareheaded, and she could see that his face looked most startlingly pale, that also pain and bewilderment were in it, and that he scarcely seemed to see her. Something in his looks and manner rooted Clare to the spot.

"Fred—Fred—Wilmot!" she cried, in a low voice, but, without stopping, he gave her one sad glance expressive of pity and love, sorrow and pain, and passing on towards the tomb, left her alone—alone and bewildered, while a new sense of great fear that she could not analyse, caused her to rush towards the house she had so lately quitted.

At the door she met her husband, full of excitement and agitation.

"You abroad, Clare," he exclaimed, with grave surprise; "have you then heard what has happened—ah, your white face tells me that you have?"

"What has happened, Cecil?" she asked, in a low, breathless voice.

"Poor Wilmot—God forgive me if I have wronged him!—has just been murdered and robbed by his native servant, a Patan scoundrel named Aloodeen."

"Murdered?"

"Yes—just as the sunset gun was fired."

In a swoon Clare fell at his feet like one who was dead.

He had been stabbed to the heart! Who, or what was it in his likeness that Clare had seen at the place they were to meet? She was saved from her great temptation—saved to remain a sorrowing and innocent wife. She never again saw the face of Wilmot, even in a dream, though often in the years to come she decked his lonely grave with flowers.

THE GREAT SEA SERPENT.

From all we have read and heard of a singular sea-monster that has been seen from time to time in various parts of the ocean, it is difficult to doubt that some such creature, or creatures rather, may exist; though the reiterated allegations of "old salts," that they *do* exist, may be but a relic of that dark superstition known as serpent-worship, which once prevailed over a great part of the world, and which still lingers in India, particularly among the Nagas, and of which snake-charming is a remnant.

How long this singular worship lingered in Western Europe we may gather from the "Atlas Geographus," published in 1711, which says, "there are *still* remains of this idolatory" in Lithuania, where the Boors keep adders in their houses, and pay them profound respect while professing Christianity; and also, that few families in Samogitia, are without serpents as house-hold gods.

Some years before this time, Sigismund, Baron of Herbestein, tells us, in his commentaries on Muscovy, that at Troki, eight miles from Wilna, his host ac-

quainted him, that he had chanced to buy a hive of
bees from one of the serpent-worshippers, whom he
persuaded, with much reluctance, to worship the true
God and kill his serpent. A short time after, in passing that way, he found the poor fellow miserably
tortured and deformed, his face wrinkled and twisted
away; and inquiring the cause, he answered, "That
this judgment had come upon him for killing his god,
and that he would have to endure greater torments if
he did not return to his former worship."

In the sacred writings, but more particularly in the
8th chapter of Jeremiah and the 58th Psalm, are allu-
sions to the taming or keeping of serpents; and Dr.
Thomas Shaw found the same superstition prevailing in
Barbary in 1757 (Travels).

Indian serpent-charming to this day, as we have
said, is no doubt a remnant of that form of worship
which spread all over the world, it may be from some
dim tradition of the serpents of Eden and of Aaron's
rod, that we have the Scandinavian *jormagundr*, among
the fictions of the Edda, and to which Scott refers
as—

> " That sea-snake, tremendous curled,
> Whose monstrous circle guards the world."

The serpent and the circle were alike the emblem of
eternity, and Odin was supposed to have at times the
power of taking the aspect of the former; and a remnant
of the same superstition is still to be found in Scotland

in the knot-work upon Celtic crosses and Highland dirk-hilts.

In June, 1721 (as we are told in the "Historical Register" for the following year, sold by T. Norris, at the *Looking-Glass* on London Bridge), there appeared a terrible snake off the coast of Naples, not far from the Ponte-della-Maddalena, under which the river Sebeto flows into the sea, and it devoured a fisherman in presence of many of his friends, who had barely time to effect their escape.

The latter, fearing that the presence of this monster might destroy their fishery, and anxious to avenge their companion, made several weapons (harpoons?) of iron, and large hooks, and, putting to sea on the 6th of June in strong boats, discovered the great fish, and baited their lines with large pieces of horse-flesh, and ran a strong rope with a slip from the stem to the stern of a ship.

Rushing furiously at the boat, the snake was caught into the slip-knot, and ultimately drawn on shore, when, on being measured, it was found to be " twenty Neapolitan palms long. His mouth was excessively wide, having three rows of teeth in the form of a saw in the upper jaw, and but one row in the under. He weighed sixteen *coutares*, or about four hundred-weight. In the stomach were found the skull of a man, two legs, part of the backbone and ribs."

These were supposed to have been portions of the unfortunate fisherman, whom he had devoured some days before. By order of the Council of Health it was burned, lest it might infect the air.

The writer adds, that Johnson (to whom we shall refer presently) mentions similar fish—one that weighed eight hundred-weight; another that weighed four thousand pounds, and in the stomach of which was found a man, in a complete suit of armour!

It is a curious fact that recent scientific research has revealed the existence in the sea, at the greatest depths, of most minute and wonderfully formed organisms, the beauty and rarity of which necessarily secure our admiration; but instances of animals of enormous size being met with beyond those already known, are few and far between. This fact may be accounted for by the circumstance, that while it is easy to construct instruments for capturing the smaller creatures living in the deep, it is a very different matter to entrap and secure an unseen monster, whose very size must endow him with enormous strength. The whale, so far as we know, is the largest denizen of the deep. Whether it is possible that it can be equalled by giants of some other order or race, is the point which public curiosity is very keen to have settled.

The appearance of great snakes at sea is recorded by more than one old voyager; but it would seem to have been only of late years that the idea of their existence has been generally confined to one, familiar to us all as the "Great sea-serpent."

In *Opuscula Omnia Botanic Thomæ Johnsoni*, 1629,

we have an account of a great serpent captured off Sandwich by two men, who found it stranded among the
shoal water by the sea-shore. It is described as being
fifty feet long, and of a fiery colour. We are also told
that they conveyed the carcase home, and after *eating* it,
stuffed the skin with hay, to preserve it "as a perpetual
remembrance of the fact."

In David Crantz's "History of Greenland," published
in 1766, we have an extract (illustrated by a drawing)
concerning the *kraken*, from the narrative of a Captain
Paul Egede, supposed to be the brother of a famous
Danish missionary of the same name. The kraken, it
is however necessary to remark, is the northern name
for a giant cuttle-fish, the existence of such a monster
being now a matter of scientific fact.

"On the 6th of July, 1734," says this old seaman,
" as I was proceeding on my second voyage to Greenland, in the latitude of the Cape of Good Hope, a
hideous monster was seen to raise its body so high
above the water that its head overtopped our main-sail.
It had a pointed nose, and spouted out water like a
whale; instead of fins it had great broad flaps like
wings; its body seemed to be grown over with shell-
work, and its skin was very rugged and uneven; when
it dived into the water again, it threw up its tail, which
was like that of a serpent, and was at least a whole
ship's length above the water; we judged the body to
be equal in bulk to our ship, and to be three or four
times as long."

Eric Pontoppidan, Bishop of Bergen, celebrated in his days as a naturalist, though he never actually saw it or met any one who *had* seen it, believed implicitly in the great sea-serpent existing somewhere; and in his writings has a good deal to tell us about its ways and habits; and it is upon record that Sir Lawrence de Ferry, commander of the old castle of Bergen, not only saw the monster, but shot at it on the high seas, wounded it, was pursued by it, in its pain and fury, so closely that he narrowly escaped with his life.

In 1801 there was cast ashore on the coast of Dorsetshire a snake twenty-eight feet in length and twenty feet in circumference; but this has since been alleged to have been a Basking-shark; and the same has been said of a great snake-like carcase that was beaten to pieces by a tempest, and cast ashore on one of the Orkney Isles in the autumn of 1809, and some fragments of which, the *Scots Magazine* for that year states, were lodged in the Museum of the Edinburgh University.

A very distinct description of the sea-serpent occurs in Dr. Hooker's *Testimony* respecting it, and communicated to Dr. Brewster's *Journal of Science*. About half-past six o'clock on a cloudless evening at sea, the doctor heard suddenly a rushing noise ahead of the ship, which at first he supposed to be a whale spouting, but soon found to be a colossal serpent, of which he made a sketch as it passed the vessel at fifty yards' distance, slowly, neither turning to the right nor left. "As soon as his head had reached the stern, he gradually laid it down in a horizontal position with his body, and floated along like the mast of a vessel. That there was upwards of sixty feet visible, is shown by the circumstance that the length of the ship was a hundred and twenty feet, and that at the time his head was off the stern, the other end had not passed the main-mast. His motion in the water was meandering, like that of an eel; and the wake he left behind him, was like that occasioned by a small craft passing through the water.

The humps on his back resembled in size and shape those of a dromedary."

Dr. Hooker states further, that the description precisely accorded with that of a serpent seen five years before by Captain Bennett of Boston. At a later period, three officers in Her Majesty's service—namely, Captain Sullivan, Lieutenant Maclachlan, and Ensign Malcolm of the Rifle Brigade—beheld a similar creature gambolling in the sea near Halifax; but they asserted that it was at least one hundred and eighty feet in length, and thicker than the trunk of a moderately sized tree. Nor must we forget the official account which was transmitted in 1848 to the Lords of the Admiralty, by Captain Peter M'Quhae of Her Majesty's ship *Dædalus*, past which, he and his crew saw the great sea-serpent swimming merrily—a document which produced, or provoked, a learned paper in the *Westminster Review*; while Professor Owen asserted that what was seen from the deck of the *Dædalus*, would be nothing more than a large seal borne rapidly southward on a floe or iceberg.

Recently, the appearances of the serpent have been amusingly frequent and clearly detailed. He has been seen in the north seas and the south seas, and in many places nearer home; in the Frith of Forth, off Filey Bay and the North Foreland, off Hastings and the Isle of Arran, the Menai Strait and Prawle Point; and in 1875, a battle between it and a whale was viewed from the deck of the good ship *Pauline* of London, Captain Drevar, when proceeding with a cargo of coals from Shields to Zanzibar, destined for Her Majesty's ship *London*. When the *Pauline* reached the region of the trade-winds and equatorial currents, she was carried out of her course, and after a severe storm, found herself off Cape Roque, where several sperm-whales were seen playing about her. While the crew were watching them, they suddenly beheld a sight that filled every man on board with terror. Starting straight from the bosom of the deep, a gigantic serpent rose and wound itself twice in two mighty coils round the largest of the whales, which it proceeded to crush in genuine boa-constrictor fashion. In vain did the hapless whale struggle, lash the water into foam, and even bellow, for all its efforts were as nothing against the supernatural powers of its dreadful adversary, whose strength "may be further imagined," says a leader in the *Daily Telegraph*, "from the fact that the ribs of the ill-fated fish were distinctly heard cracking one after the other with a report like that of a small cannon. Soon the struggles of the wretched whale grew fainter and fainter; its bellowings ceased, and the great serpent sank with its prey beneath the surface of the ocean."

Its total length was estimated at fifty yards, and its aspect was allowed to be simply "terrific." Twice again it reared its crest sixty feet out of the water, as if meditating an attack upon the *Pauline*, which bore away with all her canvas spread. Her crew told their terrible story. But critics there were who averred that what they had seen was no serpent at all, but only a bottle-nosed whale attacked by grampuses !

In a letter to the London prints concerning this affair, we have another description of our old friend the serpent, as he appeared off St. David's Head, to John Abes, mate of a merchantman, in 1863. "I was the first who saw the monster, and shouted out. A terrible-looking thing it was! Seen at a little distance in the moonlight, his two eyes appeared about the size of *plates*, and were very bright and sparkling." All on board thought his length about ninety feet ; but as he curled and twirled rapidly, it was a difficult matter to determine. Captain Taylor ordered him to be noosed lasso-fashion with a rope, which John Abes tells us he got on the bowsprit to throw, but in the attempt threw himself overboard. "The horror of my feelings at the moment I must leave you to imagine," continues this remarkable epistle (which is dated from Totterdown, Bristol, September 19, 1875). "The brute was then within a few yards of me, with its monstrous head and wavy body, looking ten times more terrible than it did on

board the brig.   I shiver even now when I think of it.
Whether the noise made by throwing the ropes over to
save me scared him, I cannot say; but he went down
suddenly, though not more so than I came up.   After a
few minutes he appeared some distance from us, and
then we lost him."

When next we hear of the sea-serpent after his adventure off Cape Roque, he was beheld by the crew of
no less a ship than Her Majesty's yacht the *Osborne*, the
captain and officers of which, in June, 1877, forwarded
an official report to the Admiralty, containing an
account of the monster's appearance off the coast of
Sicily on the 2nd of that month.   "The time was five
o'clock in the afternoon.   The sea was exceptionally
smooth, and the officers were provided with good tele-
scopes.   The monster had a smooth skin, devoid of
scales, a bullet-shaped head, and a face like an alligator.
It was of immense length, and along the back was a
ridge of fins about *fifteen* feet in length and *six* feet
apart.   It moved slowly, and was seen by all the ship's
officers."

This account was further supplemented by a sketch in
a well-known illustrated paper, from the pencil of Lieutenant W. P. Hynes of the *Osborne*, who, to the above
description, adds, that the fins were of irregular height,
and about forty feet in extent, and " as we were passing
through the water at ten and a-half knots, I could only
get a view of it 'end on.' "   It was about fifteen or
twenty feet broad at the shoulders, with flappers or fins

o

that seemed to have a semi-revolving motion. "From the top of the head to the part of the back where it became immersed, I should consider about fifty feet, and that seemed about a third of the whole length. All this part was smooth, resembling a seal."

In the following month, the Scottish prints reported, that when the Earl of Glasgow's steam-yacht *Valetta* was cruising off Garroch Head, on the coast of Bute, with a party of ladies and gentlemen on board, an enormous fish or serpent, forty feet in length and about fifteen in diameter, suddenly rose from the sea. Under sail and steam the *Valetta* gave chase. A gentleman on board speared it with a salmon " leister :" on which the serpent dived, and after a time reappeared with the iron part of the weapon sticking in its back. The monster scudded along for some minutes, again dived, and was not seen afterwards. There is little doubt, however, that the animal which figured in this instance was a very large basking-shark (*Selache maxima*).

An animal of exactly similar shape and dimensions was reported as being seen in the subsequent August by twelve persons in Massachusetts Bay ; and soon after on three different occasions in the same quarter by the crew of a coasting vessel.

In May, 1877, the " sea-serpent " would seem to have shifted his quarters to the Indian Ocean, which it must be remarked is the habitat of the true sea-snakes. On the 21st of that month, in latitude 2° north and longitude 90° 53′ east, the monster was alleged to have been seen by the crew of the barque *Georgina*, bound from Rangoon to Falmouth. It seemed to be about fifty feet long, " grey and yellow in colour, and ten or eleven inches thick. It was on view for about twenty minutes, during which time it crossed the bow, and ultimately disappeared under the port quarter." A second account of this affair stated, that " for some days previously the crew had seen several smaller serpents, of from six to ten feet in length, playing about the vessel."

Strange as all these stories seem, it is difficult to suppose they are all quite untrue, for, nautical super-stition apart, we have the ready testimony of various men of education and veracity. That there is only one serpentine monster in the ocean, is an idea which the great disparity in the various descriptions would seem to contradict; and certainly the most astounding aspect presented by this supposed and most ubiquitous animal, was his form and size when seen by the officers of the Queen's yacht off the coast of Sicily; though it is some-what singular that these gentlemen made no attempt to kill or capture the mighty fish, or whatever it was they saw.

By way of conclusion to these remarks we may briefly summarise the chief facts presented by " sea-serpent tales " as they appear under the light of scientific criti-cism. There is, it must firstly be remarked, nothing in the slightest degree improbable in the idea that an ordi-nary species of sea-snake, belonging to a well-known group of reptiles, may undergo a gigantic development

o 2

and appear as a monster serpent of the deep. The experience of comparative anatomists is decidedly in agreement with such an opinion. Largely developed individuals of almost every species of animals and plants occasionally occur. Within the past few years new species of cuttle-fishes—of dimensions compared with which the largest of hitherto known forms are mere pigmies—have been brought to light. And if huge cuttle-fishes may thus be developed, why, it may be asked, may not sea-snakes of ordinary size be elevated, through extraordinary development, to become veritable "leviathans" of the deep? That there is a strong reason for belief in the veracity of sea-serpent tales, is supported by the consideration of the utter want of any motive for prevarication, and by the very different and varied accounts given of the monsters seen. That the appearances cannot always be explained on the supposition that lifeless objects, such as trees, sea-weed, &c., have been seen, is equally evident from the detailed nature of many of the accounts of the animals, which have been inspected from a near distance. And it may also be remarked that in some cases, in which largely developed sea-snakes themselves may not have appeared, certain fishes may have represented the reptilian inhabitants of the ocean. As Dr. Andrew Wilson has insisted, a giant tape-fish viewed from a distance would personate a "sea-serpent" in a very successful manner; and there can be no doubt that tape-fishes have occasionally been described as "sea-serpents."

On the whole, if we admit the probability of giant-developments of ordinary species of sea-snakes, or the existence (and why not?) of enormous species of sea-snakes and certain fishes *as yet unknown to science*, the solution of the sea-serpent problem is not likely to be any longer a matter of difficulty.*

* Since writing the above, the *Daily News*, of September, 1873, reported the appearance of the serpent, "twenty metres long and two-thirds of a metre in diameter," off Aalesund, on the coast of Norway.

MILITARY "FOLK LORE."

―――◆―――

CHAPTER I.

THE RED COAT; A FEW NOTES CONCERNING ITS ORIGIN AND HISTORY.

" *Red*, of the colour of blood, one of the primitive colours," we are told by Walker; "red-coat, a name of contempt for a soldier," he adds unpleasantly below; but Colonel James in his Military Dictionary renders it more probably, as " the familiar term for a British soldier."

Colonel Mackinnon (in his "History of the Cold-stream Guards") and other writers have attributed the introduction or adoption of the British uniform to William III.; but there are sufficient proofs of its having been common alike to England and to Scotland long before the revolution in 1688.

That red was originally deemed a warlike colour, though now worn only by the British and, till the Holstein war, by the Danish troops, there is abundant evidence.✳

――――――――――

✳ The red of the Danish army was darker than ours. In 1702, their cavalry, line, and militia, wore iron-grey, with green stockings; but

Bellona, the sister of Mars, is depicted by ancient painters and described by the poets as being clad in garments stained with blood, and the planet which bears the name of the warlike god is known by its ruddy appearance. This hue arises simply from the atmosphere, and hence the bards of classical antiquity named the planet after the god of battles. To show that in savage lands some of those old ideas still prevail, Colonel James Grant in his "Walk Across Africa," with the gallant and lamented Speke, mentions that his valet Uledi told him, "that in his native country of Uhiao, the people imagined that all foreigners eat human flesh, and that cloth was dyed *scarlet* with human blood."

In heraldry, *gules* is the vermilion colour in the arms of commoners; but without elaboration, our present object is to trace the origin and the gradual adoption of our national uniform, "the old red rag (as our soldiers call it) that tells of England's glory."

The colour was deemed eminently martial and warlike by the Romans, among whom the *paludamentum*, the military robe or cloak of a general, was scarlet, bordered with purple. Juvenal (vol. vi.) mentions officers

---

there were some exceptions. The first named force had buff coats, and in warm weather rode with hats, their helmets hanging at their saddle bows. Lobat's dragoons were clad in red, lined with white ; the regiment of Jutland wore white, lined with red, red breeches and black cravats ; and the Queen's own Guards wore fine scarlet.— *Travels in the Retinue of the English Envoy, in* 1702.

clad in a scarlet dress, and according to Livy, such was also the attire of the lictors who attended the consul in war.

Scarlet is mentioned among the colours used by the Britons for dyeing their skins in the time of Julius Cæsar; but their favourite herb was glastum, or woad, called *glas* by the Celts, *i.e.*, blue,.that they might look dreadful in battle.

The *red* uniform of the British Army was adopted simply from the circumstance, that it was the royal colour of the kingdoms of England and Scotland, centuries before the union of the crowns or of the countries; red and blue being the royal livery of England, red and yellow the royal livery of Scotland. In the latter country, red has ever been the judicial colour, worn by the Lords of Council and Session, the magistrates of Edinburgh and other cities, as well as by the students of some of the universities.

The Royal Crowns of England and Scotland were always lined with scarlet, though James IV for a time adopted imperial purple. The surcoat of the Knights of the Garter is crimson; and in the apparel of those of the Bath we find the surcoat, breeches and stockings all red, as directed at the revival of the Order by George I. in 1725.

Scarlet faced with blue was the uniform of the City Guard of Edinburgh, a corps which existed from the days of Flodden until those of Waterloo.

In England, scarlet and blue had long been the two

chief colours of the cloth directed for the array of the king's troops; in the time of the Crusades the English wore white crosses; but Henry VIII. had troops in white with a red cross. From the commencement of the fourteenth century the Scots wore blue surcoats with white St. Andrew's crosses thereon. Scotch and English soldiers were wont in those days to taunt each other as *Blue-coat* and *White-coat.*

The Memoirs of Kirkaldy of Grange record an instance of this kind in a sham fight.

In the afternoon of the 2nd March, 1571, a party of Sir William Kirkaldy's soldiers were marched from Edinburgh Castle, which they approached again at 8 p.m., with white English surcoats over their armour. On drawing near they were challenged thus:

"Who are ye that trouble the Captain in the silence of night?"

"The army of the Queen of England," replied the mock assailants with a discharge of arquebusses. Blank volleys promptly responded from the walls, during which they freely bestowed upon each other the taunts and scurrility which the Scots and their Southern neighbours used in battle as liberally as hard blows.

"Begone, ye lubbards! Away, *Blue-coats!*

"I defy thee, *White-coat!* dyrt upon your teeth! Hence, knaves, to your mistress—her soldiers shall not come here," &c. The cannon were then discharged, upon which the mock Englishmen took to flight, after an hour's skirmish in the dark, which filled the peaceable portion of the citizens with dismay, and drew forth some prophetic remarks from John Knox, who heard the clamour from his house in the Netherbow.

The favourite colours of the House of Tudor were green and white. At the battle of St. Aubyn, Sir Edward Wydeville was slain at the head of a vast body of Bretons, whom, to deceive the enemy, he had clad in *white* English doublets with red St. George's crosses thereon.

White and red were the colours worn by Richard II. as his livery, and during his reign they were favourites with his courtiers and the citizens of London, a large company of whom, headed by the mayor, all wearing these, the king's colours, met him and the queen on Blackheath, and conducted them in state to the Palace of Westminster. At the coronation of Henry IV we find the English peers wearing a long scarlet tunic, called a *houppelande*, with a cape above it; the knights and esquires present wore the same kind of tunic, but without the cape.

In 1432, when Henry IV returned from France, he was met at Eltham by the Lord Mayor of London, who was arrayed in crimson velvet with a baldrick of gold, attended by three henchmen dressed in suits of red spangled with silver, and by the aldermen wearing gowns of scarlet with purple hoods. Then in 1535 we find Henry VIII. donning a crimson velvet jerkin with purple satin sleeves, and among the items of his voluminous wardrobe are enumerated, "a cloke of skarlette with a brodegarde of right crymson velvetto; a dublette of carnacion coloured sattin embrowdered with damaske gold; a jacquette of the same," and several other "dublettes" and "clokes" of similar sanguinary hues; and during his reign we find the first decided approach to the uniform of the future British Army.

"Henry VIII. passed to Bulloigne with an army divided into three battalions," says a curious work, printed at London in 1630.* "In the vantguard were 12,000 footmen and 500 light-horsemen, cloathed in blew jackets, with red guards. The middleward (where the King was), consisted of 20,000 footmen, clothed with red jackets and yellow guards. In the rereward was the Duke of Norfolk, and with him an army like in number and apparell to the first, saving that therein served 1000 Irishmen, *all naked*, save their mantles and their thicke-gathered skirts." This indicates a costume like that of the Highlanders.

On this occasion, in 1544, Henry was attended by his Body-Guard of Pensioners, each of whom "was accompanied by three mounted men-at-arms, dressed in suits of *red and yellow* damask, the plumes of themselves and steeds being of a like colour." ("Account of the Gentlemen-at-arms.") In battle they wore complete armour, their horses being "barded from counter to tail," *i.e.*, with a spiked frontlet for the head, criniere to guard the mane, a poitrinal or breast-plate, and a croupiere or buttock-piece.

* "Relations of the most famovs kingdoms, throwout the world."

Contemporaneously we find his nephew, James V of Scotland, having a body-guard established in 1532, consisting of 300 men of Edinburgh, clad in scarlet doublets faced with blue, with blue bonnets, gilt partizans and daggers.

Henry's " Bulleners," as they were named, were conspicuous in their scarlet dress at the battle of Pinkie, in 1547, where they were commanded by the Lord Gray, and where they were driven back in confusion, leaving the staff of the royal standard in the hands of the Scots. In Patten's quaint account of this battle, he mentions, incidentally, that "Sir Miles Patrick being nigh, espied one in a *red doublet*, whom he took *thereby* to be an Englishman."

In a letter of Sir John Harrington's, we find the pay and clothing of Queen Elizabeth's troops in Ireland detailed at some length, but the colours are not stated. For an officer in winter, "a cassock of broad cloth, with bays, and trimmed with silk lace, 27s. 6d. A doublet of canvas, with silk buttons, and lined with white linen, costing 14s. 5d. Two shirts, three pairs of kersey stockings, three pairs of shoes of neat's leather, at 2s. 4d. per pair, and one pair of Venetians, of broad Kentish cloth with silver lace, at 15s. 4d."

On the 23rd July, 1601, 1500 of her men arrived from England, clad in *red cassocks,* to share in the siege of Ostend.—(History of the Siege.) Of these, says Stowe, 1000 were Londoners, and they are now represented by Her Majesty's 3rd Foot, or Kentish Buffs.

We find no trace of the national colours at the coronation of Charles I. as King of Scotland, in 1633, at Edinburgh, where he was escorted by the Gentlemen Pensioners, under the Earl of Suffolk, and the Yeomen of the Guard, under the Earl of Holland. We are told by Spalding that he was accompanied by "his ordinary English Guards, clad in his livery, having *brown velvet* coats, side (*i.e.*, close) to their hough, and beneath with boards of black velvet, and His Majesty's armes wrought in raised and embossed work of silver and gold upon the back and breast of ilk coat. This was the ordinary weed of His Majesty's Foot Guards." Those furnished by Edinburgh were clad in "white satin doublets, black velvet breeches, silk stockings, hats, feathers, and scarfs. These gallants had dainty muskets, pikes, and gilded partizans." On this auspicious occasion, all the Scottish peerage wore their usual robes of crimson velvet. In this King's reign, David Ramsay, who was an officer of Gustavus Adolphus, when appearing to fight a duel with Lord Reay, wore a coat of scarlet (according to Sanderson's "History of England"), so thickly laced with silver that the ground of the cloth was scarcely visible.

Singularly enough, scarlet was early adopted among the grim Scottish Covenanters. At the battle of Kilsythe, where Montrose routed their troops with great slaughter, we find that "the red-coat musketeers" were cut to pieces by Viscount Aboyne and his Gordons. It may be worth mentioning here that the chequer on

the bonnets of our Highland regiments was first adopted
by the clans under Montrose, as significant of the *fess-
cheque* of the House of Stuart.   The great Marquis
wore scarlet at his barbarous execution in Edinburgh,
in 1650; and in the course of that year we find Sir
James Balfour recording, in his " Memorialls of Church
and Staite," that an English ship was made a prize by
the Scots, who found in her " eleven hundred elles of
broad clothe, seven hundred suttes of made clothes, and
als many *read cottes*, 250 carabines, 500 muskets, with
powder and matches," being supplies for the troops of
Cromwell, several of whose regiments appear, however,
to have been clad in blue.

Balfour, at this period, mentions on several occa·
sions the " four-tailled " coats of the Scottish infantry
and artillery, which must have been something like
the old Highland doublet now worn by our Highland
corps.

At the Restoration, when forces were established in
England and Scotland, each country having its separate
guards, line, and artillery, scarlet was the colour almost
uniformly adopted, save in one instance, when the King
clothed in blue, faced with red, the Royal Regiment of
English Horse Guards, which was embodied on the 26th
August, 1661, under Aubrey, Earl of Oxford.   These
colours it still retains; but a corps of marines raised
about the same time, oddly enough, wore yellow coats—
the old Dutch uniform.*

* William III. had a regiment of Dutch Horse in London, styled the

On the 2nd April in the same year, 1661, the
Scottish Life Guards rode through the city of Edinburgh "in gallant order," says Nicol the Diarist,
"their carbines upon their saddles, and swords drawn
in their hands. It pleased His Majesty to clothe their
trumpeters and the master of the kettle-drum in very
rich apparel." Colours were presented, and soon after
the King gave to each gentleman a buff coat.

In February, 1683, General Sir Thomas Dalzell obtained from the Privy Council at Edinburgh a licence
permitting the manufacturers at Newmills " to import
2536 ells of *stone-grey* cloth from England," for his
dragoon regiment, the *Scots Greys*, which had been
raised two years before—hence their costume, as well
as their grey horses, may have led to their present well-
known appellation. This grey cloth cost five shillings
an ell.

In May of the same year, Colonel John Grahame of
Claverhouse imported from England 150 ells of red
cloth, 40 ells of white, and 550 dozen of buttons, for
the use of the Life Guards, and the Council ordained
that the uniform of the Scottish infantry should be " of
such a dye as shall be thought fit to distinguish sojours
from other skulking and vagrant persons, who have
hitherto imitated the uniform of the King," and red was
the dye so universally adopted that in 1685 we find

Blue Horse Guards ; they returned to Holland on the 20th March,
1689, after which the present Oxford Blues got that appellation
permanently.

300 ells of it ordered by Captain Patrick Grahame for the City Guard of Edinburgh.

The Cavalier trooper, Captain Crichton, writes of the Scottish cavalry in *red* in 1676; and in 1684 we find that the dress of the Coldstream Guards was a red coat lined with green, red stockings, red breeches, and white sashes.* "The colonel and other officers, when on duty, to wear their gorgets."

In Sir Patrick Hume's account of Argyle's descent upon Scotland (printed in Rose's Observations upon the historical works of Mr. Fox), among the Scottish forces led by the Earl of Dumbarton, he says, "wee saw in view a regiment of red-coat foot, too strong for us to attacque." This was the Scots Royals, or 1st Regiment of the Line. Before the victorious charge at Killie-crankie, Viscount Dundee is said to have substituted a green for a scarlet uniform over his buff coat; and the former colour is *yet* considered ominous to those of his name who wear it.†

Some years before the Revolution, Grenadier companies had been added to the English and Scottish establishments.

Charles II. having resolved to introduce hand-grenades, on the 13th April, 1678, issued a warrant for a company of one hundred men to be added to the Holland regiment, under the command of Captain John Bristoe, to be armed with those explosives, and to be

* Royal Orders, &c.
† Browne's "History of the Highlands."

styled Grenadiers. A similar company was soon added
to every other corps in both countries. These soldiers
carried fusils with bayonets, hatchets, and swords.
Their uniform was different from that of the musketeer
and pikeman; the two latter had round hats with broad
brims turned up on one side, the former a fur cap with
a lofty crown; they also wore cravats "of fox tailes."

"In 1678," says Evelyn in his Diary, "were brought
into the service a new sort of soldiers called Grenadiers,
who were dextrous at flinging hand-grenades, every one
having a pouch full; they wore furred caps with coped
crowns like Janizaries, which made them look very
fierce, and some had hoods hanging down behind.
Their clothing being pybald, yellow, and red." Such
was the origin of our "British Grenadiers" of immortal
memory!

According to Fosbroke, after throwing the grenade,
on receiving the words "Fall on," they rushed on the
enemy with hatchets, which they wore in addition to
muskets, slings, swords, and daggers.

The Scottish Government, in 1702, raised a corps of
Horse Grenadier Guards, afterwards incorporated with
the United forces, and now represented by the Life
Guards.

Towards the close of the 17th century, the clothing of
the British troops varied; hence, we find, that in the
year 1685, when the North Lincolnshire (now 10th)
Regiment of Foot was raised by John, Earl of Bath, it
wore blue coats, which were lined with red, and the

P

men had waistcoats, breeches, and stockings all of red,
and round Cavalier hats with broad brims, which were
turned up on one side, and ornamented with red
ribbons. The companies of pikemen * alone wore red
worsted sashes. Shortly after the Revolution in 1688,
the 10th Foot were clothed in scarlet, like the rest of
the British Infantry.

In 1687, the "old Tangier Regiment," or, Queen's
Own Foot (now the 2nd Regiment), which was raised
in 1661, for the defence of that portion of Africa which
was ceded to Britain as the dowry of the Infanta of
Portugal, wore a red frock coat with skirts turned back,
loose green knickerbockers, white stockings, black
broad-brimmed hats, looped up on one side, and shoes
with rosettes. In the buff belts were long rapiers and
fixing daggers, while a collar of bandoliers was worn
across the chest.

William III. ordained in 1698, "that no person
whatsoever should presume to wear scarlet or red cloth
for livery, except such as are in His Majesty's service,
or the Guards," yet, for all that, scarlet was, and is
still, the livery of more than one noble family in Scotland.

The 3rd, or Kentish Buffs, were so called from the
circumstance of their being the first corps whose ac-

* The *last* pike perhaps used in the British Service we saw carried
by a sergeant of Captain Wyatt's Company of the Royal Artillery in
1835, when marching for embarkation for Britain, out of Signal Hill
Barracks in Newfoundland.

coutrements were made of leather prepared from the
hide of the buffalo. Their waistcoats, breeches, and
facings were, however, all of the same buff colour in
1665, according to Captain Grose. For nearly the same
reason, the 31st, or Huntingdonshire Foot, raised in
1702, call themselves the "Young Buffs." In the
Army List, the 78th Highlanders are styled the Ross-
shire Buffs; and in some old lists, the 56th, or
West Essex Regiment, raised in 1755, figured by their
pet name of *Pompadours*, their facings being then, as
now, purple, the favourite colour of Madame's gown and
fontange. While on the subject of uniform and equipment, we may mention that in the Memoirs of Sergeant
Donald Macleod, " who having returned wounded, with
the corpse of General Wolfe, was admitted an out-pen-
sioner of Chelsea in 1759, and is now * in his 103rd
year," we have an absurd statement to the effect, that
when he enlisted in the 1st Royal Scots, " as a boy in
the Scottish service under King William III.," they
were accoutred with steel caps, bows and arrows (?).
He might as well have added scalp locks and war paint.
Singular to say, this nonsense has been reproduced by
Miss Strickland in her Life of Queen Anne. Long prior
to the time given, the regiment wore its orthodox red
coat, faced and lined with blue, and was armed with
good match-lock muskets, the "cocked lunts" of which
revealed their whereabouts, in the dark, to Monmouth's
cavalry on the night before the battle of Sedgemoor.

* 1791. Published by Sewell, Cornhill.

p 2

Of old, the London militia, though all dressed in scarlet, were known by their facings, and not by numbers.

In the list of officers, commissioned for the City, on the 24th December, 1698, we have those of the orange, yellow, white, red, green, and blue regiments; and concerning these corps the following interesting proclamation was posted up throughout London, when the Highlanders under Prince Charles were advancing on Derby.

"Notice is hereby given, that every officer and soldier in the six regiments of militia, without waiting for beat of drum, or any other notice, do, immediately on hearing the said signals, repair with their arms and the usual quantity of powder and ball, to their respective rendezvous; the *red* regiment upon Tower-hill, the *green* regiment in Guildhall-yard, the *yellow* in St. Paul's Churchyard, the *white* at the Royal Exchange, the *blue* in Old Fish-street, and the *orange* in West Smithfield." *

It is hence that in Foote's humorous farce, " The Mayor of Garratt," Major Sturgeon is made to say that he had served under Jeffery Dunstable, knight, Lord Mayor of London, and Colonel of the *yellow*.

Prince Charles Edward was partial to the national uniform, and frequently wore it. He is represented in red, in the miniature which he gave to his secretary,

---

* In 1759 this corps was ordered by its Colonel to adopt blue clothing.

Murray of Broughton, one of nine painted on copper, as gifts to his principal adherents. His Life Guards, under Lord Elcho, wore blue faced with red; but, in his small and gallant army, the Duke of Perth's regiment, wore scarlet uniforms. (Vide Spalding Club Miscell., vol. i.)

A scarlet uniform worn by Cardinal York, before he took holy orders, and probably when he commanded a body of French and Irish troops at Dunkirk, in 1745, is now preserved at Inzievar House, Fifeshire, having been preserved by Edgar of Keithwick, who was long attached to the last of the Stuarts, in the capacity of secretary.

Like the light cavalry, most of the militia corps would seem to have been originally dressed in blue. According to an old ballad, the Lothian regiment were so clad at the Battle of Bothwell-bridge in 1679.

The uniform of the first-named force has frequently varied. In 1784, the clothing of the 17th, and similar corps, was changed from scarlet to blue. They wore blue in the Peninsula, and in 1830 were clad in scarlet again, when the moustache, which they and other corps had adopted, was ordered to be shaved off. (Records of the 17th Lancers.)

The old Scottish Guard of the French kings wore hoquetons of white, "in token of their unspotted fidelity," but the other Scottish troops in the French service, the Gendarmes Écossais, who took precedence of all the household troops, and the Infanterie Écossais,

which took rank after the 12th regiment of the old
French line, wore blue, while scarlet was the dress of
the Irish brigades of the Louis' in later years.

Our Chasseurs Brittaniques, a foreign corps, consisting in some instances, of deserters from every army in
Europe, wore the national uniform, and thus, when on
duty, frequently caused confusion and mistakes by their
ignorance of the English language.

In 1742, the coats and breeches of the line were
tightened, and the hats were looped up on three sides,
and in that year, the 7th, or South British Fusiliers,
and the 21st, or North British Fusiliers, figured in the
high conical cap which came into vogue with the
Prussian tactics. Their coats had no collars, the skirts
were buttoned back and faced with blue. Numbers
were first put on the coat buttons in 1767.

Red and yellow being, as we have stated, the royal
livery of Scotland, the facings of Scottish regiments
have generally been of the latter colour, and many that
now wear blue, had yellow when first embodied.

The whole infantry of the East India Company wore
the national colour, and it is greatly to be regretted that,
on the commencement of our Volunteer movement, the
Government did not enforce the adoption of scarlet,
instead of permitting the endless varieties of silly
colours and costumes now worn by many corps throughout the United Kingdom.

The statistics of European wars show us that the
French, who are clad in *blue*, suffered a greater loss in

proportion than the British, who wear *red*, when under fire. An old Peninsula officer, whose letter is before us, mentions, "When our Light Company, and the company of the 60th Rifles (green), attached to our brigade, were skirmishing on the same ground (against the enemy), the latter lost more than we did, although composed chiefly of Germans, who are proverbially cautious skirmishers. This is an important subject. I saw, at the Battle of Vittoria, the wonderful effect of the imposing appearance of the British line on the enemy. After they had been driven from their position and completely scattered, many glorious attempts were made by their officers to rally them on some heights behind the ridge on which our line was advancing. It became an object with the officer commanding the Light Companies, which were scattered in pursuit, to get them arrayed for the attack of a column which formed on one of those heights at some distance in our front, and thus became a rallying point to the thousands who were flying from the ridge in helpless confusion.

"Before we had a sufficient number of the pursuers collected to attack this formidable column, it broke and bolted, its soldiers disappearing among the racing mobs who threw away their arms and fled towards the Pyrenees. While wondering what had caused so sudden a panic among men who, but a moment before, seemed ready to adhere until death to their officers, we—the skirmishers—looked back to the ridge, and saw a sight which I shall never forget. The whole British line crowned the mountains, from wing to wing, looking like a wall of fire, their bayonets glittering in the sun, as they moved steadily, silently, and presenting a glorious picture of power and order. This sight it was which struck the enemy to the heart, and made him fly from his new position in sudden panic. No army, although double the number, if clad in sombre uniform, could ever make such an appearance, or produce such an effect as this." *

Our uniforms have frequently varied according to the climate in which corps have been stationed. The kilt has generally proved too warm for Indian service, and white trousers are substituted. In the Caffre war the 74th Highlanders wore short dark blouses, tartan tunics, and hummal bonnets, i.e., without feathers. In Canada the King's Dragoon Guards lately wore busbies of fur, blue pea-jackets, and long boots lined with sheep-skin in winter. The Ashanti uniform is still remembered.

Save the Blues, all our cavalry wore scarlet, until the middle of George III.'s reign, when blue was adopted for the Light corps; but silver-grey, with red facings, was worn by all dragoons, while serving in India, until 1820. Eleven years after, scarlet was resumed for all corps except the Horse Guards and Hussars; but blue was ordered again for all Lancers and Light Dragoons in 1840.

---

* At the commencement of the Volunteer movement, this letter was addressed to the author of this paper, who was then actively engaged in the formation of a corps now wearing *grey*.

Blue has always been worn by the Royal Regiment of Artillery, which was first embodied in England in the year 1750, by Colonel William Belford, who commanded that arm of the service at the battle of Culloden, four years before.* The facings, vests, and breeches were all scarlet.

Hussars were first introduced in our service in 1793, and Lancers after the battle of Waterloo; but so early as 1794 we had a corps of Lancers, named the British Uhlans, formed out of the remains of the French Royalist army, and which, with the Hussars of Choiseul, Salm, and Rohan, perished in the fatal expedition to Quiberon in 1796.

Uniform has ever been considered a badge alike of honour and service; thus, in the *Gazette* for June, 1867, we find that Her Majesty was graciously pleased to permit a retired Captain of the Edinburgh, or Queen's Own Regiment of Militia, "to retain his rank and *wear his uniform* in consideration of his long service in that corps."

We have had the pleasure of knowing more than one brave veteran officer, who treasured affectionately "the old red rag," in which he had followed Picton, Grahame, or the Iron Duke, and in which he had been wounded on the glorious fields of Spain or in the crowning victory of Waterloo; and in every age there has been some eccentric enthusiast who stuck manfully to fashions that had departed.

In 1808, many an old officer would as soon have cut

off his head as his pigtail when the Horse Guards
ordered the army to be shorn of that remarkable ap-
pendage. Old Sir Thomas Dalyell, of Binns (first
Colonel of the Scots Greys), who rode yearly to London
to kiss the hand of King Charles II., adhered to the
close-sleeved doublet of the days of James VI. This,
with his portentous vow-beard (which he had sworn
never to cut after the execution of Charles I), " when he
was in London never failed to draw after him a great
crowd of boys, who constantly attended him at his
lodgings, and followed him with huzzas as he went to
Court and returned from it. As he was a man of
humour, he would always thank them for their civilities
when he left them at the door to go to the King, and
would let them know exactly at what hour he intended
to come out again and return to his lodgings." (Memoirs
of Captain Crichton, the Cavalier Trooper.)

General Preston, who commanded the same regiment
in the Seven Years' War, and who died colonel of it, at
Bath in 1785, was the last British officer who wore a
buff coat. An officer who served with him records that
at the capture of Zerenberg, Preston received more than
a dozen of sword-cuts, which fell harmlessly on his
" buff-jerkin."

Old Colonel Charles Donellan, who commanded the
48th, and was wounded at Talavera (mortally, we
believe), was the last officer who adhered to the antique
three-cornered Nivernois hat; and there was a General
Cameron, in the same campaign, who adhered to the

Highland bonnet, and never would adopt the cocked hat.

At Dettingen, George II. appeard in the same red coat which he had worn when serving under Marlborough. Thackeray says, " On public occasions he always displayed the hat and coat he wore on the famous day of Oudenarde, and the people laughed, but kindly, at the odd old garment, for bravery never goes out of fashion." At Minden, in 1759, we find the luckless Lord George Sackville leading the cavalry in the same red coat which he had worn as a youth at Fontenoy ; and the same sentiment has prevailed in the humbler ranks of the service.

An aged soldier, named Robert Ferguson, who died at Paisley in 1811, in his ninety-seventh year, preserved to the last, as a precious relic, the old red coat of the 22nd Foot (Handysides, wherein Sterne's father was a captain), in which he had been wounded at the battles of Dettingen and Fontenoy, just as future years may see some veteran preserving the faded and perhaps bloodstained tunic which he wore with Raglan at Sebastopol, or with Havelock at Lucknow.

We have thus attempted to trace the history of that scarlet uniform, which is so inseparably connected with the past, the present, and the future glory of the British Isles. It is the garb which first fires the enthusiasm and ambition of our youth, and is ever kindly and affectionately remembered by our white-haired veterans in old age, for there is something almost filial in the

emotion with which an old soldier recalls the uniform,
the facings, and badges of his regiment, whatever its
number might have been, from the 1st Royal Scots to
the Rifle Brigade. There is not a battle-field, honourable to Britain, or a portion of the globe where our
drums have beaten, but where it has formed the shroud
of many a noble and gallant heart—so all honour, say
we, to "the old Red Coat, that tells the tale of England's
glory ! "

<hr />

CHAPTER II.

FURTHER NOTES ON ITS HISTORY AND ON REGIMENTALS.

In the preceding chapter, the origin of the British
uniform was plainly deduced from the fact of scarlet being
the Royal livery alike of England and of Scotland, and
hence its adoption as a general national colour. To
these notes we purpose to add a few more on the
gradual progress of badges and distinctions in the
service.

The red cross of St. George was the general badge of
England from the Crusades, till the time of Edward IV.,
and by an act of the Scottish Parliament passed in
1385, during the reign of Robert III., every soldier was
ordained " to wear a white St. Andrew's Cross on his

back and breast, which, if his surcoat was white, was to be broidered on a circle or square of black cloth."

In the time of Henry VIII., a red St. George's cross on a white surcoat was adopted as the distinguishing badge of English troops; and in an order to raise men for the service of Mary I., in the northern counties, she directs, that "they be clothed in whyt, with redde-crosses on ye arme, in ye olde maner."

These red crosses were destined to figure soon after, at the battle of Ancrum in 1544, when, as the ballad has it, the stream

> " Ran red with English blood,
> For the Douglas true and the bold Buccleugh,
> 'Gainst keen Lord Evers stood."

When the English were routed, 700 Scottish outlaws of broken border clans, who had joined them, threw aside their red crosses, and joining their countrymen, made a merciless slaughter of the fugitives with axe and spear, shouting to each other the while, "Remember Broomhouse!"

Love of the sanguinary colour seems to have spread rapidly, and so, as some one has it, "no true English-man can either fight, or hunt, to his satisfaction, save in a red coat," but badges were speedily added thereto.

Stowe records in his Survey of London, that " Robert Neville, Earl of Warwick, with 600 men all in red jackets, embroidered with *ragged staves* before and behind, was lodged in Warwicke Lane; in whose house there was oftentimes six oxen eaten at a breakfast, and every tavern was full of his meat, for he that had any acquaintance in that house, might have as much of sodden or roasted meat as he could prick and carry away on a long dagger."

The proposal that the medical officers of all European armies should wear one great distinguishing badge, by which their profession might be known, is not a new one, for we find Ralph Smith, in the time of Elizabeth, after telling us that military "surgeons should be men of sobrietie, of good conscience, and skillfull in that science, able to heal all scars and wounds, especially to take out a pellet, &c., must wear their Baldricke, whereby they may be known in time of slaughter, as it is their charter in the field."

In this reign the Cavalry wore scarlet cloaks; but in the stirring times of Cromwell, with red and blue, a reddish-brown was much used by both horse and foot; hence he says in one of his letters, " I had rather have a plain russet-coated captain, that knoweth what he fights for, and loves what he knowes, than that which you call ' a gentleman,' and is nothing else."

Of all the colours for uniforms, the most absurd were some of those adopted by our Rifle Volunteers, in their too wary desire to be unseen. A battalion of the Italian Legion, raised during the Crimean war, was clad in silver grey ; and it was admitted by all competent judges to be the colour best adapted for riflemen, and, moreover, when handsomely laced and trimmed, it was very becoming. This was the favourite colour of the Indian Light Cavalry.

When contrasted with the tight tunics, tiny shackos, and plain trousers of the present day, the equipment of a corps of the last, or the preceding century, in its amplitude and variety, must have presented a very different and very picturesque aspect. On the 8th, or King's Own Regiment, being raised for King James, by Richard, Lord Ferrars, the captains were armed with pikes, the lieutenants with partisans, the ensigns with half-pikes, the sergeants with halberds; thirty rank and file of each company were pikemen, seventy-three were musketeers, and all carried swords. The waist-coats and breeches were yellow; the uniform, scarlet lined with yellow; the stockings and cravats white; the hats were *à la* cavalier, turned up on one side, and ornamented with flowing yellow ribbands. (Records 8th Foot.)

Ten years before this time, each company consisted of thirty pikes, sixty muskets, and ten men armed with light fusils, and "the tallest men were always culled out as pikemen." (*Bruce on Military Law*, 1717.)

The following description of a deserter, from the 22nd Foot, in those days, is rather amusing, as to costume :—

"Run away, out of Captain Soames' Company, in his Grace the Duke of Norfolk's regiment of Infantry, quartered at Newport, in Shropshire; Roger Curtis, a barber surgeon, a little man with short black hair, a little curled; round visage, fresh-coloured, in a light coloured coat, with gold and silver buttons, red plush breeches and white hat; he lived formerly at Downham Market, in Norfolk. Whoever will give notice to Francis Baker, agent to the said regiment, in Hatton Garden, so that he may be secured, shall have two guineas reward."*

A spectator of the Camp of the Household Brigade, on Putney Heath, in October, 1694, describes the three regiments of Guards as wearing scarlet, of course; the 1st, faced with blue; the 2nd, or "Cole-stream," with green; the 3rd Scots, with white; the officers being distinguished by white scarves worn over the left shoulder, and fringed with the colour of the regimental facings. The Holland Regiment (Buffs), are described as wearing red, faced with flesh-colour; the Queen's or Tangier Regiment, red, faced with sea-green; the Lord Admiral's Regiment of Marines, raised in 1664 (and afterwards incorporated by William III., with the 2nd Foot Guards), in doublets and breeches of yellow.

Until the reign of Her present Majesty, red was worn by all the drummers and buglers of the regiment of Artillery; but although, from the earliest period, it was deemed the great national colour of our forces, it is somewhat remarkable that it was not adopted by the English or Irish Militia, until the year 1759, and a song of that period begins :—

* "London Gazette," 1689.

' Ye mounseers, give ear, we have nothing to fear,
  For the Militia are now clothed in RED, Sirs !
They have hearts that are stout and will never give out,
  With Rockingham bold at their head, sirs !
You may brag and may boast, upon your own coast,
  And parade it from Dunkirk to Calais ;
But have a care now, how you venture too far,
  In your flat-bottomed boats to make sallies."

Long denied a militia force, in dread of Jacobite in-
fluences, Scotland had none from 1746 till the close of
the last century, when, ten years after the death of her
" Bonnie Prince Charlie," ten battalions were raised,
and their colours and insignia (most of which are now
deposited in the Castle of Edinburgh) were designed by
the Court of the Lyon King of Arms, then Robert, Earl
of Kinnoull, with whom the applications for such were
lodged.

In our former chapter, the uniforms of the Irish and
Scottish regiments which belonged to the French Line,
during the last century, were referred to. These corps
(according to the " Liste Historique des Troupes de
France," 1758,) were numbered as the 92nd, 93rd,
94th, 98th (Gardes de Jacques II.), 99th, and 109th,
all Irish ; the 107th Royal Écossais under the Duke of
Perth, and the 113th Écossais under Lieutenant-General
Lord Ogilvie, who died in Scotland in 1803.

The two Scottish regiments wore coats and vests of
blue, and their hats were bound with gold. All their
Irish brother exiles wore scarlet, with white vests generally, and carried on their colours black or yellow

Q

crosses, with the " Couronne d'Angleterre," which had
no braver or more bitter enemies, as the terrible day of
Fontenoy attested ; and where they seem to have acted
true to the spirit of the Fenian song :

> " Oh, if the colour we must wear,
>   Is England's cruel red,
>   Let it remind us of the blood
>   That Ireland has shed ! "

And when our troops landed at Cancalle Bay in 1758,
they were surprised to find themselves stoutly opposed
by entire battalions in scarlet ; and no wonder was it
that they were so, for it was the Irish Brigade, whose
ranks were manned and officered by the sons and grand-
sons of the adherents of King James, the same gallant
Irish Brigade which was welcomed to the British Establishment in 1794, and, unfortunately, was soon after
reduced.

In our service, the White Horse of Hanover is borne
on the colours of the 3rd Dragoons, the 7th, 14th,
23rd, and 27th Foot, &c. This badge is as old in
history as the Welsh Dragon of the 10th Hussars and
12th Lancers, having been the ancient cognisance of
Saxony or Westphalia,—a White Horse, on a field
gules—borne for centuries by the House of Brunswick.
Henry the Proud, Duke of Bavaria, in consequence of
his marriage in 1123, with Gertrude, the lineal descendant of Wittekind, last of the Saxon Kings, assumed
the armorial bearing of that Sovereign, if a barbarian
so weak and savage deserve the title. The banner of

Wittekind originally bore a black horse, which, on his compulsory conversion to Christianity, under the sword of Charlemagne, was changed to white, as emblematic of his new and purer faith. Hence our White Horse of Hanover and its motto *Nec Aspera Terrent*, which appears on the colours of the regiments above mentioned. It made its appearance in our service about the same time as the hideous black leather cockade, so long retained in loyal opposition to the White Rose of the Stuarts, and which is seen now only on the hats of footmen.

But the badge borne for the longest period in succession by the same unbroken body of men, is undoubtedly the St. Andrew's Cross of the 1st Royals, who represent alike the Scottish Guard of St. Louis (the comrades of "Quentin Durward" under Louis XI.), and the Green Brigade of Scots, who served Gustavus Adolphus, a corps whose almost fabulous antiquity was long a jest in the French service, as well as our own, being twitted in both as the Guards of Pontius Pilate, who slept on their post

A very remarkable instance of love of the "Old Red Coat" occurred when the Scots Greys marched from Carlisle in April, 1766. A troop-quartermaster named Robert Mackenzie, then in his eighty-eighth year, was left behind, totally prostrated by age and infirmity. He was born in Scotland in 1688, had joined the Greys in 1705, when Lord John Hay was colonel, and was proverbially known as "the oldest soldier in the service."

The sound of the trumpets had scarcely died away homeward on the north road, when the hand of death came on the old enthusiast, and feeling that the hour of his dissolution was come, he insisted on being clad in his full uniform, his boots were drawn on, his sword girt about him, and thus accoutred, he expired, of sheer " disappointment at his inability to proceed. He was carried to his grave by six invalids; the pall being supported by six sergeants of recruiting parties in the town, and the Cumberland Militia fired six platoons at his interment."

An old enthusiast of a similar kind, though of higher rank, was the amiable General Charles O'Hara, the comrade of Granby and Ligonier, Lieutenant-Colonel of the 22nd, somewhere before 1788, and who, in the first year of the present century, died Governor of Gibraltar. He was the last British officer who adhered to the uniform of the Minden days, and to that remarkable style of cocked hat introduced by the great Austrian Marshal, with its tall straight feather and large black rosette on the dexter side; hence O'Hara was known in the service as "the last of the Kevenhullers."

At Gibraltar "he was buried with all the honours due to his rank," wrote an officer of the 29th, who was present. "I had never before seen the funeral of a general officer. There was his horse—the well-known charger on which we had so often seen him mounted— bearing the boots and spurs of his departed master; on the coffin lay other mournful insignia, the sword, the

sash, and not the least prominent memorial, the Keven-
huller hat, with its tall, unbending feather, and I gazed
on it for the last time."

He was succeeded in his command by the father of
her present Majesty.

But in the quaint adherence to the costume of a past
age, there are few cases like one recorded by O'Keefe,
the player, whose recollections were published in 1826,
and who mentions that in his day, there was an aged
captain, John Desbrissay, who walked about the streets
of Dublin, "unremarked," in the Cavalier dress of the
reign of Charles II. This, however, was before the
time of the notorious Wilkes. This eccentric veteran
lived in Corkhill, Dublin, and his name appears in the
Army Lists for 1747, as agent for the 5th Horse, 5th
Royal Irish Dragoons, 12th Foot, and several other
corps stationed in Dublin.

County designations were not given until 1786, but
numbers had been introduced, and badges, pretty
generally adopted for all corps of Horse and Foot, on
their colours, buttons, or belt-plates, prior to the first
year of George the Third's reign.

In 1759, when Colonel John Hale (who came to
London with the news of Wolfe's fall, and the conquest
of Canada) raised the 17th Light Dragoons (now Lancers), it was ordered that "on the front of the men's
caps, and on the left breast of their uniform, there was
to be a death's head and cross-bones over it, and under
the motto, "or glory;" and this grim device (the

badge of the famous Black Brunswickers in later times)
they still retain, like the old Pomeranian Horse,
who, since the days of Gustavus Adolphus, have worn
skulls and cross-bones on their high fur caps, and in
Sweden are now known as the King's Own Hussars.

It was not until 1764 that the swords of the Grenadiers were abolished, and the arms of the foot soldier
were confined to the musket and bayonet; and it was
in that year when the officers and men of our cavalry
first wore the epaulette (in lieu of the old aiguilette)
on the left shoulder; at the same time, the jack-boots
were abolished, and the horses were ordered to have
long tails. The 8th Light Dragoons, however, had
long the peculiar favour of wearing cross-belts for the
pouch and sword. Having annihilated a corps of
Spanish Horse at Almenara in 1710, and equipped
themselves with the Spanish belts as trophies, they wore
them in memory of that event until January, 1776,
when they were abolished, and, at the same time the
helmets were substituted for the cocked hats.*—(" Records, 4th and 8th Hussars.")

Singularly enough, the 90th Light Infantry (still
affectionately remembered in Scotland as Sir Thomas
Graham's Perthshire Greybrecks), when serving under
Abercrombie, in Egypt, wore helmets of brass, and
being taken for dismounted Dragoons, were vigorously

---

* It was in 1794 that the Blues resumed for a time the cuirasses,
which the Corps had not worn since their march to Salisbury in
1688.

charged by the French cavalry at the battle of Alexandria. In the *mêlée*, their Lieutenant-Colonel, old Lord Hill of gallant memory, received a ball on his helmet, which brought him to the ground, though it failed to penetrate the brass metal, of which it was composed.

In these brief memoranda on uniforms and equipment, to enter elaborately on the dress of our Highland regiments, or its antiquity and advantages, would take up too much space.

Apart from written history, song, or tradition, there are in Scotland many records of vast age carved in stone, such as the Cross at Dupplin and the tomb at Nigg—both works prior to the eighth century,—which represent the Caledonian Warriors kilted to the knee, exactly like our Highland regiments now ; and on the last-named memorial, the figure has a purse or sporran.

The first regiments of Highlanders embodied were two battalions raised, among other Scottish levies, by the government of Mary Queen of Scots, in 1552, to aid Henry II. of France in his wars. Each man would seem to have provided his own kilt or tartans, as the Scottish Privy Council ordain that they shall be "sub-stantiouslie accompturit, with jack and plait, steilbonett, sword and buckler, new hose and new doublett of can-vouse, at the least, and sleeves of plait or splints, with one speir of sax ell long or thereby." These men were chiefly drawn from the same glens, and by the same noble family, which in later years enrolled the 92nd Gordon Highlanders of Egyptian and Peninsular fame.

The early Highland corps were remarkably jealous of any alteration or innovation in their costume, real or fancied, and hence a dangerous mutiny broke out among the West Fencibles, in Edinburgh Castle, in 1778, in consequence of some changes that were proposed, particularly in the adoption of a cartridge-box, which they oddly alleged "no Highland regiment had ever worn before." A portion of the battalion was ultimately surrounded on Leith Links (where they had flung their pouches mutinously at the feet of the General), and compelled, by the 10th Light Dragoons, to adopt them at the point of the sword; but the remainder in the Castle broke out into open revolt, raised the drawbridge, and threatened to turn the guns on the city; nor did the matter end, until one Fencible was sentenced to be shot, and another to receive a thousand lashes, punishments which were, however, commuted.

In the following year occurred the dangerous mutiny at Leith, when seventy recruits for the 42nd and 71st, on a rumour being mischievously spread that they had been betrayed into a Lowland corps, which wore trousers, fought with the South Fencibles, till forty-five of them were shot down and bayonetted.

In 1811 we had two Greek regiments raised in the Ionian Isles, the 1st and 2nd Light Infantry, which were kilted, and wore the full Albanian costume.

All these various distinctions in uniform, badges, and insignia which we have briefly noted, and others, such as the Sphinx of Egypt, the Tiger of India, the Lion of Nassau, the Dragon of China, the Eagle of France, the Elephant of Assaye,* the Castle and Key of Gibraltar (*Montis insignia Calpe*), and all the other noble emblems borne on the colours of our various regiments, are the historical HERALDRY of the service, and are worthy of the highest consideration.

They are eminently calculated to produce the *esprit de corps*, a just pride and honourable rivalry; and, by the past glories they represent, to inspire in our army that heroic virtue of which the elder Pitt spoke so eloquently in Parliament, when he said of our troops, in the debate upon pay :—

" To the virtue of the British Army we have hitherto trusted; to that virtue, small as the army is, we must still trust; and without that virtue, the Lords, the Commons, and the people of England may intrench

---

* The 74th and 78th Highland Regiments are entitled to carry a third colour for Assaye. The antelope was bestowed on the 6th Foot, in the war of the Spanish Succession, with the motto *vi et armis*, which they seem to have relinquished till 1873, though it used to be painted on the knapsacks, as on an old one possessed by the Corps in 1825, remained to testify. The Scots Greys, who forgot their old motto "SECOND TO NONE," resumed it in 1871. The origin of it seems scarcely known; but Colonel Darby Griffith, who so gallantly led the Greys at the battles of Balaclava, Inkermann, and the Tchernaya, in a letter to the author on the subject, says, "It is well authenticated that the Greys were raised in Scotland before the 1st Dragoons were raised in England, as also were the Coldstream before the Grenadier Guards. The English Regiments were accorded the No. 1, as taking precedence; but as a kind of atonement, both the Coldstream and the Scots Grey have the motto 'SECOND TO NONE.' Aldershot, 15th May, 1865."

themselves behind parchment up to the teeth; but the sword will find a passage to the vitals of the constitution!"

Hence it is, that even the lace, the buttons, and other insignia of a corps are so carefully shorn from the uniform of the unhappy soldier who is disgraced, nd rendered incapable of bearing arms again; and when writing of those things, perhaps we cannot do better than close this article by an anecdote which records one of the most startling instances of wholesale disgrace that ever occurred in a European army.

THE DEGRADATION OF THE REGIMENT OF ABO.

In all armies corps have frequently been punished *en masse*, by being sent on foreign service or hazardous duty out of their turn, for the crimes of individuals, for general discontent, or for mutiny. Some have been exterminated, like the Janizzaries and the Mamelukes; decimated, like the Chapelgorris, or Red Caps, a battalion of 800 Guipuzcoan Volunteers, famous in the army of the Queen of Spain; or, like that Carlist Regiment, which, for sundry acts of sacrilege, was formed in line, and had every tenth file, with his coverer, taken out and shot.

In the "Art of War, 1720," we are told that during the campaign in Holland, a captain and his entire company, belonging to an Italian regiment, were hanged in line for desertion at Emerich, in the Duchy of Cleves; and in later times, in our own service, the 5th Royal Irish Dragoons, a fine old corps, consisting originally of nine troops, embodied under Colonel James Wynne, in the winter of 1688, with the Harp and Garter on their colours,—a corps that was brigaded with the Greys on the extreme right in the campaigns of Marlborough, and which, after serving with characteristic bravery in all our wars till those of the French Revolution, was disbanded in 1798 (for alleged sympathy with the Irish Insurgents), when General Lord Rossmore was their colonel; and since when, as a mark of the royal displeasure, their place and number remained vacant in the Army List for sixty years, until the present 5th Royal Irish Lancers were embodied in 1858; but in no instance was there ever a wholesale disgrace inflicted on a corps such as that to which the King of Sweden, Gustavus III., subjected the unfortunate Regiment of Abo.

When in the year 1788 he suddenly attacked Russia, victory remained undecided in a naval engagement between his fleet under the Duke of Sudermania and that of the Empress under the Scoto-Russian Admiral Greig, and his nobles who served in the Marine refused to act further in a war, which seemed to have no cause but the will of the King. Gustavus was inflamed by this opposition; he wished an object on which to vent his wrath and pride, and soon found one in the Regiment of Abo.

A brief armistice had ensued, during which he

summoned a diet at Stockholm, where, on the 22nd
February, 1789, by a preponderance of three inferior
states, a declaration placed in his hands unlimited
power, and he still resolved to prosecute the hopeless
war against Russia.

In the army, at the head of which he placed himself,
was this Regiment of Finlanders from Abo, a province
which comprehends a part of Eastern Bothnia and the
Aland Isles, whose inhabitants are a hardy and indus-
trious race.   The regiment fought with all the heredi-
tary bravery of the old Finns, and served at the capture
of several small towns; but the arms of Gustavus were
unsuccessful by land, where his measures were discon-
certed by an event which he could not have foreseen.

After making all his preparations to storm the strong
fort and town of Fredericksham, which had been
ceded to the Empress Elizabeth in 1743, and the re-
possession of which would have opened to him the
gates of the Russian capital, his officers, and chiefly
those of the Finnish Regiment of Abo, flatly refused
to pass the frontier, alleging as a reason, "that the
constitution of the Swedish kingdom would not permit
them to be accessory to foreign war which the nation
had not sanctioned."

This put an end to what was named the Finland
Expedition; it gave the enemy time to put themselves
in a perfect state of defence, and filled Gustavus with
fresh fury; but despite the attempts of the Russians
to intercept him, he reached Borgo, an old seaport in

the district of Nyeland, where he established his headquarters, and where his first act was to assemble the
whole Swedish Army, under arms, on the 8th of June,
1789, in front of the town, and along the margin of
the river, which there flows into the Gulf of Finland.

A hollow square of contiguous close columns of
Horse, Dragoons and Infantry was then formed; the
whole were ordered to prime and load with ball-car-
tridge. The Artillery were unlimbered and loaded
with round and cannister shot, in case of resistance,
though none, save a very few, knew precisely what was
about to ensue.

Then the fated Regiment of Abo, which had taken
so marked a part in the defection before Fredericksham, was marched in a solid close column of companies into the centre of this vast hollow square, with
its colours flying; and a hum of expectation and
surprise, not unmixed with dismay, pervaded the whole
assembled masses.

By Gustavus, a king whose ruling passions were
heroism and selfishness, vanity and ambition, they
were ordered to " ground their arms," which were at
once taken away, with all their swords, bayonets, and
accoutrements.

They were then ordered to strip off their regimental
coats, and appear in their shirts and breeches. The
officers were deprived of their epaulettes and commis-
sions, and were cashiered on the spot.

Their colours were then rent from the poles and torn

to pieces, the poles being broken under foot, while the drums were defaced by persons appointed to do so.

The whole battalion then passed from the right of companies out of the hollow square by single files, while a general hiss was maintained by the whole army until the last man had quitted it; and the united sound of this unpleasant expression of contempt rising into the still air, by the sea-shore, is said to have had a very singular and remarkable effect on those who heard it.

Though thus broken up and disbanded, the Corps was not set adrift; for the whole of the privates were drafted into the different battalions of the Artillery, and long after the fiery Gustavus had perished by the hand of the regicide Ankerström, it was a bitter taunt in the Swedish army to have belonged to " the degraded Regiment of Abo."

CHAPTER III.

FAMOUS AND ANCIENT BANNERS.

In all ages and in all armies, the greatest veneration has ever been manifested by soldiers for their ensigns and standards, as being the veritable representation and embodiment of the national glory and honour, or it might be of a righteous cause. In the ages of classical antiquity, the religious care taken of these emblems was extraordinary. The soldiers worshipped them, and swore by them, as some European troops still do. The Roman Legionaries incurred certain death if they lost them in battle; and Livy tells us, that to animate them, the standards were sometimes thrown among the enemy, that they might be recaptured at all hazards.

In all armies at the present day, regimental standards are consecrated by a religious ceremony, have the highest military honours paid to them, and when too old for use, are solemnly deposited in a church, or sometimes burned, or buried with all the honours of war; and by the Queen's Regulations (Section VII.) are finally marched from their last parade, to the air of "Auld lang Syne."

Among the most famous banners of antiquity, may be enumerated the Labaram of Constantine, the Oriflamme of France, those of Otho IV., of Philip Augustus, of Bayard, Joan of Arc, and Mahomet.

Like most ancient banners, the origin of the Labaram was alleged to be miraculous, and surrounded by fables, though the reign of Constantine was so glorious, that it required not the meretricious aid of prodigy. When on his march against Maxentius, he is said to have seen in the heavens a cross of flame like the Greek letter X inverted in the form of a square cross, and in Greek around it, the words *Conquer by this.* Eusebius further relates, that next night, the Saviour appeared to him, and ordered him to make a military standard, in the form of the cross he had seen, which he did, and was always successful in war. Its name has not unfrequently been written Laborum, to signify that the cross should put an end to the *labours* and persecutions of the Christians; and it was supposed the guards to whom this miraculous banner was intrusted, were always invulnerable in battle.

At the battle of Bouvines, the imperial standard of Otho IV., like that of the English—the banner of St. John of Beverley on the field of Northallerton—was hoisted from a frame, raised on four wheels. Upon it was painted a dragon, above which was a gilded eagle. On that day the royal standard of France was a gilded staff, with a white silk colour, powdered with fleurs-de-lis, which had become the national arms. "The old crowns of the kings of Lombardy," says Voltaire, "of which there are very exact prints in Muratori, are mounted with this ornament, which is nothing more than the head of a spear, tied with two other pieces of crooked iron."

The banner used by the Chevalier Bayard, when he gallantly took command of Mézierès, and defended it against 40,000 Spaniards under Charles V., is still preserved in the Hôtel de Ville of that place.

Joan of Arc, bore with her in all her battles and sieges a consecrated banner, which was believed to be miraculous, and was revered as holy. It was white silk, and bore a figure representing the Supreme Being, grasping the world, and surrounded by fleurs-de-lis.

Clad in white armour, with this standard in her hands, she entered Orleans on the 29th of April, 1429, in the face of a vastly superior English force, and lodged it with herself, in the house of Jacques Bouchier. She had previously declared, at the moment when Dunois, repulsed, was sounding the retreat, that when her standard touched the city wall, the assailants should enter. "It was touched. The assailants burst in. On the next day the siege was abandoned and the force which had conducted it withdrew in good order to the north." Joan bore this standard, also, at the capture of Jargeau, when Suffolk was taken prisoner and his garrison put to the sword, and it was in her hand, at her crowning glory, the coronation of Charles VII. at Rheims. She stood with it before the high altar, says Lord Mahon. "It had shared the danger," she observed, "and it had a right to share the honour."—(Monstrelet, &c.)

When tried as a witch and heretic by the Bishop of Beauvais and other tools of the English, they asked her "why she put trust in her standard, which had been consecrated by magical incantation?" But she replied that she put trust alone in the Supreme Being, whose image was impressed upon it. Then they demanded why she carried in her hand that standard at the anointment and coronation of Charles at Rheims; and again she answered, that the person who shared the danger was entitled to share the glory.

But the most famous banner in Europe or Asia

at one time was undoubtedly that of the Knights of the Temple. It was formed of cloth, striped black and white, called in old French *Bauseant*, a word which became the battle cry of the Templars. It bore on it the red cross of the order, with the humble and pious inscription, *Non nobis, Domine, sed nomini tuo, da gloriam* (Not unto us, O Lord, not unto us, but to Thy name give the glory !)

Bauseant was in old French the name for a piebald horse, or a horse marked black and white (Roquefort-Ducange, &c.) ; and the word is still preserved and used in its original sense in Scotland as *bawsent*, as any reader of Burns's poems may remember. At the commencement of a battle the Marshal took the standard of the order from the sub-marshal, and unfurled it in the name of God. He then named from five to ten of the brotherhood to surround and guard it ; one of these he made a knight-preceptor, who was to keep close by him with another banner furled on a spear, to be instantly displayed if any mishap befell the *Bauseant*. In the event of the Christians being defeated, the Templar, under penalty of expulsion from the order, was not to quit the field so long as the banner of the order was flying ; should no other red-cross flag be seen, he was at liberty to join that of the Hospitallers, and was only to retire, as well as he could, when the *Bauseant* and every other Christian banner should have disappeared.

In "Ivanhoe" Scott spells the name of the banner *Beauseant.*

In referring to the banner of the Templars, it is impossible to forget that one so often displayed against the Christians, the standard of the Prophet Mahomet, the unfurling of which was so frequently threatened at the commencement of the Russo-Turkish war, a ceremony which only takes place on gravest emergencies or occasions of state.

The origin of this standard is remarkable. When the Prophet lay on his death-bed at Medina, while his mind was full of his projected conquest of Syria, he summoned the chiefs of his host around him to hear his last orders and wishes. While listening to his dying utterances in silence and awe, Ayesha, the most beautiful and best beloved of his wives, rushed into the room, and, tearing down a green curtain which screened one end thereof, threw it before the chiefs, and desired them to display it as the holy banner of Islam, and this was actually done in many subsequent wars against the Christians and others. By some it was said to have been the curtain that hung before the apartments of Ayesha; and it has been permanently lodged in the Seraglio at Constantinople, and is generally brought forth on the occasion of a new sultan being girt with the sword of Osman, or Othman; but it may shrewdly be doubted whether this banner—the present *Tanjak-Sherif*—is the same that was unfurled at Bedr, and which was upheld by nine hundred and fifty of Mahomet's disciples against the whole power of Mecca, at Ohod, a mountain northward of Medina, when Hamza, the uncle of the Prophet, fell.

Though unvarying faith and tradition carry it back to
the days of Mahomet, there can be little doubt that it is
the identical banner which, in 1683, Kara Mustapha,
nephew of the great Cuprogli, hoisted on the walls of
Vienna, though that city was not completely conquered.
Its display is always attended with much pomp and
ceremony When unfurled it is always handed to the
Scheik-ul-Islam, or Grand Mufti, who combines in his
own person the supreme power of the law with the
highest office of religion, who mounted on a caparisoned
steed, and, attended by the Sultan, bearing a drawn
scimitar, rides in procession through the streets of Constantinople, escorted by the *Ulemas*, whose duty it is to
proclaim that war has been declared against the un-
believers. The scheik then assigns it to the commander-
in-chief, whose duty it is to see that it is always borne
in front in battle.

It is a veritable banner of blood, denying mercy to
man, woman, and child, on the display of which, as the
Koran has it, " the earth will shake, the mountains
sink into dust, the seas blaze with fire, and the hair of
children grow white with anguish ; " but for more than
three generations it has never been brought forth in
hostility—at least, not since the Empress Catharine
sought to reinstate the Christian Empire at Constantinople. Upon it is the dubious motto, " All who draw
the sword in the cause of Faith shall be rewarded with
temporal advantages."

The Turks and Tartars were wont to make use of

horses' tails for their ensigns, and the number of these
denoted the rank of their commanders—the Sultan
having seven, and the grand vizier only three, &c.

The alleged origin of the holy banner of Persia is
curious. It is said that during a battle which lasted
three days between Saade and Rustam, the usurper—
the same who assassinated the reforming Sophi in
1499—the standard of the monarchy was captured, a
circumstance that caused excess of grief on one side and
of joy on the other—one party feeling that their *prestige*
had departed, and the other—that of the usurper—
deeming it a sure presage of future victory. This warlike relic was simply the leathern apron of a blacksmith,
who in some remote time had been the William Wallace
of Persia, for the mastery of which the Saracens so long
contended with the Turks; but the badge of heroic
poverty was disguised, and almost concealed, by the
profusion of gems which covered it.

Undoubtedly, the banner which had the most distinct
and glorious history was the Oriflamme of France, first
adopted in person by Louis VI. in 1110, and which
continued to be borne by the French sovereigns, in
addition to the Royal Standard, down to the time of
Charles VII., and the accounts of which have been
entirely overlooked by British historians and antiquaries.
Before the time of Louis VI., the Comtes de Vexin were
bound by the charter of their lands, which they held of
the Abbey of St. Denis, to protect the domains of the
latter, and accordingly, on the approach of any danger

or invasion, they assembled their vassals and appeared before the Abbey, where they received its banner, or gonfanon, which was borne before them in battle in defence of the lands of the church. At a later period the county of Vexin having been annexed to the crown, the kings of France followed the pious example of the ancient counts, to whom they had succeeded, and thus, in time, the oriflamme, as a royal standard of France, supplanted that which had been hitherto borne, the alleged cloak of St. Martin, of Tours—or rather the half thereof, as, according to the Bollandists, he gave the other portion to a shivering beggar at the gate of Amiens.

He to whom the care of the banner was confided at the head of the army, had the title of *Porte-Ori-flamme*, and had the command of its chosen guard, noble chevaliers and men-at-arms. He was ever a man of prudence and approved valour, and his post led to higher honours. We find in history, under Charles V of France, a gentleman styled Marshal of France, who was its bearer. It was an office for life, and for death too, as his oath obliged him to perish rather than abandon the *Oriflamme*.

Louis IX. lost it on his expedition to Egypt, as it fell, for a time, into the hands of the infidels; and "the Oriflamme has not been in use in our armies," says the *Dictionnaire Militaire*, 1758, "since the English were absolute masters of Paris, after the death of Charles VI."

The Oriflamme was of flame-coloured silk—hence its name—uncharged, and divided at the lower extremity into three portions ending in green tassels. It was hung from a cross-yard, with two cords of silk and gold to keep it from swinging in the wind, on the march, or when in battle.

The first *named* in history as its bearer is Anscieu Seigneur de Chevreuse, in 1294, under Philip le Bel. He had predecessors in the time of Louis le Gros ; but René Moreau is the last who, in 1450, was commissioned with the real dignity of *Porte-Oriflamme*. Though usually, till the first Revolution, lodged at St. Denis, it was occasionally left for a time in the custody of its bearers ; hence the families of D'Harcourt and Beavron long affirmed that they were in possession of the real Oriflamme, as successors of Pierre de Villiers de Lisle Adam, who had been its bearer, and whose daughter married the brave Jean Garencière.

Louis VII. took it with him in his voyage to the Bosphorus and his march through Hungary and Thrace. Philip Augustus had it displayed in 1183, in the war against Philip of Alsace, Count of Flanders ; Galois, Seigneur de Montigné, bore it at the battle of Bouvines, and Louis VIII. unfurled it in the war against the Albigeois in 1226.

Louis IX. had it with him in the war against Henry III. of England in 1262, and, as stated, in his crusade against the infidels in Egypt ; De Chevreuse bore it under Philip in 1304 ; and the bearers were

successively, Raoul, surnamed *Herpin*, Seigneur d'Erquery
in 1315; Miles de Noyers de Vilbertin in 1328; Geoffry
Lord of Charny in 1355; Arnoul d'Andrehon in 1388;
the Seigneur de L'Isle Adam in 1372; Sire de la
Trimoille and Guillaume de Bordes in 1383; Pierre
d'Aumont, surnamed *Hutin*, in 1397; and Guillaume
Martel de Bocqueville in 1414.

Louis XI. received the banner from the hands of
Cardinal d'Alby in 1465, in the ancient church of
St. Catharine *du Val des Écoliers* at Paris, prior to the
war against the Burgundians, and after that, we hear
no more of the famous Oriflamme, which must have
perished at the sack of St. Denis in 1793; but a
modern red-flag supplies its place behind the altar there,
at the present day.

The so-called Raven-banner of Hubba the Dane,
which was captured near Northam in Devonshire, when
he was slain in battle by the Saxons, in 869, and where
his tomb is still shown, was simply a stuffed black bird,
probably of the raven species, which remained quiet
when defeat was at hand, but clapped its wings
vigorously before a victory.

The royal ensign of the West Saxons was a golden
dragon; and thus we hear often of the Dragon of
Wessex in the fierce old fights during the time of the
Heptarchy.

It was not until after the Synod of Oxford, in 1220,
that the Red Cross of St. George supplanted the
martlets of St. Edward, up to that date the patron of

England. The Scottish Cross of St. Andrew has a fabulous history exactly similar to that of the *Labarum* of Constantine, and dating back to the ninth century; but in neither England nor Scotland has a banner of any antiquity been preserved, unless we may enumerate as such the banner given to the citizens of Edinburgh by Margaret of Oldenburg, Queen of James III., in 1482, and still preserved there, under the local name of the Blue Blanket, or Banner of the Holy Ghost, on the displaying of which, not only the craftsmen of Edinburgh, but those of all Scotland, were bound to appear in arms, under the Convener of the Trades. The fragment of it that remains, shows that its colour was blue, crossed by the white saltire of St. Andrew.

CHAPTER IV

FAMOUS AND ANCIENT CANNON.

HISTORY shows us that in past ages there has ever and anon been in most countries a fancy for forging or casting ponderous cannon, even as there has been often in a spirit of rivalry, a fancy for building great ships; and the result has very generally been that, in both instances, there has been a mistake; for the great ships have been almost invariably cast away, and the great guns have proved useless, even for battery pur-

pose; and it is not improbable that such may be the
result eventually with our " Woolwich Infants " and
our eighty-one ton guns.

Though cannon are mentioned as having been used
in a sea fight between a Moorish King of Seville and
a King of Tunis in the 13th century, they first marked
the inauguration of a new era in war when Edward III.
of England brought with him to the field of Cressi in
1346, five small pieces, made by whom is quite unknown; but there can be little doubt that they were
constructed in the mode of all early cannon, of iron bars
fitted together, hooped with rings and charged with
stone shot—not iron balls.

Prior to Cressi, however, cannon had undoubtedly
been used in sieges. In 1338 there was one used at
Cambrai from which cross-bows were discharged, and
several small guns of the same kind were used in the
following year at the investment of Quesnoy; again at
the siege of the then Moorish town of Algesiras, near
Gibraltar, in 1342; and old annals tell us of the
overwhelming terror their explosion excited among the
enemy.

Iron balls were first cast in the reign of Louis XI. in
1461; but stone were in common use for a hundred
years later.

As time went on, cannon, though primitively formed
as described, increased in size that prodigious balls
might be expelled from them against walled places, in
imitation of the ancient machine which they had super-

seded; thus they soon became of enormous bore, until
they attained the dignity of bombardes, like Mons Meg in
Edinburgh Castle; but the difficulty of managing these
pieces, and the growing knowledge that iron shot of
much less weight could be impelled further by the use
of better powder, gradually introduced the cast metal
cannon used at the present day.

The five little cannon used at Cressi, to the wonder
of the French who had *none*, were doubtless the same
that Edward used at the siege of Calais in the following
year.

In 1366 the Venetians, when besieging a town now
named Chioggia in Lombardy, had with them two
small pieces of artillery having leaden balls, worked by
Germans, according to Le Blond's " Elements of War,"
dedicated to Louis of Lorraine; and battering guns were
used by the Turks against the Christians at Constantinople in 1394; but the great bombardes were at their
zenith when, in 1451, Mahomet II. began his march
against the same city, with fourteen gigantic guns,
which threw stone shot seventy-eight inches in circumference, weighing 800 lbs. In the siege, traces of
which remain to this day, the Christians are supposed
to have been without cannon, as they omitted to de-
molish the great bridge of boats which was constructed
by the Turks and conduced so much to the reduction of
the city.

For more than four centuries the guns of Mahomet II.
protected the Dardanelles—the gate of the Eastern

Empire; and, as an old traveller relates, that as they were shotted when fired on holidays, land was usually to be had very cheap on the opposite side of the straits.

Though practically these great pieces of artillery have given place to Krupp and other guns, they still remain on their old sites; but cannon of this description can only be discharged with effect when the object passes their line of fire, as they are not mounted on carriages but built into a wall. Some of those at the Dardanelles carry balls 26½ inches in diameter, and lie flat on a paved terrace near the level of the water, where they opened on our fleet in 1808, when Admiral Sir John Duckworth forced the passage of the Straits.

By a granite shot from one of these, when the fleet returned, H.M.S. *Royal George* had her whole cutwater carried away; by another, the mainmast of the *Windsor Castle* was cut in two like a fishing-rod; another carried away the wheel of the *Repulse*, at the same moment killing and wounding twenty-four men, and rendering the ship so unmanageable, that but for the noble seamanship of her crew, she must have gone on shore.

A granite ball burst through the bows of the *Active*, and rolling aft destroyed all in its career, till it was brought up abreast of the main hatchway; a second tore away the whole barricade of her forecastle and fell into the sea to starboard; a third lodged in the bends abreast of the main-chains, and then tumbled overboard. ("Duckworth's Dispatches," &c.)

Baron de Tott tells us that he had seen one of these

guns, which had been cast in the reign of Amurath, fired. Its ball weighed eleven hundredweight, and required a charge of powder amounting to 330 pounds. At the distance of 800 fathoms he saw this enormous globe divide into three pieces, which crossed the strait and rebounded from the rocks opposite.

One of these guns was sent to Woolwich, in exchange for an Armstrong breech-loader, and bears the inscription—

" Help o Allah ! Mahomet Khan, the son of Murad !"

Louis XII. of France had a bombarde cast which is said to have thrown a ball of 500lbs. from the Bastile to Charenton ; but the guns of these times were destitute of trunnions, dolphin-rings, or breech-buttons.

Another enormous cannon of Mahomet II. is still to be seen at Negroponte, used at its capture by him from the Venetians in 1470. It defends the south side of Kastro, and is the most remarkable monument there.

There is now preserved in the Castle of San Juliao da Barra, ten miles from Lisbon, a gun that was captured at the siege of Diu, on the southern coast of Gujirat, in 1546, by a gallant Portugese cavalier, Dom John de Castro, which is destitute of the appliances named, and is of some remarkable metal. It bears upon it a Hindoo inscription to the effect that it was cast in 1400. It is 20 feet 7 inches long ; its external diameter at the centre is 6 feet 3 inches, and it discharges a ball one hundredweight.

In ancient times there was a fondness for bestowing
upon these great guns some peculiar and dignified name.
Twelve brass cannon cast in 1503 for Louis XII., being
all of remarkable size, he named after the greatest peers
of France.   The Spaniards and Portuguese named them
after certain saints; thus, when the Emperor Charles V
departed to attack Tunis, his bombardes were named
after the Twelve Apostles.

In the Malaga there is still an 80-pounder of great
antiquity named the "Terrible." Two very curious
60-pounders in the arsenal at Bremen are each named
"The Messenger of Bad News;" an 80-pounder at Berlin,
now in the Royal Arsenal, is named "The Thunderer;"
at Milan there is a 70-pounder called the "Pimontelle"
(or the little spicer); and another at Bois le Duc is styled
Le Diable.   A third in the Castle of St. Angelo at Rome,
made of the nails which fastened the copper-plates com-
posing the roof of the ancient Pantheon, bears upon it
this inscription—

"*Ex clavis trabalibus porticus Agrippæ.*"

Many of the cannon of the sixteenth and seventeenth
centuries were remarkable for their beautiful and ornate
character.   A decorated Spanish cannon now preserved
in the Paris Museum, is a fine example of these florid
pieces, which were always cast of brass or mixed
metal.

Diego Ufano, in his treatise on Artillery, published in
1614, shows us the metallic mixtures of copper, tin,

and brass, and the proportions of these, then used for
cast pieces of cannon.

The Russian arsenals are very rich in great and
ancient cannon and others of historical interest.

In front of the first arsenal at the Kremlin, are ranged
a wonderful memorial of Napoleon's terrible retreat
from Moscow, in the shape of no less than 875 pieces
of captured ordnance; of these 365 are French, 189
are Austrian, 123 are Prussian, and the remainder bear
the royal insignia of Italy, Naples, Bavaria, Saxony,
Westphalia, Hanover, Spain, Würtemberg, Holland, and
Poland. Many of these (says Sutherland Edwards) are
inscribed with pretentious names that contrast strongly
with their present humble position, such as the "Invincible," the "Conqueror," the "Eagle," and so forth.

In front of the second arsenal is a wonderful collec-
tion of colossal cannon, ranged in a long line, with the
shortest in the centre; thus their muzzles present a
complete arc. The largest of these is a 4800-pounder,
weighing, however, only forty tons! It has never
been fired, and is only remarkable as a piece of
casting.

An inscription on it tells that it was cast by the
Russian master-founder named Chokoff, in 1586, by
order of the Czar Feodor, who in that year conquered
Siberia (the way to which was discovered by the
Cossack warrior Jermack), and of whom a clever representation, on horseback, with crown and sceptre, appears
close to the muzzle. Beside it are six other large pieces,

the smallest of which weighs nearly four tons. —(" The
Russians at Home.")

About the end of the fifteenth century the following
guns were in universal use :—

The Cannon-Royal		48 pounder.
,, Bastard-Cannon .	.	36 ,,
,, Half-Carthoun	.	24 ,,
,, Culverin .	.	18 ,,
,, Demi-Culverin	.	9 ,,
,, Falcon .	.	6 ,,
,, Saker .	.	6, 5, 8 ,,
,, Basilisk (also)	.	48 ,,
,, Serpentine .	.	4 ,,
,, Aspik .	.	2 ,,
,, Dragon .	.	6 ,,
,, Syren	.	60 ,,
,, Falconet	3, 2, 1 ,,
,, Moyenne .	.	12 ounces.

By the middle of the seventeenth century, the largest
cannon generally used in the field were 24-pounders,
or others like the culverins of Nancy (18-pounders), so
called from being first cast in that city; while the
smallest were 6 and 3-pounders.

Mortars were first used to expel red-hot balls and
large stones, long ere shells were known. They are
believed to have been of German origin, and were used
at the siege of Naples by Charles VIII. in 1135; but
shells were first thrown out of them at the siege of
Wachtendonk in Gueldres, by the Count of Mansfield.
Shells were first invented by a citizen of Venloo, who, at a
festival in honour of the Duke of Cleves, contrived, unfortunately, by the explosion of them, to reduce nearly the

whole city to ashes. Maltus, an English engineer, first taught the French how to use them at the siege of La Motte in 1634. (Le Blond.)

The howitzer differs from the mortar, being mounted on a field carriage, like a gun; the chief difference being that the trunnions of the first are at the end, and of the other in the middle. The invention of the howitzer is subsequent to that of the mortar, as from the latter it originated.

The first man who invented the spiking of artillery was Gaspar Vimercalus of Bremen, who thus nailed up the artillery of Sigismund Malatesta.

Rifled cannon are by no means a modern invention, and can be traced far back into antiquity, as the *arquebuse-rayée* of the French.

No kind of gun has been more universally known and used all over Europe and America than the carronade, or "smasher," as it was called. Cast at the Carron Works in Scotland (hence their name), they were the invention of General Robert Melville, an officer who served under Lord Rollo of Duncrub, at the capture of Dominica in the West Indies. Peculiarly constructed, and having a chamber for powder like a mortar, they were shorter and lighter than ordinary cannon.

Cast in mighty numbers for more than seventy years at Carron, they were employed by the fighting and mercantile marine of all Europe and America, till the time of the Crimean War. The first of them was presented by the Carron Company to the family of General

s

Melville, with an inscription on the carriage, which records that the guns were cast "for solid, ship, shell or carcase shot, and were first used against the French fleet in 1799."

Mr. Smiles, in his "Industrial Biography," tells us that when cannon came to be employed in war, the vicinity of Sussex to the Cinque Ports gave it an advantage over the iron districts of the north and west of England, and for a long time the iron works of that county had a monopoly in the manufacture of guns. The stone balls were hewn from quarries at Maidstone Heath. An old mortar, which lay on Eridge Green, near Frant, is said to have been the *first* used in England. The chamber was cast, but the tube consisted of hooped bars.

In the Tower are some old hooped guns of the date of Henry VI. The first cast-iron cannon of English make were made at Buxtead in Sussex, in 1543, by Ralph Hogge, master founder, whose principal assistant was Pierre Baude, a Frenchman. About the same time, Hogge employed Peter Van Collet, a Flemish gunsmith, who, according to Stowe, "caused to be made certain mortar pieces, being at the mouth from eleven to nine inches wide, for the use whereof the said Peter caused to be made certain hollow shot of cast iron, stuffed with fyrwork, whereof the bigger sort has screws of iron to receive a match to carry fire, to break in small pieces the said *hollow shot*, whereof the smallest piece hitting a man would kill or spoil him."

This is undoubtedly the parent of the explosive shell which has been brought to such terrible perfection in the present day. Many of Baude's brass and iron guns are still preserved in the Tower; and perhaps from his foundry came that very beautiful gun which bears the name of Henry VIII., 1541, and is preserved now at Southampton.

Two old English guns are at present in the ducal castle of Blair, whither they had been brought by the Athole family when Lords of the Isle of Man.

One is inscribed thus:—

"Henricus Octavus; Thomas Seymoure Knighte, Receyvour of the Peel, was Master of the King's Ordynans, when John and Robert Owyn made this pese. Anno dni., 1544."

The other has the legend:—

"Henry, Earle of Derbye, Lord of this Isle of Man, being here in May, 1577; named *Dorothe*. Henry Halsall, Receyvour of the Peele, bought this pese, 1574."

This was the fourth Earl of Derby, a K.G., and he had named the gun from his mother Dorothy, who was daughter of Thomas Howard, Duke of Norfolk.

The old brass gun, popularly known as Queen Anne's Pocket Pistol, was once called Queen Elizabeth's, according to Colonel James. It was cast at Utrecht in 1544, and is a 12-pounder, twenty feet long, finely ornamented with figures in bas-relief.

Scotland, which is rich in military and historical

antiquities of all kinds, can also boast of several ancient cannon, extant or in her annals.

In 1430, James I. had cast for him in Flanders a cannon of brass, called the Lion of Scotland, bearing this inscription :—

> " Illustri Jacobo Scottorum principe digno,
> Regni magnifico, dum fulmine castra reduco
> Factus sum sub eo, nuncupar ego Leo."

" This," says Balfour in his *Annales*, " was the first canon or bombard of any strength or bignes, that ever was in Scotland." Among several ancient guns in the armory of the Grants of Grant in Strathspey, is one of singular beauty, covered with figures of men on horseback, and animals of the chase. It is four feet two inches long, and seems to have been a Moyenne or wall piece, and is inscribed :—

"Dominus Johannes Grant Miles Vicecomes de Invernes Me fecit in Germania. 1434."

The most ancient gun made in Britain is undoubtedly that bombarde known as Mons Meg in Edinburgh Castle. An inscription on the *new* stock, cast at Woolwich in 1835, states that the gun "is *believed* to have been forged at *Mons*, in 1486." But this is proved now to have been a gross mistake, an assertion which is utterly without warrant, as an elaborate " History of Galloway " shows from proofs indisputable that it was made by a smith of that county, in 1455, for the service of James II. (then besieging the Castle of Threave), at a place still named Knockcannon. It weighs six tons and a half, is composed of malleable iron bars hooped together, and its balls, which are all of Galloway granite, are twenty-one inches in diameter.

Two of these shots fired from it compelled the castle to surrender in the summer of 1455, and *both* were found in 1841 amid the ruins—one in the wall, the other in the draw-well; and both lay in a *direct line* from Knockcannon to the breach in the huge donjon tower. For his work, M'Kim received the forfeited lands of Mollance, pronounced in Scottish parlance, *Mowance*, and hence the tradition of "Meg" being forged at *Mons*. In 1497, it accompanied the Scottish army into England in the cause of Perkin Warbeck; to the siege of Dumbarton in 1489, and many other scenes of strife. In 1681, the gun burst, when firing a royal salute for James Duke of Albany, as two of the fractured hoops still show. On these occasions, like the old bombardes of the Dardanelles, it was generally *shotted*, as the Royal Treasurer's Accounts contain many entries of payments, for "finding and carrying *her* bullet from Wardie Mure to the Castell."

In 1509—thirty-four years before Ralph Hogge began to cast guns in Sussex—James IV employed Robert Borthwick, his master gunner, to *cast* a set of brass ordnance for Edinburgh Castle. Seven of these were named by the king the *sisters* of Borthwick—being all alike in size and beauty. They were inscribed—

" *Machina sum, Scoto Borthwick Fabricata Roberto.*"

With ten other brass field-pieces, these guns were all taken by the English at the battle of Flodden, where Borthwick was killed, and the Earl of Surrey, who saw them, asserted that there were none finer in the arsenals of King Henry.   Several of these guns were retaken by the Scots from the Earl of Hereford's army in 1544, and were long preserved in the Castle of Edinburgh, on the walls of which, in the siege of 1573, were a number of guns that bore the crowned salamander, the badge of Francis I., and had perhaps been brought from France by the Regent Duke of Chatelherault.

An old cannon named *Dundee,* which had been used in war by the Viscount of that name, was long preserved in the Castle of Kilchurn; but has now disappeared.

In the heart of British India there was, singular to say, found an antique Scottish cannon, which is now shown in Edinburgh, and the story of which is remarkable.   At the siege of Bhurtpore in 1826, among the guns on the ramparts was one of great calibre and destructive power, popularly known among our soldiers by the absurd name of "Sweet-lips," which was taken at the point of the bayonet by H.M. 14th Foot.

Beside it was found a Scottish brass cannon, an 18-pounder, inscribed : —

"*Jacobus Menteith me fecit, Edinburgh, Anno Dom.,* 1642."

It at once attracted the attention of Captain (afterwards Colonel) Lewis Carmichael, an old Peninsular officer.

then aide-de-camp to Sir Jasper Nicolls. On the day before the storm, with six grenadiers of the 59th and four Ghoorkas, he had made a gallant dash into one of the breaches, to reconnoitre it for the desperate work that was to come, and he asked for the old Scottish cannon as a reward. It was at once given, by order of the Governor-General, and he brought it with him to Edinburgh, where it is preserved in the Museum of Antiquities, with several other ancient guns, some of which belonged to Sir Andrew Wood of Largo, Admiral of James III., and captain of *the Yellow Frigate ;* but how it came to be so far up country in India, among the Jauts, it is difficult to conjecture, unless it had belonged to one of the ships of the old and ill-fated Scottish East India Company, which was ruined by the enmity and treachery of William of Orange.

British India has produced many pieces of ordnance, great in calibre and remarkable in history; among them may be enumerated the great gun of Hyder and Tippo, and the enormous cannon found at Agra, when that place was captured by Lord Lake in 1803. It had trunnions, and was furnished with four rings, two at the breech and two at the muzzle. It was of brass, says Thorne, " and for magnitude and beauty stands unrivalled. Its length was 14 feet 2 inches; its calibre 23 inches; the weight of its ball, when of cast iron, 1500 lbs. ; and its whole weight 86,600 lbs., or a little above 38 tons."

Though called brass, it was, according to common

report, composed of a mixture of precious metals.   The *Shroffs*, or native bankers, were of that opinion, as they offered £12,000 for it, merely to melt down.   Lord Lake preferred to send it as a trophy to Britain, and proceeded to have it transported to Calcutta on a raft.   It proved too heavy for the latter, and capsizing sunk in the waters of the Ganges.

Another curious piece of ordnance, locally known as *Jubbar Jung*, fell into our hands at Ghuznee in 1842. It was of brass and beautifully ornamented; it carried 64-pound shot, and these being of hammered iron whizzed as they passed through the air.   It made some havoc among the tents of our 40th Regiment, and the Huzarehs, followers of Ali, who joined General Nott at the siege, implored him to destroy " Jubbar Jung," for which they appeared to entertain a deep religious horror.

There are at this hour cannon at Bejapore, beside which our " Woolwich Infants" and Armstrong 100-ton guns sink into insignificance.   One of these, called the *Mulk-e-Meidan*, or "Sovereign of the Plains," cast by Roomi Khan, "the Turk of Roumelia," or first Monarch of Bejapore, an Ottoman of Constantinople, weighs forty tons; and, to crown all, Major Rennell mentions an old iron cannon at Dacca, which threw a shot 465 pounds in weight!

The last great gun actually used was King Theodore's huge bombarde at Magdala in 1868, for which he had an enormous number of stone balls made, and which he believed to be the Palladium of Abyssinia. It was shattered to pieces among his troops, on their first attempt to use it.

The last and most remarkable invention in artillery is a much needed fire-arm, which may supersede our boasted steel mountain ordnance, "the jointed gun" of Sir William Armstrong, which can be unscrewed into three separate pieces, each of which is light enough for conveyance on the back of a horse, and when put together form a powerful and long-range cannon, similar to the present field-piece.

Such a gun would have been invaluable in Ashantee, or among the mountains of Abyssinia; and the want of some such fire-arm was sorely felt at times during the Indian mutiny, especially about its close, when our moveable columns pursued the rebels in the deserts of Bekaneer, where the gun carriages of even the flying artillery at times sunk axle deep in the dry heavy sand, rendering them almost useless for service.

In Europe, this is peculiarly the age of enormous cannon. "Armour of two feet in thickness," says a recent writer, "and guns of one hundred tons in weight being now accomplished facts, and ships already bigger than the *Inflexible* being already in hand, we may well ask ourselves, *What will be the next step?*"

STORY OF A MERCHANT CAPTAIN.

ABOUT the time of the accession of George III. to the throne, few domestic events made a greater sensation in the papers and periodicals of the day than the adventures and fate of a sea-captain named George Glass, especially in connection with a mutiny on board the brig *Earl of Sandwich*. This remarkable man, who was one of the fifteen children of John Glass, noted as the originator of the Scottish sect known as the Glassites, was born at Dundee in 1725. After graduating in the medical profession, he made several voyages, as surgeon of a merchant-ship (belonging to London), to the Brazils and the coast of Guinea; and in 1764, he published, by Dodsley, an interesting work in one volume quarto, entitled *The History of the Discovery and Conquest of the Canary Islands, translated from a Spanish manuscript.*

He obtained command of a Guinea trader, and made several successful voyages, till the war with Spain broke out in January, 1762. Having saved a good round sum, he equipped a privateer, and took command of her as captain, to cruise against the French and Spaniards; but he had not been three days at sea, when his crew mutinied, and sent him that which is called in sea-phraseology a round-robin (a corruption of an old French military term, the *ruban rond*, or round ribbon), in which they wrote their names in a circle ; hence none could know who was the leader.

Arming himself with his cutlass and pistols, Glass came on deck, and offered to fight, hand to hand, any man who conceived himself to be wronged in any way. But the crew, knowing his personal strength, his skill and resolution, declined the challenge. He succeeded in pacifying them by fair words ; and the capture of a valuable French merchantman a few days after put them all in excellent humour. This gleam of good fortune was soon after clouded by an encounter with an enemy's frigate, which, though twice the size of his privateer, Glass resolved to engage ; and for two hours they fought broadside to broadside, till another French vessel bore down on him, and he was compelled to strike his colours, after half his crew had been killed and he had received a musket-shot in the shoulder.

He remained for some time a French prisoner of war in the Antilles, where he was treated with excessive severity ; but upon being exchanged, he resolved to embark the remainder of his fortune in another privateer and " have it out," as he said, with the French and Dons. But he was again taken in action, and lost everything he had in the world.

On being released a second time, he was employed by London merchants in several voyages to the West Indies, in command of ships that fought their way without convoy; and according to a statement in the *Annual Register*, he was captured no less than *seven* times.   But alter various fluctuations of fortune, when the general peace took place in 1763, he found himself possessed of two thousand guineas prize-money, and the reputation of being one of the best merchant captains in the Port of London.

About that time a Company there resolved to make an attempt to form a settlement on the west coast of Africa, by founding a harbour and town midway between the Cape de Verd and the river Senegal.   In the London and other papers of the day we find many statements urging the advantage of opening up the Guinea-trade ; among others, a strange letter from a merchant, who tells us he was taken prisoner in a battle on that coast, and that when escaping he " crossed a forest within view of the sea, where there lay elephants' teeth in quantities sufficient to load one hundred ships."

In the interests of this new Company Glass sailed in a ship of his own to the coast of Guinea, and selected and surveyed a harbour at a place which he was certain might become the centre of a great trade in teak and cam woods, spices, palm oil and ivory, wax and gold. Elated with his success, he returned to England, and laid his scheme before the ministry, among whom were John Earl of Sandwich, Secretary of State, and the Earl of Hillsborough, Commissioner of Trade and Planta-tions.

With truly national patience and perseverance he underwent all the procrastinations and delays of office, but ultimately obtained an exclusive right of trading to his own harbour for twenty years. Assisted by two merchants—the Company would seem to have failed— he fitted out his ship anew, and sailed for the intended harbour; and sent on shore a man who knew the country well, to make propositions of trade with the natives, who put him to death the moment they saw him.

Undiscouraged by this event, Captain Glass found means to open up a communication with the king of the country, to lay before him the wrong that had been done, and the advantages that were certain to accrue from mutual trade and barter. The sable potentate affected to be pleased with the proposal, but only to the end that he might get Glass completely into his power; but the Scotsman was on his guard, and foiled him.

The king then attempted to poison the whole crew by provisions which he sent on board impregnated by some deadly drug. Glass, by his previous medical knowledge, perhaps, discovered this in time; but so scarce had food become in his vessel, that he was compelled to go with a few hands in an open boat to the Canaries, where he hoped to purchase what he wanted from the Spaniards.

In his absence the savages were encouraged to attack the ship in their war-canoes; but were repulsed by a sharp musketry-fire opened upon them by the remainder of the crew, who, losing heart by the protracted absence of the captain, quitted his fatal harbour, and sailed for the Thames, which they reached in safety.

Meanwhile the unfortunate captain, after landing on one of the Canaries, presented a petition to the Spanish governor to the effect that he might be permitted to purchase food; but that officer, inflamed by national animosity, cruelly threw him into a dark and damp dungeon, and kept him there without pen, ink, or paper, on the accusation that he was a spy. Being thus utterly without means of making his case known, he contrived another way of communicating with the external world. One account has it that he concealed a pencilled note in a loaf of bread which fell into the hands of the British consul; another states that he wrote with a piece of charcoal on a ship-biscuit and sent it to the captain of a British man-of-war that was lying off the island, and who with much difficulty, and after being imprisoned himself, effected the release of Glass. The latter, on being joined by his wife and daughter, who had come in search of him, set sail for England in 1765, on board the merchant brig *Earl of Sandwich*, Captain Cochrane.

Glass doubtless supposed his troubles were now over; but the knowledge that much of his property and a great amount of specie, one hundred thousand pounds, belonging to others, was on board, induced four of the crew to form a conspiracy to murder every one else and seize the ship. These mutineers were respectively George Gidly, the cook, a native of the west of England; Peter M'Kulie, an Irishman; Andrew Zekerman, a Hollander;

and Richard H. Quintin, a Londoner. On three different nights they are stated to have made the attempt, but were baffled by the vigilance of Captain Glass, rather than that of his countryman, Captain Cochrane; but at eleven o'clock at night on the 30th of September, 1765, it chanced, as shown at their trial, that these four miscreants had together the watch on deck, when the *Sandwich* was already in sight of the coast of Ireland; and when Captain Cochrane, after taking a survey aloft, was about to return to the cabin, Peter M'Kulie brained him with "an iron bar" (probably a marline-spike), and threw him overboard.

A cry that had escaped Cochrane alarmed the rest of the crew, who were all dispatched in the same manner as they rushed on deck in succession. This slaughter and the din it occasioned, roused Captain Glass, who was below in bed; but he soon discovered what was occurring, and, after giving one glance on deck, hurried away to get his sword. M'Kulie, imagining the cause of his going back, went down the steps leading to the cabin, and stood in the dark, expecting Glass's return, and suddenly seized his arms from behind; but the captain, being a man of great strength, wrenched his sword-arm free, and on being assailed by the three other assassins, plunged his weapon into the arm of Zekerman, when the blade became wedged or entangled. It was at length wrenched forth, and Glass was slain by repeated stabs of his own weapon, while his dying cries were heard by his wife and daughter—two unhappy beings who were ruthlessly thrown overboard and drowned.

Besides these four victims, James Pincent, the mate, and three others, lost their lives. The mutineers now loaded one of the boats with the money, chests, and so forth, and then scuttled the *Sandwich*, and landed at Ross on the coast of Ireland. But suspicion speedily attached to them; they were apprehended, and, confessing the crimes of which they had been guilty, were tried before the Court of King's Bench, Dublin, and sentenced to death. They were accordingly executed in St. Stephen's Green, on the 10th of October, 1765.

THE STORY OF RENÉE OF ANGERS.

Though it occurred so long ago as the time of Henry IV of France, the story we are about to relate formed one of the most remarkable *causes célèbres* before the Parliament of Paris, when Renée Corbeau, a young demoiselle of Angers, in Normandy, by her eloquence in a court of justice, and by her singular self-sacrifice, saved the life of a false and dastardly lover, to whom she was devotedly attached.

In the year 1594, when Henry IV., justly surnamed the Great (though his passions betrayed him into errors and involved him in difficulties), was on the throne of France, a young man named M. Pousset, a native of Tées, an old episcopal city of Normandy, was studying the Civil and Canon Law at the University of Angers, in those days a famous seat of learning. While thus engaged, M. Pousset was introduced to Mademoiselle Renée Corbeau, the daughter of a citizen. She is described as having been a girl of great beauty of person and with great modesty of manner, though witty and lively in spirit, *folatré et caressante*, and full of nameless graces. Everyone loved and admired Renée,

T

and when but a youth Pousset sighed for her. He soon
learned to love her passionately, and we are told "that
he no longer lived but to see and converse with her."

She in turn became deeply attached to Pousset, who
proposed marriage, and gave her, in writing, a document to that effect, though her parents were in circumstances so limited that he dared not consult his own
(who were people of wealth, rank, and ambition) on
this important subject. So the lovers dreamed on, and
on the faith of the written promise, Renée, it would
appear, yielded too far, and fell, as her mother Eve fell
before her; and then repentance came when too late.

The unfortunate Renée had, in time, to make a con-
fidante of her mother, who in her grief and anger revealed all to M. Corbeau. He heaped the most bitter
reproaches on their daughter, but agreed that some
plan should be adopted to bring Pousset, who was now
studiously absenting himself, to reason and a sense of
justice. It was arranged that he and Madame Corbeau
should feign a journey to a little country mansion they
possessed not far from Angers, and that Renée should
press Pousset to visit her, when they should take advantage of the occasion to surprise him; a project
which was executed with complete success.

Thrown completely off his guard by this unexpected
stratagem, the lover said with much apparent candour:

"Monsieur Corbeau, be not alarmed for the error
which our love for each other has led us into; but
pardon us, I beseech you. My intentions are still most

honourable, and I shall be but too happy to espouse your daughter.''

The incensed Corbeau was somewhat comforted by this prompt promise of reparation, and sent immediately for a notary, his friend, who lived close by. The latter drew up a formal contract of marriage in legal form, and to this, with Renée, M. Pousset appended his signature and seal, after which he took a tender farewell of the weeping girl, and retired with the view of, reluctantly, breaking the matter to his family; but so true is it that "affection is the root of love in woman, and passion is the root of love in man," that from the hour in which he signed the—to him—fatal contract, all his regard for Renée evaporated.

Her beauty and her sorrow alike failed to impress him now, and the faithless Pousset repented him so bitterly of what he angrily deemed a legal entanglement, that he hastened to Tées and unfolded the whole of the affair to his father in a story artfully coloured and fashioned to suit himself.

M. Pousset the senior, who possessed a magnificent estate, never doubted but that his amiable and facile son had been entrapped by an artful girl and her parents, and sternly told him that he could never approve of his marriage with one whose portion was so small, and desired him to commit her, the contract, and the whole affair, to oblivion. While the document, signed and sealed existed, this, however, proved impossible ; so young Pousset, either by his father's

advice or his own inclination, took refuge in the bosom
of the Church, and was somewhat too speedily ordained
sub-deacon, and then deacon, thinking thereby to
vitiate the power of the contract, and to create for life
an invincible barrier between himself and Renée.

With all the grief and horror a tender and affectionate heart could feel when love is so repaid by black
perfidy, she heard these tidings, and her soul seemed to
die within her; but her old father, who was filled with
just indignation, and whose sword the ordination of
Pousset kept in its scabbard, raised a civil action against
him before the principal court at Angers for having
deluded, and then declined, to marry his daughter in
the face of the notary's contract.

The recreant was compelled to appear; but he
appealed against the order, and denied the jurisdiction
of the court; hence the cause was brought before the
Parliament of Paris. Before this tribunal, then, were
brought the wrongs of Renée Corbeau, and the whole
affair seemed so cruel and odious to the judges—especially the fact of Pousset having taken holy orders (and
thereby degraded them) to evade the contract of
marriage—that they condemned him to espouse Renée
or *lose his head* by the sword of the executioner.

He urged that the sanctity of holy orders utterly
precluded the former reparation. On this the court
unanimously declared that he must undergo the latter.
He was accordingly replaced in the Bastile; the priest
who was to attend in his last moments came to prepare

him for death, and as all sentences were summarily executed in those days, already the headsman awaited him.

The heart of the poor girl, who loved him still, was now wrung with new anguish and pity, and she accused herself of being the cause of his approaching doom. Crushed by that dreadful conviction, in her anxiety to save him, or at least have his sentence mitigated in some manner, she conceived the idea of taking all the guilt of his position upon *herself*.

Hastening to the old Palais de Justice, she entered the great hall, the centre of which was then occupied by the famous marble table which Victor Hugo describes as being of a single piece, so long, and so broad and thick, that it was doubtful if in the world there was such another block of marble. Imploring the astonished judges to hear her, she knelt before them, and while scarcely daring to raise her eyes from the floor, she told them in trembling accents that in condemning her lover-husband, for such she deemed him, they had forgotten that she too was culpable; that by his death she would be sunk into sorrow and covered with ignominy; and that while seeking to avenge her, or repair her honour, they would bring upon her the opprobrium of all France!

The judges listened in bewildered silence, while in a low and still more tremulous voice, Renée continued thus:

"Messieurs—I will no longer conceal my crime.

Remorse of conscience now forces me to declare that, thinking you might compel M. Pousset to marry me, I concealed the fact that I snared him into loving me— that I loved him first, and was thus the source of all my own sorrow! You deem it a crime that he took refuge in holy orders to avoid the fulfilment of his contract; yet, messieurs, that was not *his* doing, but resulted from the will of a proud and avaricious father, who is, in that matter, the real criminal. Spare him then, I implore you—spare him to the world, if not to me! He has declared that his orders preclude his marrying me; and for that declaration you ordain that he must die. Oh, what matters his asserting that he would formally espouse me if he could; and because he cannot, you condemn him to die, after giving him *a choice.* Who here can doubt that he would marry me in spite of his deacon's orders? Though I am but a weak and foolish girl, I know that we may yet be wedded, could we but obtain the dispensation of his Holiness Clement VIII. Daily we expect in Paris his Legate, who possesses sovereign powers. At his feet I will solicit that dispensation; and oh, be assured, messieurs, that my love and my prayers will obtain it. Suspend your terrible sentence, then, till he arrives."

After a pause, during which she was overcome with agitation, she spoke again:

"Think of all he has endured since his sentence has been delivered, and of all that I am enduring now! Should I have among you but a few voices for me, ought these not to win me some favour of humanity over the rest, though they be more in number! but alas! should all be inflexible, permit me, in mercy at least, to die with him I love, and by the same weapon."

It is recorded that the unhappy Renée's prayer met with a very favourable reception, and that the remarkable tone of her self-accusation, of having "ensnared" M. Pousset, gave a new colour to his alleged crime. "The judges," we are told, "lost not a word of her oration, which was pronounced with a clear sweet voice, and her words found a ready echo in their hearts, while the wonderful charms of her person, her tears and her eloquence, were too powerful not to melt, if they failed to persuade, men of humanity."

She was requested to withdraw while they consulted, and the First President, M. Villeroy, after collecting their votes, found himself enabled to grant a *respite* for six months, that a dispensation might be obtained if possible; and on this being announced, the plaudits of assembled thousands made the roof of the Palais de Justice ring in honour of Pousset's best advocate, Renée Corbeau.

Ere long the Roman Legate (Cardinal de Pellevé) came to Paris; but, on hearing the ugly story of Pousset, he conceived such indignation against him, for the whole tenor of his conduct, that he constantly turned a deaf ear to every application in his favour. Soon the last month of the respite drew to a close, and the fatal day was near when Pousset must be brought forth to die!

The unexpected hostility of the Legate cast Renée once more into despair, an emotion all the more terrible that the announcement of M. Villeroy had given her brilliant, perhaps happy, hopes. These, however, did not die. She obtained an audience of Henry IV soon after he had stormed the town of Dreux and made his public entry into Paris, and, as he was cognisant of her miserable story, on her knees at his feet she once more sought an intercession for her doomed lover, if he could be termed so still.

Henry had too often felt the passion of love not to be moved by the singular beauty of the suppliant, by her sorrow, and the eloquence with which affection endowed her. He raised her from the floor and besought her to take courage, as he would now be her friend and advocate.

The Cardinal de Pellevé could not decline the prayer of such an intercessor as Henry the Great, and, as the luckless Pousset had not received the higher orders of the priesthood, his Eminence granted a dispensation in the name of Clement VIII. The marriage ceremony was duly performed, in fulfilment of the contract signed at Angers, and Renée Corbeau and the lover she had rescued "lived ever after in the most perfect union; the husband ever regarding his wife as his guardian angel, who had saved his life and honour."

ANNA SCHONLEBEN.

THE BAVARIAN POISONER.

THIS singular wretch, a woman of a nature so fiendish, and with whom the destruction of human life by secret poisoning became a veritable passion, was beheaded in the ancient city of Nuremberg, in Bavaria, in April, 1810, after a protracted trial, that brought to light the long catalogue of her iniquities.

It would appear that she was born in Nuremberg in 1760, during the reign of Maximilian Joseph—the same who concluded the famous treaty with Maria Theresa—and was left an orphan by the death of both her parents in 1765; but, as she was the heiress to some property, she remained under guardianship, and was carefully educated till her nineteenth year, when she was married—against her inclination, it is asserted—to a notary named Zwanziger.

Young, pretty, and accustomed to much gaiety in the house of her wealthy guardian, the lonely life she felt herself condemned to pass in the house of her husband formed an unpleasant contrast, all the more so, as

Zwanziger, when not absent on business, devoted his whole time to the bottle and became a confirmed bibber.

Anna meanwhile strove to forget her gloom and her griefs by novel reading, her favourite works being the " Sorrows of Werter " and those of Pamela ; but the dissipation of Zwanziger, his neglect of his profession, on one hand, and his lavish extravagance on the other, soon brought them to wretchedness and ruin ; and she, having considerable personal attractions, though she appeared hideous and repulsive at the time of her arraignment, " now attempted to prop the falling establishment by making the best use of them ; " and amid this miserable state of affairs, Zwanziger died suddenly, leaving her to continue her life, which was now one of deception and licentiousness, alone.

Her fortune wasted, her prospects blasted, she became filled with a hatred of mankind, and with rage and bitterness at her fate. All the better sympathies which her nature may have possessed in girlhood faded out, and their place was taken by a stern and grim resolution to better her now destitute condition at all risks and hazards.

It does not seem to be clearly known when the idea of systematic poisoning occurred to her, but it was eventually suspected that she had disposed of her husband by this means, and before she was received as housekeeper into the family of Herr Justiz-Amptman Glaser. She had then spent many years as a wanderer, was fifty years of age, and without a trace of her former charms.

This was in 1808, when Glaser was residing at Pegnitz in Upper Franconia, but was living apart from his wife. Anna Schonleben (for she seldom seems to have taken her husband's name), having her own ends in view, adopting the rôle of friendship, effected a reconciliation between Glaser and his wife, who returned to his home, and within a month after was seized by a sudden and mysterious illness, of which she died in the greatest agony.

As there was no appearance of Glaser wishing her to take the place of the deceased, Anna quitted his service for that of the Herr Justiz-Amptmann Grohmann, who was unmarried and only in his thirty-eighth year. He was in delicate health; thus she had every opportunity for studying to please him, by care, attention, and an affectionate regard for his comforts; but age was against her; her apparently unremitting attention won her no favour from Herr Grohmann, who received all his medicines from her own hands, and among them some dose, suggested by revenge, as he died on the 8th of May, 1809, " his disease being accompanied by violent internal pains of the stomach, dryness of the skin, *erbrechen*," &c.

She acted her part so well, she appeared so inconsolable for his loss, and won among his friends a character so high and valuable as a careful and gentle sick-nurse, that she was almost immediately received into the household of the Kammer-Amptmann Gebhard, in that capacity. On the 13th of May, only five days after the death of Grohmann, Madame Gebhard was delivered of a baby. Both mother and child were doing well till the 16th, when the former was seized with precisely the same symptoms before named, and after seven days of agony—during which she frequently asserted that she had been poisoned—she expired.

The funeral over, the widower found himself unable to manage his household and family, and not unnaturally thought he could not do better than retain in his service, for that purpose, Anna Schonleben, who had nursed his wife, as she had done his deceased friend, in their last hours; so she remained in his house invested with all the authority of *haushalterin*, though some of his friends hinted at the inexpediency of having as an inmate one whom some fatality seemed to attend.

Gebhard laughed at this as superstitious; but there was one friend, in particular, who recurred to this matter again and again so pertinaciously—though upon what grounds he never precisely explained—that he came to the resolution of acting upon his advice, and to Anna he broke the subject of her impending dismissal, but as gently as possible, for she had acquired a certain ascendancy over him.

She merely expressed her surprise and regret, and the subsequent day was fixed for her departure to Bayreuth; but prior to that event she resolved on a terrible revenge. She arranged all the rooms as usual, and filled the *salzfasten* in the kitchen, saying the while, that "it was always the custom for those who left to fill it with salt for those who came in their place;" and when the droski for her conveyance came to the door, she took in her arms the infant child of Gebhard—the infant whose mother she had poisoned, and which was now five months old—and while feigning to caress it, she placed between "its boneless gums" a soft biscuit soaked in milk.

Then she drove away, but she had not been gone an hour, when the child and every servant in the house became seized with spasms, pains, and violent sickness. In this instance none, however, died; but Gebhard, recalling the advice of his friend, now became full of alarm and suspicion. The *salzfasten*, which Anna Schonleben had been seen so fussily to fill, was examined, and a great quantity of arsenic was found to be mixed with the salt. The barrel from which the latter was taken was also submitted to chemical analysis, and arsenic was found therein.

It now came suddenly to the knowledge or memory of the simple and confiding Kammer-Amptmann, that on one occasion, in the August of 1809, two gentlemen who had dined with him, were seized by the same symptoms as his servants ere the cloth was well off the table; that one of the servants, named Barbara Waldmann, with whom she had frequent quarrels, was seized in the same fashion after taking a cup of coffee from her hands; that she had once offered a lad named

Johann Kraus a glass of brandy in the cellar, which he declined on seeing something white permeating through it; that on another occasion, the deliverer of a message to whom she had given a glass of white Rosenhourr, was sick and ill for days after, barely escaping death; and, though last not least, Herr Gebhard remembered that on the occasion of a dinner party, given on the 1st of September, after partaking of the wine which *she* brought from the cellar, he and all his guests, five in number, were seized by the usual spasms and sickness.

Gebhard and others were astonished now, that the series of sudden deaths and violent illnesses occurring to all who took anything from the hand of the woman Schonleben, had not excited their suspicions before. The bodies of those who had died were quietly exhumed; the contents of the stomach of each were subjected to chemical analysis, and the conclusion come to was that two of them at least had been poisoned by arsenic; and reports were drawn up and depositions made, while the culprit, all unaware of the Nemesis that was about to overtake her, was living at Bayreuth, from whence she had the hardihood to write to the Kammer-Amptmann more than one letter, in which she bitterly reproached him for his base ingratitude in dismissing from his service one who had been as a mother to his motherless child.

It is supposed that the object of these epistles was to procure her reinstatement in his household, but on the 19th of October, to her consternation, she was suddenly arrested, and on being searched, three packets of poison—two being arsenic—were found upon her person. After being brought to trial, she protested her innocence, and acted with singular obstinacy and ingenuity combined, till the 16th of April, 1810, when she fairly broke down, and admitted having murdered Madame Glaser by two doses of poison; but the moment the confession left her lips, according to Feuerbach, she fell as if struck by a thunderbolt, and in strong convulsions was removed to her dungeon, under sentence of death.

It is stated, that she had committed and attempted so many murders, that they had lost all character of horror to her; that she merely viewed them as petty indiscretions, or the punishing of those who offended her or who stood in her way, till at last, to poison became almost a pastime or a passion; hence, when the poison taken from her at Bayreuth was shown to her some weeks afterwards, in the old castle of Plassenburg at Culmbach, her eyes sparkled and her whole frame seemed to vibrate with delight, as if she saw again, in that deadly white drug, an old and valued friend or servant; but she admitted, that fly-powder was what she chiefly used to revenge herself upon her fellow-servants by mixing it with their beer; and that prior to quitting the house of Gebhard she had frequently poisoned the coffee, wine, and beer of such guests as she chose to dislike. She declared openly, that her death was a fortunate thing for many people, as she felt certain she could not have left off poisoning as long as she lived.

She steadily ascended the scaffold, bowed to the people, with a smile on her old, wrinkled, and, then, hideous face, laid her head on the block, and without shrinking or moving a muscle, had it struck off by the axe of the public *scharfrichter*, or executioner; and so ended this German *cause célèbre*.

LAURA WENLOCK'S CHRISTMAS EVE.

CHAPTER I.

"It cannot be that you are about to be married!" exclaimed Jack Westbrook passionately as he held the girl's hands half forcibly and gazed into her shrinking eyes; "I will not believe it—even from your own lips."

But the girl, silent and sad, hesitated to reply.

The glory of an April sunset lay over all the sweet Kentish landscape; a little tarn between two white chalk cliffs shone like molten gold, with black coots swimming, and the pearly clouds reflected on its surface; the emerald green buds were bursting in their beauty in the coppice and hedgerows, where the linnet and the speckled thrush were preparing their nests; the unclosing crocus and the drooping daffodil were making the cottage gardens gay; and everywhere, there were coming "fresh flowers and leaves to deck the dead season's bier."

It was a period of the opened year when unconsciously the human heart feels hopeful and happy, even the

hearts of the old and the ailing; but the souls of those
two who lingered, near the old Saxon *lichgate*, roofed
with ancient thatch and velvet moss, and by the old
worn stile that led to the village church of Craybourne,
were sad indeed; they were on the eve of parting, and
—for ever!

"It cannot be, Laura, that you are about to be
married, after all," repeated Jack Westbrook, a soldier-
like young fellow, not much over five and twenty,
dark, handsome and clad in that kind of grey tweed
suit, which looks so gentlemanly when worn by one of
good bearing and style, and such Jack certainly was.

"It is but too true—too true, Jack," replied Laura,
while her tears fell fast, and she strove to release her
trembling hands from her lover's passionate clasp.

Laura Wenlock was more than merely handsome;
in her soft face there was a singular and piquante
charm, a loveliness that was more penetrating and of
a higher order than mere regularity of feature, as its
expression varied so much—a charm that would have
delighted an artist, while it would have baffled his
powers to reproduce it. Her eyes were violet blue; her
hair was auburn, shot with gold, and ruddy golden it
seemed ever in the sunshine.

"You don't mean to say that you are about to marry
for money?" said Westbrook impetuously.

"Far from it, Jack—oh! don't think so meanly—so
basely of me," urged Laura piteously.

"What then?"

" *With* money—sounds different, doesn't it, Jack, dear ? " said the girl with a sob and a sickly smile.

Westbrook gnawed his thick brown moustache, and eyed her gloomily, then almost malevolently and, anon, pleadingly, for his fate was in her hands.

" From all I have heard," said he, " I feared it would come to this ; but oh, no, no, surely it cannot be—that I am now to lose you ! "

" It must be ; the fatal papers have already been prepared."

" The settlements ! "

" Yes ; debts beyond what we could ever have anticipated, have overtaken my father, and you know that his vicarage here at Craybourne is a poor one, Jack, a very poor one, and his poverty would be the ruin of my two brothers. My marriage will be the saving of them all—the Colonel is so rich."

" Philip Daubeny, of Craybourne Hall ? "

" Yes," replied Laura, with averted eyes.

" I saw him struck down by the sun on the march between Jehanumbad and Shetanpore ; and I would, with all my heart, he were there still ! "

" Don't say so, Jack," urged the girl ; " Colonel Daubeny is good, and brave, and generous—oh, most generous ! God knows, Jack, if you would take me as I am, without a shilling, I would become your wedded wife to-night," added Laura, blinded with tears ; " but you want me to wait for you, Jack, and I cannot wait, for the fate of those over there—at home—is in my power," continued Laura, turning towards the old thatched vicarage, the lozenged casements of which were glittering in the sunshine between the stems of the trees.

"To wait, of course," said he, huskily, and relinquishing her hands in a species of sullen despair; "I have but little to live on just yet, since I had to sell out of the Hussars after that infernal loss on the Oaks, and, of course, I cannot supply you with equipages and luxuries as Daubeny can do. But do have patience with me, Laura."

"I cannot—I cannot!" wailed the girl; "the dreadful *why* I have told you a thousand times."

"You never loved me truly."

"You wrong me; no one has ever been more dear to me than you, Jack."

He laughed bitterly.

"Yet you will marry Philip Daubeny? Have you thought how shameful is a mercenary marriage?"

"I have, indeed, God knows how deeply, how bitterly and prayerfully, in the silent night, when none could see my tears, save Him! Take back your ring, dear Jack, and let us part friends;" and drawing the emblem from her tiny finger, she touched it with her trembling lips, and restored it to him.

"Friends!" he exclaimed, bitterly and scornfully, while in his fine dark eyes there shone a flash of light, where evil seemed to rival love and sorrow, as he flung the golden hoop, with its pearl cluster, into the tarn, and left her without another word or glance! He strode away down the sequestered path that led to the churchyard stile, crushing, as if vengefully, under his feet the wayside flowers, the tender blossoms and sprays of spring; and the girl watched him till his retreating figure disappeared in the shady vista of the lane.

Then she interlaced her slender fingers over her auburn hair and cast her eyes upwards, full of sorrow and intense compunction for the pain she had been compelled to inflict; but there was no despair in her expression, nor was there in her heart, we hope.

"God bless you, dear—dear Jack; you will forget me in time. All is over now!" she murmured.

But the memory of Westbrook's harassed face, and the winning sound of his voice haunted her in the hours of the night as she lay feverish, restless, in a passion of bitter weeping; and full of sad and terrible thoughts, tossing from side to side, sleepless on her pillow.

CHAPTER II.

THE marriage day came, and the chimes were ringing merrily in the old square tower of the little vicarage church, scaring the swallows from their nests amid the leaves and the clustering ivy, and, aware of the event,

numbers of the parishioners and of Colonel Daubeny's
tenantry, in their holiday attire, were toiling up the
steep and picturesque pathway that led through shady
dingles to the quaint edifice which overlooked the Cray.
The humble old-fashioned organ gave forth its most
joyous notes; and what was wanting in splendour or
decoration in a church so old and rural, was amply
made up by the masses of flowers, many of them the
rarest exotics from the conservatories of Colonel Daubeny, and these garlanded the round chancel arch and the
short dumpy Saxon pillars, while the altar in its deep
recess was gay with them; when Laura, leaning on the
arm of her father, the old thin-faced and silver-haired
Vicar, and followed by her six bridesmaids, all lovely
little girls, relatives of both families, dressed alike, and
attended closely, too, by her two brothers, the thought-
less lads, whom she had sacrificed herself to serve and
advance in life, was led slowly up the church, the cyno-
sure and admiration of every eye, for all the people
knew and loved her.

The gift of the bridegroom—a handsome, grave, and
manly-looking fellow, whose hair, though only in his
fortieth year, Indian service had slightly streaked with
grey, and whose best man was his old chum and comrade, Charlie Fane—her bridal dress, priceless with
satin and lace, shone in the successive rays of sunlight as she passed the painted windows, her bridal
veil floated gracefully and gloriously around her, by
its folds hiding the ashy pallor of her charming face,

and her eyes that were aflame with unshed tears, and
trembled to look up, lest they should encounter those
of Jack Westbrook, full of upbraiding and bitterness;
but Jack was at that moment miles away occupying
his mind with very different matters, though he well
knew what was then being enacted at Craybourne
Church.

She stood and knelt as one in a dream side by side
with Philip Daubeny at the altar rail before her father,
and it certainly *did* strike the former with something of
alarm rather than surprise, that when she was ungloved
by a fussy and blushing little bridesmaid, and when she
placed her hand steadily and without a tremor in his,
it was icy and cold, as that of Lucy Ashton on her ill-
omened bridal morn.

She uttered all the words of the service in a low and
distinct voice, yet never once were her dark blue eyes
raised to those of the earnest and generous Philip
Daubeny, whose glances, moderated of course by the
knowledge that they were so closely observed, were
full of love and tenderness; and, in truth, even at that
solemn moment, Laura felt that though he had her
highest respect and her genuine esteem, she did not love
him, and could only pray to Heaven, in her silent heart,
that the time might come when she should do so as a
wedded wife.

Laura bore up nobly. If she clung to her husband's
arm, and thus sent a thrill to his heart as they quitted
the gloomy fane, with its earthy odour, for the sun-

shine of the churchyard, where the cheers of assembled hundreds greeted them, it was only because she felt weak, and wondered when the time would come that would see her laid in yonder vault, where all the Daubenys of past ages lay—the vault, with its ponderous door, mildewed and rusty, and half-hidden by huge fern leaves and churchyard nettles—and on reaching the Vicarage she nearly fainted, greatly to the terror of Daubeny and the anxiety of all.

Avoiding the former, she clung to her father.

"Kiss me, papa," she said again and again. "Kiss me, papa; are you pleased with me—pleased with your poor Laura *now*?"

"Yes, my darling, yes," replied the old Vicar, folding her in his arms. He had heard much of Jack Westbrook: but thought that, so far as himself and his family were concerned, "matters were now, indeed, ordered for the *best*" in her marriage with the Squire of Craybourne.

A man of the world—one who had seen twenty years of dangerous military service in the East—Phil Daubeny was one of whom any woman might be proud, handsome, wealthy, and well-born, and all thought that Laura was as happy in her choice as in her heart; but the image of Jack Westbrook, of whom he knew *nothing*, stood—and was for a time fated to stand—as a barrier between her and the man she had vowed to "love, honour, and obey;" and most earnestly in her soul did she pray, as the carriage bore her from her beloved home for ever, that never more in this world might Westbrook's path cross hers; but not that she feared evil would come of it, for Laura was too wifely, too pure, and too good for such an idea to occur to her.

CHAPTER III.

AMID the congratulations of friends, under the radiant smiles of her husband, even when her head nestled on his shoulder and his strong arm went lovingly round her; amid all the innumerable gaieties of Paris, of Brussels—a new world to her—this ghost seemed morbidly to haunt her; yet the honeymoon glided away, and the second month found them, amid all the charms of midsummer, located in their luxurious home at Craybourne Hall, from the upper oriels of which she could see the smoke, from the old clustered chimneys of the Vicarage, curling about the leafy coppice.

Daubeny had missed something responsive, he knew not what, in his wife, whose general listlessness, with a certain far-seeing expression of eye, began to pain and bewilder him. He kept his thoughts to himself; yet his brave and loving nature craved ever for some secret sympathy which Laura failed to accord him, and so there gradually began to yawn between them a chasm which neither could define, and the existence of which they would stoutly have denied. To Daubeny it became a source of keen and growing misery. But one night the scales fell from his eyes.

Finding himself alone and idle in London, he turned into the back stalls of the opera. The piece had not commenced; the orchestra were at the overture; the gas was somewhat low; and by some heedless fellows who were sitting in front of him he heard *his own name* mentioned once or twice in conversation, and was compelled to listen thereto.

"Jack Westbrook has got over it all now," one said. "Of course the *sting* of wounded self-esteem, at being thrown over for rich old Phil Daubeny, rankled for a time. The fair Laura was his first love—never saw such a pair of spoons in all my life, don't you know—privately engaged, and all that sort of thing."

"And now I have no doubt she will flirt with any man who will flirt with her. Of course, it is always the way—and she don't care for Daubeny, poor devil!"

"I don't think she *will* flirt," said the first speaker.

"Bah! every woman has some weak point, if you can only find it out."

"Most men, too, I suspect; but the fair Laura is clad in the armour of virtue."

"Jack Westbrook might find some weak points in that armour, too; and he won't drop out of the hunt perhaps."

Then followed a reckless laugh that stung the soul of

Daubeny to madness. The Opera stalls were no place
for that which is so abhorrent in "society"—a scene;
so instead of dashing their heads together, as he felt
inclined to do, he softly left the place just as the overture ceased and the act-drop rose; and he went forth in
a tempest of that kind of rage which always becomes
the more bitter for having no immediate object to
expend itself on; and even the speed of the night
express seemed a thousand degrees too slow as it bore
him homeward to Craybourne Hall. She had been
engaged, had a lover—her first lover, too—and all unknown to him!

He had both seen and heard of Westbrook; but not
in *this* character. Her first love—her only love! How
many uncounted kisses had, of course, been exchanged,
of which he knew naught (and had no business with
then)? How much of the bloom had been worn off the
peach ere it became his? He was full of black wrath,
and saw much now that he saw not before, and could
quite account for all her coldness. Yet, although he
knew it not, the girl who had always esteemed was now
learning to *love* him as she had never even loved Jack
Westbrook!

Late though the hour—the first of morning—he proceeded at once to his wife's dressing-room, where she
was awaiting his return in a charming blue robe that
made her fair beauty look more charming still, for there
were colour and brightness in her face and a love-light
in her eyes at his approach, till the abruptness of his

entrance and the set sternness of his white visage
startled her.

" Philip ! "

" Can it be true what I have heard to-night, Laura,
that you loved Westbrook, of the Hussars," he demanded, " and, while loving him, married *me* for my
money, and what I might do for the old Vicar and his
sons ? Is it truth that, when he gave you to me at the
altar of yonder church, your marriage vow was a black
lie and your false heart teemed with love for another ?
Speak ! " he thundered out ; but she could only lift her
timid eyes to him imploringly, and spread her little
white hands in deprecation of the coming malediction.
Her voice was gone. " Your silence affirms all I have
heard," he continued, in accents that trembled with
jealousy and sorrow. " Oh, God, what a fool and dupe
I have been ! "

" I know not what you have heard, Philip ; but, as
He hears me, I have been a true and faithful wife to
you."

" In playing a part you did not feel," he cried scornfully, " but I will aid your play no more. From this
hour we meet never again on earth. Here, in this
house, for which you sold yourself, I shall leave you,
with all its luxuries, till such time as a more regular
separation can be brought about ; and the sole sorrow
of my heart is now, that I cannot leave you free to wed
this fellow Westbrook, the cause of all your incom-
patibility and coldness to me."

He flung away, and left her in a gust of fury.

" Philip, Philip ! " she exclaimed, but she heard the hall door close ; and then, as his steps died away in the distance, she fell on the floor, overcome by her sudden and terrible emotions—startled, shocked, and conscience-stricken.

CHAPTER IV

Days passed on—days of sorrow, anxiety, and futile watching for a footfall that came no more. Whither he had gone she knew not, nor could she discover, and she was left to her tears and unavailing grief, amid the splendour of Craybourne Hall. She saw now how erring she had been ; that, while nursing a mere fancy, she had lost the true love of a good and generous man, whose last words had been the first harsh ones he had ever addressed to her.

Gone ! gone ! She felt how much she really loved him now, and all the more that a secret tie was coming, and must come ere Christmas, to bind them stronger together. She must let him know of this dear hope ; but how ? *Where* had he gone ? To death, perhaps, and she might have a child in her bosom that Philip could never, never see !

The weeks became months, and the heart of the strangely-widowed wife grew sick and heavy as lead

with hopeless waiting, watching, and agonising yearning—dead even to the speculations of those around her,
to whom the absence of her husband seemed, of course,
most unaccountable, if not unkind and cruel.

But for the sake of her child she wished that she
might die when it saw the light. Surely, then, Philip
would forgive her when he saw its little face, and she was
laid within the vault, the mildewed and rusted door of
which she had regarded with a shudder on her marriage
morning—the vault where all the dead Daubenys lay.

So in the fulness of time her baby was born—a little
fairy boy—and her father named it Philip, for him who
was still so strangely absent, and hot and burning were
the tears with which Laura bedewed its tiny face as it
nestled in her bosom; and amid the new emotions
awakened by maternity she prayed God to forgive her
for having longed to die; for no baby in the world
could be like hers, that lay so round and soft and
warm in her white bosom, and was fast growing *so*
like papa !

But where was he wandering? Why was he not
with her? Surely he would return *now?* Yet the days
still rolled monotonously on, and winter drew nigh.
The trees in Craybourne Chase were leafless; the fern,
amid which the deer made their lair, was turning red,
and the uplands became powdered with snow.

" To what a dreary and dreadful Christmas do I look
forward, papa!" she exclaimed to the sorrowing old
Vicar, "and I do so love him! Philip, Philip, come

back to me, and do not leave me thus to die!" she would wail, ever and anon, in her helplessness.

And now there came a day which she was fated never, never to forget! Her husband's firm friend and old comrade, who had been his groomsman, the stout hearted and gallant Charlie Fane, arrived at Craybourne with a face as white as the snow in the Weald of Kent—the bearer of terrible tidings, which he had heard that morning at the club, and these he had to break—he knew not *how*—to Laura, though they had been broken abruptly enough to himself.

Jack Westbrook had raised his head from the morning paper just as Fane entered the room.

"By Jove! look here, Charlie!" exclaimed Westbrook in an excited tone, "there has been a dreadful accident to the train between Paris and Calais, and among the killed—mangled out of all shape—the report says, is Colonel Philip Daubeny, a British officer. His card-case was found in his pocket."

"My God! Poor Laura, poor Phil!" exclaimed Fane, as he took the paper in his trembling hands, and in ten minutes after was *en route* for Craybourne Hall.

"Poor devil!" thought Westbrook, as he lit a cigar; "who knows but I may get the reversion of the widow, with her tin, after all?"

CHAPTER V

It was Christmas Eve at Craybourne Hall, as elsewhere all over the Christian world; but the stillness as of death reigned there, and Laura, a widow now in heart indeed, lay tossing restlessly on her laced pillow, fighting, as it were, with the grim King, and forgetful even of her infant. Never had that old hall, ever since the Tudor days, seen a more sorrowful Christmas Eve. All the landscape around it wore a shroud of ghastly white. The Cray was frozen in its bed, and all the shrubs and trees seemed turned to crystal, that sparkled with diamond lustre in the light of the moon and stars. Over the snowy waste the Christmas bells in the old Vicarage church rang out " Peace on Earth— Peace on Earth, and goodwill towards men ; " but there was no peace—peace of the heart, at least—in the stately hall; yet such a winter had not been seen for years, and great things, the old Kentish folks said, were sure to occur, for never had the holly been so covered with scarlet berries. What a Christmas for Laura !

In her chamber, dimly-lit and closely watched, she lay helpless and stunned by the depth of her woe, and honest Charlie Fane, who had seen much of human suffering in his time, watched her like a brother; and, in that chamber, there was no sound heard but the sighs of the sufferer and the chimes of the distant bells.

Suddenly there was a noise of feet and voices in the corridor without. A figure entered—was it the phantom of Philip Daubeny?

No! the strong grasp that tightened on the hand of Fane forbade that idea; and, in a moment more, the husband, looking pale and rather worn, was bending over the wife who had fainted in his arms. In Philip's face there was no sternness now, but passionate love, pity, and tears, and agony, too, till Laura revived.

" Not killed—not even injured, Philip?" exclaimed Fane.

" No, thank Heaven! but a poor fellow was to whom I lent my Ulster when hurrying homeward. Do you forgive me, darling Laura—forgive my cruel desertion?"

" Oh, yes, my love—my own Philip—all—all! And is the little fellow not a darling too—and *so* like you, Philip?" said the broken, half-hushed voice.

And as Philip, with a bursting heart, hung over his wife and child, he could hear more merrily than ever the joyous bells that told of the promise given 1800 years ago to the Chaldean shepherds as they watched their flocks by night in Judæa.

BRADBURY, AGNEW, & CO., PRINTERS, WHITEFRIARS

HENRY H VOSE

GEORGE ROUTLEDGE & SONS' CATALOGUE.

NOVELS AT TWO SHILLINGS.

AINSWORTH, W. H.
Boscobel.
Manchester Rebels.
Preston Fight.

ARMSTRONG, F. C.
Two Midshipmen.
Medora.
War Hawk.
Young Commander.

BANIM, John.
Peep o' Day.
Smuggler.

BELL, M. M.
Deeds, Not Words.
Secret of a Life.

BELLEW, J. C. M.
Blount Tempest.

BLACK, Robert.
Love or Lucre.

CARLETON, William.
Traits and Stories of the Irish
Peasantry. 1st series.
————— 2nd series.

CHAMIER, Captain.
Life of a Sailor.
Ben Brace.
Tom Bowling.
Jack Adams.

COLOMB, Colonel.
Hearths and Watchfires.

COCKTON, Henry.
Valentine Vox.
Stanley Thorn.

COOPER, J. Fenimore.
Lionel Lincoln.
Borderers.
Waterwitch.
Deerslayer.
Heidenmauer.
Miles Wallingford.
Afloat and Ashore. (Sequel
to Miles Wallingford.)
Bravo.
Headsman.
Wyandotte.

*The following in double columns,
2s. each Vol. containing 4 Novels.*
1. Spy — Pilot — Homeward
   Bound—Eve Effingham.
2. Pioneers — Mohicans —
   Prairie—Pathfinder.
3. Red Rover—Two Admirals
   —Miles Wallingford —
   Afloat and Ashore.
4. Borderers — Wyandotte —
   Mark's Reef—Satanstoe.
5. Lionel Lincoln — Oak
   Openings—Ned Myers—
   Precaution.
6. Deerslayer — Headsman—
   Waterwitch — Heiden-
   mauer.
7. Bravo—Sea Lions—Jack
   Tier—Mercedes.

CROLY, Dr.
Salathiel.

CROWE, Catherine.
Night Side of Nature.
Susan Hopley.
Linny Lockwood.

NOVELS AT TWO SHILLINGS, *continued.*

CUMMINS, M. S.
Lamplighter.
Mabel Vaughan.

CUPPLES, Captain.
Green Hand.
Two Frigates.

DICKENS, Charles.
Sketches by Boz.
Oliver Twist.
Pickwick Papers.
Nicholas Nickleby
Martin Chuzzlewit.

DICKENS, Charles. Edited by.
Life of Grimaldi, the Clown.
Illustrated by Cruikshank.

DUMAS, Alexandre.
Half Brothers.
Marguerite de Valois.
Mohicans of Paris.

EDGEWORTH, Maria.
Helen.

EDWARDS, Amelia B.
Ladder of Life.
My Brother's Wife.
Half a Million of Money.

EDWARDS, Mrs.
Miss Forrester.

FERRIER, Miss.
Marriage.
Inheritance.
Destiny.

FIELDING, Henry
Tom Jones.
Joseph Andrews.
Amelia.

FITTIS, Robert.
Gilderoy.

GERSTAECKER, F
A Wife to Order.
Two Convicts.
Feathered Arrow.
Each for Himself.

GLEIG, G. R.
Light Dragoon.
Chelsea Veterans.
Hussar.

GODWIN, William.
Caleb Williams.

GORE, Mrs.
Money Lender.
Pin Money.
Dowager.

GRANT, James.
Romance of War; or, The
   Highlanders in Spain.
Aide-de-Camp.
Scottish Cavalier: the Revolu-
   tion of 1688.
Bothwell: the Days of Mary
   Queen of Scots.
Jane Seton: A Scottish His-
   torical Romance of James V.
Philip Rollo.
Legends of the Black Watch
   (42nd Regiment).
Mary of Lorraine.
Oliver Ellis; or, The 21st
   Fusiliers.
Lucy Arden; or, Hollywood
   Hall.
Frank Hilton; or, The Queen's
   Own.
Yellow Frigate.
Harry Ogilvie; or, The Black
   Dragoons.
Arthur Blane; or, The 100
   Cuirassiers.
Laura Everingham; or, The
   Highlanders of Glenora.

NOVELS AT TWO SHILLINGS, *continued.*

GRANT, James, continued.

Captain of the Guard; or, The Times of James II.
Letty Hyde's Lovers: A Tale of the Household Brigade.
Cavaliers of Fortune.
Second to None; or, The Scots Greys.
Constable of France.
Phantom Regiment.
King's Own Borderers; or, The 25th Regiment.
White Cockade.
Dick Rodney: Adventures of an Eton Boy.
First Love and Last Love: A Tale of the Indian Mutiny.
The Girl He Married: Scenes in the Life of a Scotch Laird.
Lady Wedderburn's Wish: A Story of the Crimean War.
Jack Manly: His Adventures by Sea and Land.
Only an Ensign: The Retreat from Cabul.
Adventures of Rob Roy.
Under the Red Dragon.
Queen's Cadet, & other Tales.
Shall I Win Her.
Fairer than a Fairy.
The Secret Dispatch.
One of the Six Hundred.
Morley Ashton: A Story of the Sea.
Did She Love Him?
The Ross-shire Buffs.
Six Years Ago.
Vere of Ours.
Lord Hermitage.
Royal Regiment.

"GUY LIVINGSTONE,"
Author of.

Guy Livingstone.
Barren Honour.
Maurice Dering.
Brakespeare.

Anteros.
Breaking a Butterfly.
Sans Merci.
Sword and Gown.

HALIBURTON, Judge.

Sam Slick, the Clockmaker.
The Attaché.
Letter Bag of Great Western.

HANNAY, James.

Singleton Fontenoy.

HERING, Jeanie.

Through the Mist.

HOOK, Theodore.

Peregrine Bunce.
Cousin Geoffry.
Gilbert Gurney.
Parson's Daughter.
All in the Wrong.
Widow and the Marquess.
Gurney Married.
Jack Brag.
Maxwell.
Man of Many Friends.
Passion and Principle.
Merton.
Gervase Skinner.
Cousin William.
Fathers and Sons.

HUGO, Victor.

Les Misérables.

JAMES, G. P. R.

Brigand.
Morley Ernstein.
Darnley.
Richelieu.
Gipsy.
Arabella Stuart.
Woodman.
Agincourt.
Russell.
King's Highway.
Castle of Ehrenstein.
Stepmother.

NOVELS AT TWO SHILLINGS, *continued.*

JAMES, G. P. R., *continued.*
Forest Days.
Huguenot.
Man at Arms.
A Whim and its Consequences.
Henry Masterton.
Convict.
Mary of Burgundy.
Gowrie.
Delaware.
Henry of Guise.
Robber.
One in a Thousand.
Smuggler.
De L'Orme.
Heidelberg.
False Heir.
Castleneau.
Forgery.
Gentleman of the Old School.
Philip Augustus.
Black Eagle.
Old Dominion.
Beauchamp.
Arrah Neil.
My Aunt Pontypool.

JEPHSON, R. Mounteney.
Tom Bulkeley of Lissington.
The Girl He Left behind Him.

KINGSLEY, Henry.
Stretton.
Old Margaret.
The Harveys.
Hornby Mills.

KINGSTON, W. H. G.
Pirate of the Mediterranean.

L. E. L.
Francesca Carrara.

LANG, John.
The Ex-Wife.
Will He Marry Her?

LEVER, Charles.
Arthur O'Leary.
Con Cregan.
Horace Templeton.

LE FANU, Sheridan.
Torlogh O'Brien.

LONG, Lady Catherine.
First Lieutenant's Story.
Sir Roland Ashton.

LOVER, Samuel.
Rory O'More.
Handy Andy.

LYTTON, Right Hon. Lord.
Pelham.
Paul Clifford.
Eugene Aram.
Last Days of Pompeii.
Rienzi.
Leila, and Pilgrims of the Rhine.
Last of the Barons.
Ernest Maltravers.
Alice.   (Sequel to Ernest Maltravers.)
Night and Morning.
Godolphin.
Disowned.
Devereux.
The Caxtons.
My Novel.   2 vols.
Lucretia.
Harold.
Zanoni.
What will He Do with It?   2 vols.
A Strange Story.
Pausanias.
The Coming Race.
Kenelm Chillingly.
The Parisians.   2 vols.
Falkland and Zicci.

NOVELS AT TWO SHILLINGS, *continued.*

MARRYAT, Captain.
Jacob Faithful.
Japhet in Search of a Father.
King's Own.
Midshipman Easy.
Newton Forster.
Pacha of Many Tales.
Rattlin the Reefer.
Poacher.
Phantom Ship.
Dog Fiend.
Percival Keene.
Frank Mildmay.
Peter Simple.

2s. each Volume, containing 4 Novels.
1. King's Own—Frank Mild-
   may—Newton Forster—
   Peter Simple.
2. Pacha of Many Tales—
   Jacob Faithful—Midshipman Easy—Japhet.
3. Phantom Ship—Dog Fiend
   —OllaPodrida—Poacher.
4. Percival Keene—Monsieur
   Violet—Rattlin—Valerie.

MARTINEAU, Harriet.
The Hour and the Man.

MAXWELL, W. H.
Stories of Waterloo.
Bryan O'Lynn; or, Luck's
   Everything.
Captain Blake.
The Bivouac.
Hector O'Halloran.
Captain O'Sullivan.
Stories of the Peninsular War.
Flood and Field. [Highlands.
Sports and Adventures in the
Wild Sports in the West.

MAYHEW, Brothers.
The Greatest Plague of Life.
   (Cruikshank's Plates.)
Whom to Marry.   (Cruik-
   shank's Plates.)

MAYO, W. S.
Kaloolah.

MILLER, Thomas.
Gideon Giles, the Roper.

MORIER, Captain.
Hajji Baba in Ispahan.

MURRAY, Hon. Sir Charles.
Prairie Bird.

NEALE, Captain.
Lost Ship.
Captain's Wife.
Pride of the Mess.
Will Watch.
Cavendish.
Flying Dutchman.
Gentleman Jack.

NORTON, Hon. Mrs.
Stuart of Dunleath.

OLD CALABAR.
Won in a Canter.

OLD SAILOR.
Land and Sea Tales.

OLIPHANT, Mrs.
At His Gates.

PALISSER, John.
Solitary Hunter.

PARDOE, Miss.
City of the Sultan.

PORTER, Jane.
Scottish Chiefs.
Thaddeus of Warsaw.

PAYN, J.
Murphy's Master.
A Perfect Treasure.
Saved by a Woman.

RAFTER, Captain.
The Rifleman.

NOVELS AT TWO SHILLINGS, *continued.*

RADCLIFFE, Ann.
Three Novels in One Vol., price 2s.
Romance of the Forest.
The Italian.
Mysteries of Udolpho (2 parts).

REACH, Angus B.
Clement Lorimer.
Leonard Lindsay.

REID, Mayne.
Afloat in the Forest.
Boy Slaves.
Cliff Climbers.
Fatal Cord.
Giraffe Hunters.
Guerilla Chief.
Half Blood ; or, Oceola.
Headless Horseman.
Hunters' Feast.
Lost Lenore.
Maroon.
Ocean Waifs.
Rifle Rangers.
Scalp Hunters.
Tiger Hunter.
White Chief.
White Gauntlet.
White Squaw.
Wild Huntress.
Wood Rangers.

RITCHIE.
Robber of the Rhine.

ROSS, Charles H.
Pretty Widow.

REELSTAB.
Polish Lancer.

RUSSELL, Dr. W. H.
Adventures of Dr. Brady.

RUSSELL, W.
Romance of Military Life.

SANDERS, Capt. Patten.
Black and Gold : **A Tale of** Circassia.

SCOTT, Sir Walter.
Abbot.
Anne of Geierstein.
Antiquary.
Betrothed ; Highland Widow.
Black Dwarf; Legend of Montrose.
Bride of Lammermoor.
Count Robert of Paris.
Fair Maid of Perth.
Fortunes of Nigel.
Guy Mannering.
Heart of Midlothian.
Ivanhoe.
Kenilworth.
Monastery.
Old Mortality.
Peveril of the Peak.
Pirate.
Quentin Durward.
Red Gauntlet.
Rob Roy.
St. Ronan's Well.
Surgeon's Daughter.
Talisman ; Two Drovers.
Waverley.
Woodstock.

2s. each Volume, containing 4 Novels.

1. Waverley — Monastery — Kenilworth—Rob Roy.
2. Pirate — Ivanhoe — Fortunes of Nigel — Old Mortality.
3. Guy Mannering—Bride of Lammermoor—Heart of Midlothian—Antiquary.
4. Peveril of the Peak — Quentin Durward — St. Ronan's Well.—Abbot.

A WONDERFUL MEDICINE.

BEECHAM'S PILLS

Are admitted by thousands to be worth a Guinea a Box for bilious and nervous disorders, such as wind and pain in the stomach, sick headache, giddiness, fulness and swelling after meals, dizziness and drowsiness, cold chills, flushings of heat, loss of appetite. shortness of breath, costiveness, scurvy, blotches on the skin, disturbed sleep, frightful dreams, and all nervous and trembling sensations, etc. The first dose will give relief in twenty minutes. This is no fiction, for they have done it in thousands of cases. Every sufferer is earnestly invited to try one box of these Pills, and they will be acknowledged to be

WORTH A GUINEA A BOX.

For females of all ages these Pills are invaluable, as a few doses of them carry off all gross humours, open all obstructions, and bring about all that is required. No female should be without them. There is no medicine to be found to equal BEECHAM'S PILLS for removing any obstruction or irregularity of the system. If taken according to the directions given with each box they will soon restore females of all ages to sound and robust health.

For a weak stomach, impaired digestion, and all disorders of the liver, they act like "MAGIC," and a few doses will be found to work wonders upon the most important organs of the human machine. They strengthen the whole muscular system, restore the long lost complexion, bring back the keen edge of appetite, and arouse into action with the ROSEBUD of health the whole physical energy of the human frame. These are "FACTS" admitted by thousands embracing all classes of society; and one of the best guarantees to the nervous and debilitated is, Beecham's Pills have the largest sale of any patent medicine in the world.

CAUTION.—The Public are requested to notice that the words "BEECHAM'S PILLS, St. Helens," are on the Government Stamp affixed to each box of the Pills. If not on they are a forgery.

Prepared only and sold wholesale and retail by the proprietor, T. Beecham, Chemist, St. Helens, Lancashire, in boxes at 1s. 1½d. and 2s. 9d. each. Sent post free from the proprietor for 15 or 36 stamps. Sold by all Druggists and Patent Medicine Dealers in the Kingdom.

N.B.—Full directions are given with each box.

PEARS'
SOAP
A SPECIALTY FOR THE COMPLEXION

Recommended by Sir Erasmus Wilson, F.R.S., *late President of the Royal College of Surgeons of England, as*

"The most refreshing and agreeable of balms for the skin."

MDME. ADELINA PATTI writes :—"I have found Pears' Soap *matchless for the hands and complexion.*"

MRS. LANGTRY writes :—'Since using Pears' Soap for the hands and complexion, *I have discarded all others.*'

MDME. MARIE ROZE (*Prima Donna, Her Majesty's Theatre*) writes :—"For preserving the complexion, keeping the skin soft, free from redness and roughness, and the hands in nice condition, Pears' Soap *is the finest preparation in the world.*"

MISS MARY ANDERSON writes :—"I have used Pears' Soap for two years with the greatest satisfaction, for *I find it the very best.*"

PEARS' SOAP—SOLD EVERYWHERE

www.ingramcontent.com/pod-product-compliance
Lightning Source LLC
Chambersburg PA
CBHW020807060726
47498CB00017B/925